NORBY TO
THE RESCUE

Having attracted Jeff's attention, Marcel said cheerfully, "Good-bye, my American friends. I am so happy to have known you."

Jeff dashed up to the block, one hand outstretched and the other still holding the lightning rod. Before the executioner could object, he shook Marcel's hand and was embarrassed when the little prisoner clung to him, kissing him on both cheeks.

"Norby," yelled Fargo. "Take the little man and Jeff out of here. I'll be with Benjamin Franklin. Marcel, get on Jeff's back."

"Jeff," asked Norby, "is that man with the axe going to do something I wouldn't like?"

"Right!" Jeff dropped the lightning rod and grabbed Norby's hand as the robot dropped farther down.

Norby said, "Then it's time to leave."

Ace Science Fiction books by Janet and Isaac Asimov

THE NORBY CHRONICLES
NORBY: ROBOT FOR HIRE
NORBY THROUGH TIME AND SPACE

JANET AND ISAAC ASIMOV

NORBY THROUGH TIME AND SPACE

(PREVIOUSLY PUBLISHED IN HARDCOVER
AS *NORBY AND THE QUEEN'S
NECKLACE* AND *NORBY FINDS A VILLAIN*)

ACE BOOKS, NEW YORK

NORBY THROUGH TIME AND SPACE

An Ace Book/published by arrangement with
Walker and Company

PRINTING HISTORY
Walker and Company edition (*Queen's Necklace*) published 1986
Walker and Company edition (*Finds a Villain*) published 1987
Ace edition/September 1988

NORBY AND THE QUEEN'S NECKLACE

*To Marg and Bill Atwood,
with thanks*

1

Dangerous Play

"Jefferson Wells, actor?" The museum guard scowled and barred the doorway. "So *you* say. Where's your identification?"

"I haven't got it," said Jeff earnestly. "Fargo didn't give me one. That's Farley Gordon Wells, who's playing the part of the King. He's my brother. I'm in the skit, too—gentlemen-in-waiting—and I'm first on the stage. . . ."

"I don't care who you are or what you're supposed to do. You've got to have identification. That Queen's necklace we have is valuable and no one gets in who isn't authorized. And even if you had identification, you can't bring in your barrel. It would have to be checked."

The domed lid of the barrel, complete with metal brim, popped up to reveal half a head with two eyes glaring with anger at the guard. Facing Jeff on the other side of the head were two more eyes, looking just as angry.

"I go where Jeff goes, you numbskull!" The metallic voice seemed to come from the lid. As Fargo always said, Norby—the small robot that looked like a barrel—always talked through his hat.

The guard reddened and Jeff interposed quickly. "This is the teaching robot for the whole cast," he said. "His name is Norby and he's very temperamental, so you'll have to excuse him. We're all speaking French and Norby makes sure we get it right. He's absolutely necessary to the skit. So you see, *I've* got to get in. And *Norby's* got to get in."

"That's right," said Norby, sounding smug. "This skit is being put on before an audience of Federation dignitaries, in case you don't know it, Mr. Whatever-your-name-is."

1

Norby's legs telescoped out of his barrel body, so Jeff put him down.

Rocking back and forth on his two-way feet, Norby telescoped out both of his arms, grabbed Jeff's hand and said, "If we don't get in, the skit can't go on and the Queen's necklace, which is the museum's newest acquisition, can't be publicized. And everyone will want to bounce you off the wall! So just let us pass."

He tried to walk forward, pulling at a rather reluctant Jeff, who preferred to make his point by reason.

The guard threw himself in front of them, arms outstretched. "No, you don't. It doesn't matter what you say. No identification, no entrance. Those are my instructions. And it especially goes for fresh kids and barrels."

The guard was not a very tall man, and Jeff was nearly six feet tall, even though he was only fourteen. He looked down at the guard and said quietly, "Do I look like a fresh kid? I'm a Space Cadet and I'm in the skit along with my brother, Fargo, and his fiancée, Albany Jones, who's a police lieutenant and the daughter of the mayor of Manhattan. I'm afraid they're all going to have something to say to you if you don't let me pass this minute."

"Yes? Well, here comes Mayor Jones. Talk to *him*, you fresh kid."

A big man in dress tunic stepped out of an official air car at the foot of the broad steps leading to the front door of the Metropolitan Museum of Art in the nation of Manhattan (now part of the Terran Federation).

Mayor Leo Jones had a massive head with a shock of sandy hair that made him resemble a good-humored but determined lion. He bounded up the steps and clapped Jeff on the shoulder. "What's wrong, Jeff, old man? Why are you hanging about out here and keeping Marie Antoinette waiting?"

The guard gulped and backed off, but Jeff said, "No problem, Mr. Mayor. I was a little late and was just about to present my identification."

"Forget it. You're with me," said the mayor.

Norby made a sardonic little bye-bye motion at the guard with one of his hands and marched ahead into the great hall and through the Egyptian wing with an air of owning the place, while Jeff and the mayor followed at a more sedate pace.

Despite his four eyes, Norby was moving too rapidly to get out of the way of the Holovision Director as she charged out of the auditorium.

There was a collision, and the director, a formidably large woman, said, "Oof," rubbed her bruised knee, and glared first at Norby and then at Jeff.

"Jefferson," she said, "you're late, and I don't want you letting that so-called teaching robot running about on his own. He's a menace! Are you aware this show is live? We have to start on time." She looked quickly at her watch. "You have to get into your costume and makeup *now.*"

"I'm sorry," muttered Jeff. "I'll do it as fast as I can." He hauled Norby off to the dressing room where he found Fargo already elegant in an elaborate wig and a costume that was a faultless fit. Too faultless, because it was skintight and he clearly would be unable to sit in it—or even move, perhaps.

Fargo greeted Jeff with an abrupt, "Well, what kept *you?*" and then turned away in order to continue arguing with the museum's Curator of History, a thin, anxious man.

"How can I tie the blasted ribbons around her neck when I'm wearing these tight lace gloves with only part of my fingers sticking out? I can hardly move them."

The curator sighed, "It's the director's orders. She insists on absolute authenticity of costume—which is ridiculous since the entire skit is fiction. Marie Antoinette probably never tried on the necklace. And if she had, she probably would have wanted to keep it. That would have been in keeping with her thoughtlessness and would have made her almost as unpopular as the loss of the necklace did. Obviously the novel by Alexander Dumas had it all wrong—"

Fargo interrupted. "I have no time to worry about the historical accuracy of the skit. I need practical help. Can't you fix a large simple clasp on the necklace so I can slip one end into the other with a nice click and have it done? How can I maneuver slippery ribbons into a knot that will hold while I'm wearing these gloves?"

The curator looked horrified. "A *clasp* on the Queen's necklace? We'd be a laughing stock! The whole point of the skit is to publicize this valuable acquisition—"

"It's not the original," protested Fargo. "As I understand it, the original no longer exists. This is just a paste replica."

4 JANET AND ISAAC ASIMOV

"Even so," said the curator patiently, "it is an *exact* paste replica and has enormous historical value. It would be unthinkable to fiddle with it. Haven't you seen it? The necklace is an open metal bib covered with diamonds—or rather, simulated diamonds. Fastened to metal loops at each side are ribbons that are tied about the neck. That's the way it was designed, and that's the way it must be shown. No clasps!"

"Ridiculous!" said Fargo.

"What's ridiculous," snapped the curator, "is a tall policewoman playing a short Marie Antoinette and a skinny fellow like you playing a fat Louis the Sixteenth. *That's* what's ridiculous!" The curator stalked out, slamming the door behind him.

Fargo shrugged at Jeff. "Such a fuss over a skit to make publicity for the museum. And you should see the security over the necklace—as though anyone would want to steal something that has only historical value."

Jeff had now struggled into his costume and was trying not to sneeze while a young woman powdered his face and darkened his eyebrows.

A metallic grating sound issued from Norby. He was chuckling.

"Both of you look silly in satin and lace. Wouldn't you rather be in a play about the French Revolution than do this fictitious renunciation scene? Read Dickens—"

"Norby," said Fargo, "don't give me any trouble. The museum wants to publicize the necklace, not the replica of a guillotine."

"But everyone knows this replica necklace is only junk used by the jewelers, Boehmer and Bossange, as a model to show to the possible buyers of the real diamond necklace, which was stolen, broken up, and the individual stones sold. It's gone. Why the fuss about the replica?"

"Humans are sentimental about history," said Jeff, trying to adjust his too-small wig. "This paste replica is the only physical reminder of the Queen's necklace and it has a romantic story, too. It turned up in the trunk of a family whose ancestors had emigrated from France, first to England and later to the United States. There was all kinds of excitement about identifying and authenticating it and more excitement about *which* museum would get it. Having the Metropolitan acquire it was a great victory for Manhattan."

"It probably cost a great deal and it isn't worth it," said Norby. "I've seen pictures of it and I think it's ugly. The metal holding the stones is dark. It's not silver, the way the real diamond necklace is supposed to have been. I still think the beheading of Marie Antoinette would be more interesting."

"No beheading for *my* Marie Antoinette," said Fargo, shaking his head and causing his heavy powdered wig to fall off and land at the feet of the director, who had just barged in.

"Put that back on!" she bellowed (her natural tone of voice). "We're ready to begin. The necklace will be taken out of its security container as soon as you're backstage."

Fargo said politely, "Would you mind picking up the wig? I can't bend in this stupid costume."

Jeff picked up the wig quickly before the director could make up her mind whether or not to perform the menial service.

The director looked Fargo up and down and smiled toothily. "I must say you're charming in this costume."

"Too tight," said Fargo.

"Exactly," said the director. "Come along."

Backstage, Albany stood next to Fargo, her powdered wig high and looped with jewels, the bodice of her gown cut low.

"You look stunning," whispered Fargo, "much too pretty to go to the guillotine."

"Don't forget," said Albany, "the King loses his head first."

"I already have," said Fargo grinning.

Jeff said, "Norby, what's the matter?" for Norby had suddenly extruded his sensor wire from his hat.

"I don't know. They've taken the fake necklace out of the security container and this is the first time I've been able to sense it. There's something odd about it."

"Silence!" shouted the director, shoving Jeff onto the stage.

The curtain rose and Jeff stared straight ahead, trying not to think of the glittering audience of city officials before him, or of the holovision cameras. The director's music synthesizer was giving out what was supposed to be 18th century French music. Then suddenly there was a trumpet blast. Jeff pulled open a door of the stage set, bowing as Fargo entered. Fargo walked forward carefully as he tried to keep his elaborate wig in balance.

"Ah, my faithful Jacques," said Fargo in Old French. "The Queen will arrive at any moment. She does not know I have a present for her."

He held up the little jewel box, covered with purple velvet, and Jeff's sharp eyes could almost hear the distant squeak of the simultaneous translation into Terran Basic through the earpieces affixed to each member of the audience.

Out of the corner of his eye he could see Norby's domed hat peeping around a backstage curtain in the wings. Norby's hand was waving at him.

Then it seemed as though someone had pulled Norby back. And soon afterward, Albany swept past the back curtain and through the open door as Jeff bowed low again.

Jeff could not hear the opening dialogue between King and Queen because Norby was trying to speak to him softly through the thin painted back wall of the set.

"Jeff," came Norby's voice. "It's something bad—dangerous—"

"Shut up!" came the hoarse whisper of the director.

"Let me tie the necklace around you, my love," said Fargo to Albany as he opened the box and displayed its contents. "Your beauty will enhance the diamonds."

"But we can't afford it," said Marie Antoinette, with her hands behind her back, not daring to touch the necklace lest she weaken. "France cannot afford it. We drove ourselves nearly into bankruptcy helping the Americans in their fight against Great Britain."

"My ministers said it was worth it to weaken Great Britain. Is it not a beautiful necklace?"

"Incredibly beautiful, but I do not wish it."

"Is it that you object because it was originally made for my grandfather in order that he might give it to the Dubarry woman?"

The Queen's nose tilted higher into the air. "I have no love for the Dubarry, but the necklace never touched her. No, it's my concern for France that stops me. Send the necklace back to Boehmer and Bossange. Perhaps someone else will pay the one million six hundred thousand *livres*."

"But I must see it on you, even if only once," said the King.

Jeff's nose was itching, but he couldn't scratch it, and it

seemed to him that backstage Norby was still trying to make him hear some warning.

"Ah, well. Just once," said Marie Antoinette, stepping into the brightest light on stage as Fargo took out the necklace and handed the box to Jeff, who put it on a side table.

Holding the heavy necklace by its smooth and slippery ribbons, Fargo advanced to the Queen and, of course, the ribbons slipped through his fingers and the necklace fell to the floor.

"A sign from the angels that this was not meant to be," ad-libbed Fargo in his role as King. He made a negligent gesture as though the matter were of no importance, and bent down to pick up the necklace—forgetting that kings do not do that sort of thing.

There was a loud, tearing sound and Fargo suddenly paled. Jeff wondered why his twenty-four-year-old brother should look so upset. And then he saw that the seat of Fargo's satin trousers had split neatly up the seam.

Fargo held the necklace irresolutely for a moment. He was supposed to tie it around Albany's neck from the front, while she faced the audience, but that would have meant displaying his backside, something he clearly did not intend to do. For a moment, he hesitated. Then he said, "Ho, Jacques, tie this necklace around the Queen's neck. I feel clumsy today."

An anguished but suppressed howl rose from behind the scenes as the Curator of History witnessed the terrible mistake of having any male who was not the King touch the Queen in so intimate a fashion.

Jeff ignored it and took the necklace from Fargo, who grabbed Jeff's hand for a moment.

In that moment Jeff heard in his mind a telepathic message from his brother—a telepathy made possible by their earlier adventures in space.

—Jeff, you've got to tie the blasted thing because I've split my trousers.

—I know, Your Majesty.

—Don't be funny, and tie it right.

Jeff approached the Queen respectfully, quite certain she had heard the seam split and knew what was going on. One could always trust Albany's intelligence.

What one couldn't trust was the necklace. Jeff placed it on

Albany's chest and tried to tie the ribbons behind her neck. But they wouldn't tie. However he knotted them, the ribbons started to give as soon as he let go. Fargo had moved to the other side of Albany and was trying, uselessly, to help.

Jeff continued to fumble while Albany stared over his shoulder at the audience and improvised a patter of French conversation that seemed to deal endlessly with the expenses of the crown and what she would like to buy for her little Trianon palace.

Jeff, desperate, noted that the two back tassels of the necklace seemed longer and sturdier than those in front. Each ended in a big diamond from which hung a bell-like arrangement with five connecting short chains of diamonds. It was very gaudy and Jeff felt himself beginning to agree with Norby that the necklace was ugly.

He could hear some slight tittering from the audience. He was taking too long. Breathing deeply, he took the two back tassels and looped them over each other, first once—not firm enough yet to hold the necklace in place—and then—

"Jeff! Wait!" Norby's voice was clearly audible.

But the audience was beginning to laugh and both Fargo and Albany seemed unable to continue. Jeff *couldn't* wait.

Jeff looped the back tassels a second time and yanked them into a tight knot. Fargo was pulling, too. Between that and the diamonds at the end of each tassel, the new knot would *have* to hold.

"Jeff," shouted Norby. "Don't do that!"

2

Into History

What Jeff realized first was that he wasn't on the stage at the Metropolitan Museum of Art.

The stage did not have an oriental carpet on the floor. Yet one was directly below Jeff's nose because he was lying on it. He turned his head and saw a high slit of a window and beyond it, rooftops silhouetted against what looked like the pale streaks of light in an early morning sky.

He rose to his feet and saw that he was in a small, dark room, lighted only by the window and the soft glow of an oil lamp on a heavy wooden desk.

"Ow! I think I've hit somebody," said Fargo.

"Where are we?" asked Albany. She was there, too. "And who's that?"

Lying unconscious near Fargo was a small man in brown costume, a necklace clutched in his left hand. A similar necklace, much shinier, had apparently fallen from his right hand. Albany picked it up.

"These look like real diamonds!" she said, crossing her long legs under the big skirt and rising with one athletic motion. "Have we found the real Queen's necklace?" It dangled from her hand, and in the daylight it was brighter than the dull replica around her neck.

Jeff was studying a newspaper on the desk. It was French, but despite the archaic typeface and its generally ancient appearance, the paper itself seemed quite new. He said, "I think we've travelled through time somehow. If this newspaper is the real thing, we're in France, Paris probably, and this is the 18th century. In fact, if this is yesterday's newspaper, this is the morning of February 1, 1785, the day the necklace was

9

delivered to Cardinal Rohan. He'd been led to believe that the Queen wanted him to buy it for her."

"Then that's Bossange. Or Boehmer," said Fargo, rising stiffly, the cloth of his underpants showing through the rip in his satin costume. "He's just knocked out, I hope. And where is that blasted robot of yours, Jeff? He can go through time. So I suppose he's responsible for all this."

"I'm sorry, Fargo. Norby's not here. He'd be all over me if he were."

"He *must* be here. How would we have travelled through time without him? And why here, I wonder? And why now? I tell you I'll scoop out that little monster's insides and use his barrel to store mothballs."

"But, Fargo," said Albany, "Norby wasn't on stage with us when we left. He couldn't have moved us through time without making physical contact with us, could he?"

"Actually," said Jeff, "he was trying to warn me not to tie the back tassels of the necklace. Is it possible that what we were fooling with was more than just a replica of the Queen's necklace? We were all three standing close together, in contact, and perhaps the replica was a time-travel device that was invented by someone, somewhere, sometime."

Fargo leaned against the desk and flicked at the lace on his wrists. "If we're going to imagine a mysterious time-travel device, we might as well imagine magic. That would be more fun."

"Scientists say that magic is a name we use for something we don't understand," said Jeff. "Albany, maybe it would be better if you took off the necklace."

"But if it brought us here, we'd better hang on to it tightly," said Albany. "How would we get home without it as a time-travel device? And wouldn't it be nice to go back home with the *authentic* Queen's necklace? That would surprise the museum authorities right out of their socks." She held the real diamonds next to the paste stones she was wearing. "See the difference?"

"The jeweler's waking up, assuming he *is* the jeweler," said Fargo. "Shall I hit him a little bit to keep him unconscious?"

"Don't," said Jeff. "If you injure him, history may be changed. And that goes double if we try to return with the real necklace."

"It's probably changed already," said Fargo. "Once we fall into the 18th century, practically anything we do will change history. And what *will* we do? I'll have to brush up on sword play. Or maybe that will go out of fashion with the French Revolution coming in only four years. And after that there will be that young soldier named Napoleon, who rose to become Emperor of France."

The jeweler began to call out weakly, "Bossange! Bossange!"

"This one is Boehmer then," said Jeff.

While the little jeweler, Boehmer, struggled to sit up, his eyes still closed, the replica necklace in his hand slipped to the carpet.

Albany let out a startled cry and Jeff saw with horror that the replica necklace had begun to wriggle like a snake across the carpet toward her.

"That's the same thing you're wearing," said Fargo. "I think I get it now. This is an example of one object at two different time periods and it's struggling to join itself!"

Still holding the real diamond necklace, Albany touched the replica tied around her neck. She stepped hastily away from the crawling replica on the floor.

"It's horrifying watching that thing crawl," she said. "I think I'd feel safer somewhere else." And with that she suddenly seemed to blink out. The replica necklace she'd been wearing was gone. The diamond necklace she'd been holding was gone. Now only the other replica remained.

Fargo rushed to the spot where Albany had been standing. "Where did she go? How?"

The replica necklace on the floor stopped moving the moment Albany vanished, and now lay still on the floor as if it had never tried to reach itself.

Boehmer opened his eyes, looked at his empty hands, and shouted in German-accented French. "Thieves! Help! Bossange! Thieves! We are being robbed!"

His partner, Bossange, entered the room with a pistol.

"We're American visitors—" began Fargo.

"They have stolen the necklace," shrieked Boehmer. "The real one. Bossange, hold the pistol ready. We will force them to give up what they have taken. I shall call the police. We must deliver the diamonds today. The cardinal will not be happy if we delay. Nor," and he looked at Fargo and Jeff with savagery in his eyes, "will the Queen of France. It's the Bastille for you."

And it was. Nor did Jeff and Fargo enjoy it, for the Bastille dungeons were dark, damp, and dirty. And they smelled terrible.

"If only Albany hadn't picked up the real diamonds," said Jeff. He spoke in Terran Basic, for there was another prisoner in the dungeon with them. "Then the jewelers would have no charge against us except breaking and entering. Now they think we threw the necklace out the window to a confederate."

Fargo sat down on a moldy bench. "If only she hadn't disappeared with the necklace. Or if only we had the slightest idea where she was. She's probably in a different time period altogether, I suppose."

"Maybe she went back to Manhattan," said Jeff. *"Our* Manhattan."

"Maybe," said Fargo. "But without the replica and without Norby, we can't go anywhere." He sighed. "I never thought that Space Command's top secret agent would go to the guillotine."

"You won't be guillotined," said Jeff as he stared at the third person in the room in an absent way—there didn't seem to be any use at this point in making friends. "The guillotine hasn't been invented yet."

"I don't remember much of the ancient history Norby tried to pour into me," said Fargo. "What happens instead? Do they hack off your head with an axe?"

"If you're an aristocrat, they do. If we can't convince them we're aristocrats, we're hanged. Or drawn and quartered. Or broken at the wheel."

"That doesn't sound like fun."

"It isn't," said Jeff. He shivered. He wasn't shivering entirely at the thought of execution. Since it was indeed February 1, the room was cold.

The other prisoner of the room spoke up. "Pardon me, my friends. You speak a language to me unknown. Is it, then, that you do not speak French?"

Fargo said, "We are Americans, but we speak French." And he said it in French.

The other prisoner said, "Ah! Then shall we speak French?

Permit me to introduce myself." He was a middle-aged man, but he was no bigger than a large child. "My name is Marcel Oslair and I am delighted to make your acquaintance. I have not much time for making acquaintances or for keeping them now, and I will not be fatiguing you with my presence for long. I am to be executed this afternoon."

For all that had happened since Fargo, Jeff, and Albany had been dropped into the jewelry shop of Boehmer and Bossange, it was still morning.

"We will be served our one meal of the day soon," Marcel continued, "and I am afraid that in spite of there being few prisoners in the Bastille right now, the food leaves much to be desired. May I have the pleasure of knowing your names, my dear sirs?"

"I'm Fargo Wells and this is my brother Jeff. But tell us, why are you going to be executed? You don't have the appearance of a desperate criminal."

"Alas, it is not necessary to be a desperate criminal to be executed, my friends. Or necessary even to be guilty. Mine is a sad story, for I am completely innocent of any crime." Marcel's smile lit his thin, dirty face like a lamp. "All prisoners say that, of course, but in my case it happens to be true. I come from a family of clockmakers, but you have probably not heard of the Oslair clocks and automata if you are foreign spies—"

"Spies!" said Fargo indignantly.

"I crave pardon," said Marcel apologetically. "As you were being brought in, one of the guards told me I would have the honor of playing host to a pair of foreign spies. I took you to be Austrians, in league with our foreign queen."

"We are certainly not Austrians."

"I see then why I did not understand your language, for I speak a bit of German."

"We are Americans."

Marcel looked doubtful. "It is true I don't understand English, but how can you be Americans? Does not all the world know that Americans wear simple homespun clothes? And you do not have an American accent."

"Fargo," said Jeff impatiently, "let Marcel finish telling us why he's here." He turned to the little man. "When you say your family made automata, did you mean robots?"

"I do not know that word," said Marcel hesitantly. "Is it an English word?"

"Well, yes, in a way," said Jeff, reddening a bit. How could he forget that the word, robot, which was Czech in origin, would not be applied to mechanical men for another century and a third? "What I meant was, did your family make mechanical men?"

"Ah, yes, and ladies who played the harpsichord, and birds that laid eggs, and many other wonders. Some of the automata were life-sized and since I have always been small, I could get inside to work the machinery. Those were great days for my family, but alas, all of my people are gone now, and I am the last of the Oslairs." He shook his head sadly. "In a few hours I will be gone, too," he said.

"You have not yet told us how you come to be in the Bastille," Jeff said.

"You see, my friend, after I was left alone, I found no way of earning a living by myself and I was forced to sell the automata, one by one. Finally I had left but one goose and it caused my downfall."

"A mechanical goose?"

"Indeed. When my landlord grew importunate for his rent, I sold the goose, too, and, through misfortune, to a villain who filled the inside with stolen gold and shipped it to England. I was blamed both for the theft and the treachery of shipping French gold to another country. I had no bill of sale, and the man was a known criminal, though not to me. He vanished across the border. No one believed my story, and I had no family left to help me."

"Terrible," said Jeff. "Was there no trial?"

"But, of course there was," said Marcel. "We are not savages here. I was quickly convicted, however. The judges were not going to believe a little clockmaker when it was more important to show how efficient they were in convicting and punishing a criminal—whether he was a criminal or not. So now I must be ready to die. It is not so bad. I will be joining the rest of my family, perhaps, wherever they have gone. My dear father and mother—my younger brother—"

Fargo removed his heavy wig and used it as a pillow. He said, "Marcel, if we can think of a way of getting out of the Bastille, we will try to take you with us."

"My friend, you are most kind."

"But for now, I seem to have lost a night somewhere, and I must sleep a short while."

"Sleep well," said Marcel cheerfully.

Fargo could sleep anywhere and under any conditions, and was soon snoring while Jeff continued to rack his brains for a way out.

"Marcel," he said softly, "why do you think Americans dress in homespun?"

"All the world knows it," said Marcel, puzzled at the question. "And they don't wear wigs."

Jeff removed his. It was uncomfortable anyway, and it was bad enough to be dressed in tight satin clothes.

Marcel nodded. "Cher papa does not approve of wigs."

"Your late father?"

"Ah, and you insist you are an American. Do you not know that the American ambassador, Benjamin Franklin, is called 'cher papa' by the ladies of the court?"

"Franklin! Yes, he must still be here in France! I forgot."

"Monsieur Franklin does not dress as you and your brother do," said Marcel.

"Could I see him, I wonder?"

"Alas, he is old and often ill. He rarely leaves his home in Passy."

"Where's that?"

"A short distance from Paris, on the way to Versailles."

"Could someone get there with a message in a short time?"

"Less than an hour with a horse," said Marcel.

Jeff ran to the door and yelled for the guard. "I demand to see Benjamin Franklin, my compatriot! There will be trouble with the United States of America if you don't send for him!"

No one answered, and Marcel laughed. "That new country you claim as your own is very small and weak, and in no condition to take offense at anything a great power like France might want to do to foreign spies."

"But I'm not a spy. I'm only fourteen."

"Old enough and big enough to be a soldier or a spy."

Jeff sat down next to Fargo and tried to think. If he couldn't talk to Franklin, the only hope was Norby, but could the robot respond? Did he still exist?

His back was against Fargo's back and the contact allowed

the thought to cross over telepathically. Fargo yawned and said in Terran Basic, "I agree. Summon Norby. Perhaps the replica took Albany to Versailles. Perhaps it reacts to the way one is dressed. With Norby we'll be able to look for her there."

"I'm trying, but he's several centuries and almost five thousand kilometers away from us."

"He's your robot, Jeff. He tunes into you better than anyone. It's the only chance I see at the moment."

"But, Fargo, suppose our coming here has changed history and there's no Norby in the future, in our own time? Suppose *we* don't exist in our future either?"

"We exist here."

"But—"

"Jeff," said Fargo firmly. "Don't invent catastrophes. Let's pretend Norby exists, and you try to reach him. Besides, our clockmaker friend feels left out when we talk in Terran Basic."

"Sorry, Marcel," Jeff said in French. "I need to meditate—to sit in silence and think deeply. Do you know what I mean?"

"Certainly. I used to meditate while waiting for my father to give me the signal when I was inside the big automata. It made the waiting easier and made me calmer for any task ahead."

"That's what I need," said Jeff. "I have a very difficult task ahead." And he settled down to attempt it.

3

THE EXECUTIONER'S BLOCK

The dank, grey walls of the Bastille seemed to close in on Jeff. It was so hard to concentrate. Reaching Norby seemed impossible, and after half an hour, he gave up.

He began pacing up and down the miserable chamber, while Fargo and Marcel, having nothing better to do, watched him, their eyes turning back and forth.

Jeff stopped suddenly. He had an idea.

"Fargo," he said, "there's a pen in my inside jacket pocket. Do you have any paper?"

"Paper? You're kidding. This stupid costume's so tight that I had to leave everything in the dressing room."

Jeff thought for a moment and decided he didn't need his inside pocket. He ripped it out and began to write on the material, which was white cotton because the museum had not thought it necessary to line the inside of the costume with satin.

"Is that English?" asked Marcel, looking on.

"Yes, it is," said Jeff.

"The pen writes even though you haven't dipped it in ink."

"An American invention," said Fargo smoothly. "News of it has not yet spread to other countries."

"Fascinating," said Marcel.

Looking over Jeff's shoulder, Fargo said, "What kind of message is that? 'We must all hang together or, most assuredly, we shall all hang separately.' It doesn't mean anything."

"Franklin will recognize the words," said Jeff. "Now give me the top button from your waistcoat, Fargo. Mine aren't gold-colored."

"But they're only gold-colored plastic."

"Exactly why I want one to send to Franklin."

"My friends—the jailer is opening the door with our meal," said Marcel. "Can't you smell it?"

"Unfortunately, I can," said Fargo, removing his lace gloves and stuffing them into his waistcoat pocket. The ends of his fingers, which had not been covered by the gloves, were dirty and there was no place to wash. "I suppose I'll have to eat whatever slop they give us with these fingers."

Jeff stepped to the door and bowed as the jailer walked in holding a steaming bowl of something grey and lumpy. "Sir, we are wellborn Americans and we wish to send a message to Benjamin Franklin, who will surely reward you for any news concerning us. Will you send this message to him, with this button?"

"Gold!" said the jailer greedily.

"Not at all," said Jeff. "You can tell for yourself it is too light in weight. Weigh it in your hand."

The jailer did so, and spat to one side. "Painted wood! Why do you want to send this?"

"Why, as proof that they are indeed Americans in spite of their aristocratic garb," put in Marcel. "Who but these rustics from the wild western forests would dress up to visit Versailles, yet wear buttons like these. No Austrian or Frenchman would dream of it."

"That's right," said Jeff, relieved at Marcel's coming up with so pat an explanation.

"Jailer," went on Marcel with increased confidence, "in your hand you have proof that these men are undoubtedly Americans and not Viennese spies."

"So what?" said the jailer. "They still stole a diamond necklace and will be executed in a few days if the necklace is not returned. Or even if it is. And what care I? I have my wife Marie and my own children to feed, and I shall not do that long if I spend too much time talking to prisoners."

"On the other hand, you will feed your family better if you carry this message and the button to the good Franklin. Even if these men are to be executed, Franklin would still pay for the privilege of seeing them before they die. He is rich. He may pay you a year's wages. What would that sum be to him?"

"There is that possibility," said the jailer, his grimy fist closing around Jeff's scrap of cotton and the button of a material that did not exist in Franklin's time. "Now eat your nice gruel, you scum, and if this man Franklin does not pay, you spies will have a most miserable time before you die."

Fargo inspected the food after the jailer had gone. "I always did hate hot cereals, especially lumpy ones, but if we're not going to eat again until tomorrow, I suppose we ought to try to get some of it down."

Marcel produced two pieces of wood he had apparently kept as clean as possible. "My friends, here are two plates. Pray divide the food and eat as much as you wish. Since my own execution is nigh, there is no reason for me to weigh myself down needlessly with food."

"You can't tell," said Fargo, his irrepressible optimism bouncing back in spite of the food and the jailer's threat. "Better eat a good third of it, Marcel. We will persuade the good Benjamin Franklin to buy your freedom, too."

"Impossible, I'm afraid. He might send word to you, but he will not come himself. Jouncing in a carriage is very hard on the old man."

"Even a messenger might be of help."

"Agreed," said Marcel. "A message from Franklin might buy enough time for you to give the authorities a chance of finding the jewels you are supposed to have stolen. But as for me, there will be no time for help. I will be gone, perhaps, before the messenger even arrives. Nevertheless, my friends, I thank you heartily for your intended kindness to me."

All three of them worried down the gruel in silence and drank from the pitcher of stale water that the jailer had also brought.

Fargo said, "I wonder if we'll ever find Albany. I keep telling myself she's a cop, a strong, brave cop who can take care of herself, but I can't bear the thought of losing her somewhere in time."

Jeff said, "I'm sure that wherever she is, she is much safer than we are. And if she's in Versailles and hears about us she might even arrange our release."

Fargo said, "You scribbled something else on that message to Franklin before you gave it to the jailer. Did it have anything to do with Albany?"

"Not quite. It was something else. I wanted him to bring a

small lightning rod with him. I thought it might help me reach Norby."

"You mean, like an antenna."

"More or less. I'll snatch at any chance."

They had grown accustomed to speaking in French and were doing so without thought.

Marcel, who had been listening with a look of intense interest on his face, said, "My dear friends, do not be offended if I ask a question. I know well the lightning rod, which, after all, is an invention of your compatriot, Franklin. All the world knows of this and of its miraculous way of fending off the lightning bolt. But who is this Norby you speak of whom you wish to reach? Is it another powerful compatriot?"

"In a way," said Jeff. "Norby is an automaton, like those your family made, but much more advanced. I can give him orders by talking to him, even across a distance."

"You tell me this seriously? You are not amusing yourself at the expense of a poor man who is about to die?" said Marcel earnestly.

"No, no, Marcel. I tell you nothing but the truth. My automaton speaks and reasons and has marvellous abilities."

"Alas, alas. I wish to believe you, but to do so would increase my unhappiness a hundredfold. I would like to see this automaton. If it is indeed as you say, I would give my life to see it—but instead I must give my life before I see it. How sad I am!"

"If we can save your life, Marcel," said Jeff, "then perhaps you will see Norby in time. It all depends on Franklin."

"Ah, the good Franklin. He is a scientist and he is interested in automata, too. He attended one of the last exhibitions given by my father before he died. Yes, he did. Even," (here Marcel paused dramatically) "even His Majesty, Louis the Sixteenth attended and spoke graciously to my father. His Majesty is a skilled locksmith, you must know. It is indeed a great pity he was born to the kingship, having such a future as a locksmith and mechanic."

Fargo asked, "Does the King know you are in prison?"

"Would that be likely?" said Marcel. "Who would bother to tell him? But you must not concern yourself with me, but with yourselves. Will Monsieur Franklin truly recognize that the false gold button was made in America? He has not been there for many years and he may not know this new invention."

"He'll know that the button wasn't made in Europe," said Jeff. "He's a very intelligent man."

"So he is. There are those who think he is in league with the devil—did you know that? I have heard some ignorant folk say that the lightning rod is a powerful magic and dangerous to use."

Fargo said, "I hope you don't believe that."

"Not at all. My father taught me that every automaton was simply a mechanism that could be understood, even though the onlookers suspected supernatural powers. And with that, I grew firmly convinced that there is no magic. Although your pen that writes without ink is a little hard to understand. And I can't help but wonder at an automaton that responds to spoken commands. Perhaps there is a small person within Norby, someone my size?" Marcel questioned.

"No, no," said Jeff. "There's only machinery inside my Norby. He's much smaller than you are."

"Then if he can move freely, his clockwork must be quite minuscule. Would he be light enough to be lifted by balloon?"

"What kind of balloon?"

"Why, a balloon. Surely you have heard of the balloons that have recently risen, carrying people. Some say it will be the next step in transportation! But they are dangerous, I think. They are filled with hydrogen, which can easily go up in flames. Do you have balloons in the nation of the United States?"

Fargo said, "Not yet." Then, suddenly frowning, "I wish I could get into a balloon and rescue Albany. I keep thinking she's in Versailles. After all, that's where the Queen's necklace, the real one, was supposed to go."

Jeff, remembering that Albany had both the replica and the necklace with the real diamonds, wondered how the court would react to Albany's appearing in their midst. He shrugged.

Marcel said, "Careful, my friends. Sometimes these walls have ears, for there are guards who are supposed to listen when we are unwary and talk among ourselves. If you speak of jewels, then you will be beyond help. Even Franklin wouldn't save you if you have actually stolen jewels belonging to the court."

"I assure you, Marcel," said Jeff. "We have stolen no

jewels—but we can't explain what really happened. No one would believe us."

He was beginning to wonder if anything might be heard from Franklin. The old man was only a few miles away, but this was 18th-century France. There were no forms of powered transportation. The steam engine had been invented but it had not yet been added to ships or locomotives. Of course, there were no gasoline or nuclear engines, and no one had even imagined the antigrav devices that lifted cars and the hyperdrive that powered spaceships in Jeff's own century. In the France of Louis the Sixteenth, all people who wished to travel over land either walked, rode horses, or rode in vehicles pulled by horses.

Jeff had just decided that no one would come—or that if someone came, it would be too late—when the jailer's big key grated in the lock.

Fargo, never the pessimist, jumped up eagerly. "Franklin?"

But Marcel shook his head. "I fear it is only my impending doom. They have come to lead me to the execution. See—there is the executioner behind the jailer. He wears a black mask, for he does not wish to be recognized. It is a shameful occupation, though of course a most necessary one."

"You mean he's going to do it here?" said Jeff.

"Don't want to get this nice dungeon all bloody, do we?" said the second jailer—he was not the same one who had gone off with the message. He smiled evilly, for he had several teeth missing and looked as if he had fangs. "We take this condemned man out to the executioner's block. The executioner, Petit-Paul here," (he jerked a thumb at the hulking, massive man behind him) "wants to get a look at the two spies he will take care of tomorrow. He is a most conscientious worker."

"But we are not spies—we're honest Americans," said Jeff desperately.

The jailer shrugged. "Call yourselves what you wish. You will be executed as spies."

Marcel tugged at Jeff's sleeve. "There is no use arguing with the jailer, my friend. Come, let us instead ask him a favor.—Jailer, may these American gentlemen come into the inner courtyard that they may pray for me when I die? Surely you will not deny a dying man a last gift."

The jailer grinned again. "You wish these men who will die tomorrow to watch you die today? Instead of a priest? Why not? You will but go to the kingdom down below the more surely."

Jeff said, "But Marcel, we cannot bear—"

Marcel said, "Please, my friends. You have made my last hours pleasurable with your company. I will die more easily for your continued company. My only regret is that I will never see your automaton, friend Jeff."

The executioner's block was horribly stained with dried blood. Jeff wished he hadn't come, although the cold air helped to clear his mind. If only he could concentrate on Norby, all might yet be well—but all he could think of was poor shivering Marcel ready to march between the armed soldiers lined up before the executioner's block.

For some reason, Marcel was beaming. "I'm to be decapitated," he said. "But that is wonderful."

"Wonderful?" said Jeff with stupefaction.

"Indeed. How proud my father would feel if he knew. Decapitation is for aristocrats. Poor devils like myself are hanged. This is the good King's work. He did not wish a fellow clockmaker to be hanged as though he were scum. He *did* hear about me after all."

Fargo said, "It would be better if he freed you."

Marcel shrugged. "You ask too much. The Austrian Queen and her favorites would never allow it. And they have too much power over the softhearted King."

"Come," growled the jailer. "I'm not here to listen to all this fine talk. I'm a hardworking man and so is Petit-Pierre. Others wait their turn. On your knees before the block, small criminal—"

But at that moment, Jeff heard footsteps pounding through the courtyard. A plainly-dressed young man ran up to them, accompanied by a puffing fat man to whom the jailer and the executioner bowed respectfully, while the soldiers presented arms.

"I'm Benjamin Franklin's grandson," said the young man in perfect French. He looked from one prisoner to another and then addressed Fargo. "My name is also Benjamin, but I am usually known as Benny. The Lieutenant of the Bastille has permitted me to interview you in order to find out if you are really Americans."

The lieutenant said haughtily, "The United States is an ally of France. If, therefore, you are American citizens, I will place you in the custody of Mr. Franklin. If, however, the jewels are not recovered and it is clear that you participated in the theft, you will be executed—Americans or not. The King's justice is not to be overturned."

"Lieutenant," said Fargo, "we didn't steal anything. My brother and I are the famous Wells brothers, American actors and conjurers. We're in Paris to give a show."

The lieutenant snorted. "Then what were you doing at the Boehmer-Bossange establishment? Practicing levitation in diamonds?"

Fargo bestowed a brilliant smile upon him. "No, Lieutenant. I am sure the jewelers will find that they themselves have merely mislaid whatever it is they claim they have lost. The truth is—"

Jeff held his breath. He himself hated to lie and was so bad at it he had given up trying, but he had to admire Fargo's easy glibness.

"—we wanted to have an early performance today."

"Where, Sir Conjurer?"

"In the woods near Le Trianon, hoping to please the Queen."

"In the woods? In the very middle of winter?"

"We Americans are hardy people and I am of the northern forests. We hoped the Queen would see us from her window."

"And you could see the ladies, no doubt? Are all you Americans like your Franklin?"

"Be more respectful to my grandfather, Lieutenant," said Benny indignantly.

"I assure you, sir," said the lieutenant, leering, "I admire him. His popularity with the ladies, at his age—"

"And so," continued Fargo, "my brother and I were searching for a tailor, without whom we would not be able to perform."

"Why did you need a tailor?"

Silently Fargo turned around and bent over.

It was clear to Jeff that the lieutenant was impressed with the evidence of the need.

Fargo went on. "We inquired about a tailor's shop, and some lout gave us the wrong direction. He told us to bang on the back door, which we did. The door opened and we found Monsieur Boehmer lying on the floor, unconscious. Perhaps he had been robbed, but not by us. When he woke, he accused *us* of theft."

Marcel said, "That sounds convincing."

The lieutenant cast a look of disapproval at him. "Not convincing. Merely suggestive. You must convince me that you are genuinely American. Your accent is odd."

Benny interposed. "These gentlemen knew my grandfather's words to the signers of the Declaration of Independence about hanging together or hanging separately—but perhaps we need additional evidence. Can you speak English as well as write it?"

Fargo cleared his throat. "'When in the course of human events, it becomes necessary for one people to dissolve the political bands which have connected them with another...'"

Fargo's resonant tenor went on, speaking English with only a slight Terran accent. "'We hold these truths to be self-evident, that all men are created equal, that they are endowed by their Creator with certain unalienable rights, that among these are life, liberty, and the pursuit of happiness...'"

"Excellent," said Benny, "although your accent is a trifle odd. Are you from one of the wilder western territories?"

"Sort of," said Fargo, "but we are definitely Americans."

"And reciting revolutionary and seditious nonsense," muttered the lieutenant. "I understand enough English to know *that*."

"It was the American Declaration of Independence, Lieutenant, an independence your gracious king was pleased to help us achieve," said Benny. He turned to Fargo. "My grandfather was intrigued by your button and wishes to discuss it with you, but he was puzzled by your request for a lightning rod."

"Did you bring one?" asked Jeff, trying to stand between Marcel and the lieutenant and afraid each instant that the latter would suddenly order the execution to proceed.

"In this old sword-stick," said Benny, unscrewing the head of a cane he had brought. "I assure you, Lieutenant, that there's no sword in here. May I bring out the lightning rod?"

"Let him," said the executioner in a hoarse voice. "I have always wanted to see a lightning rod up close. They say they are made in the devil's workshop."

Benny took out the small lightning rod and put it in Jeff's outstretched hand.

Petit-Paul muttered, "It is only an iron stick. Is that all?" He sounded dreadfully disappointed.

"Thanks," said Jeff, putting both hands around it and closing his eyes.

"Pay no attention to him," said Fargo. "In the chaos of our arrest, we lost our wands. I can do without; I use my hands. My brother, however, insists on a wand, and with it he acts to make an automaton appear—a mere conjurer's trick, of course."

"My grandfather is most interested in automata," said Benny, "and I am quite convinced you are Americans. With the lieutenant's permission, I will take you to Passy to meet my grandfather. Do you have your automaton with you?"

"Let us see," said Fargo. "If my brother's conjuring works properly, he will come to the lightning rod, floating through the air by means of an invisible balloon."

"Incredible," said Benny. "Does it come to the lightning rod because there is a magnetic sympathy?"

The lieutenant became suddenly aware that other business was being neglected. "Get on with this execution," he roared. "Petit-Paul, we do not pay you to play the role of an ugly statue."

Petit-Paul growled deep in his throat and motioned to Marcel. "Your head down on the block, you."

Jeff thought, Please, Norby, tune into me. Then he looked up at the block to see Marcel waving at him.

Having attracted Jeff's attention, Marcel said cheerfully, "Good-bye, my American friends. I am so happy to have known you."

Jeff dashed up to the block, one hand outstretched and the other still holding the lightning rod. Before the executioner could object, he shook Marcel's hand and was embarrassed when the little prisoner clung to him, kissing him on both cheeks.

It had started to snow a bit earlier and the flakes were now coming down hard and steadily. The flakes melted on Jeff's face and the moisture hid the tears.

"Good-bye, Marcel. I tried—I'm so sorry—"

"Jeff," Marcel cried out excitedly. "Something has appeared over your head. The snow is falling about it. And now—legs—arms—oh, such happiness! It must be your automaton!"

"Norby," yelled Fargo. "Take the little man and Jeff out of here. I'll be with Benjamin Franklin. Marcel, get on Jeff's back."

Every soldier in the place—the executioner, the jailer, the lieutenant—all seemed transfixed, unable to interfere.

"The balloon is really invisible," said Marcel, jumping onto Jeff's back and staring upward. His voice was ecstatic.

"Jeff," asked Norby, "is that man with the axe going to do something I wouldn't like?"

"Right!" Jeff dropped the lightning rod and grabbed Norby's hand as the robot dropped farther down.

Norby said, "Then it's time to leave." And suddenly it wasn't snowing anymore.

4

Time Trouble

Jeff felt woozy. He could see that they had landed in someone's room, but he felt himself to be still floating. He was standing on a faded, worn rug, but it seemed insubstantial beneath his feet. All the massive furniture was carved from dark wood, as were the glass-front bookcases. Floor-to-ceiling glass doors in one wall opened onto a terrace and beyond there was a formal garden in bloom, although Jeff found it difficult to see anything clearly.

"I see everything blurry," said Norby. "Do you?"

"Everything is clear to me except you two," said Marcel. "You two seem faded, as if I can almost see through you." He was standing near a table piled with papers, and he held one up. "Everything in life has suddenly become a puzzle, so I don't mind one more. See, Jeff, this newspaper is in English, I am certain, and the date is April 16, 1896. How is that possible? Can we have moved by some powerful science into the future and into England?"

"I was trying to get home," said Norby, "but I think the necklace brought me here. It's lying on the shelf in that bookcase."

Jeff and Norby looked at the necklace. Except for being dusty, it seemed the same as the replica Albany had worn for the ill-fated skit in Manhattan.

"Please," said Marcel. "Is this travel-in-time the deed of the automation that speaks for itself?"

"I'll try to explain," said Jeff. And in as few words as possible, making use of terms he thought would be understood by a man of the 18th century, he explained about robots and about Norby's abilities. "Can you believe me, Marcel?"

Marcel looked pale. "It is very difficult, my friend. You are from still farther in the future and you make use of advanced science. I try to believe, Jeff, but thinking of it gives me a headache."

"Listen, Jeff," said Norby, "we're in danger, and we can't stay here. I've been trying to tune into our own time. The necklace replica is definitely there, but something is awfully wrong. Ever since I was near it in the museum, I've felt it pull me, but—"

"But if that's the case," said Jeff, trying to focus, "if the replica is home and is pulling you, why don't you just follow the pull and go home, Norby?"

Norby said, "Well, I think history has changed."

Jeff said, "You mean that because history has changed, there's no way we can go home? That we don't exist there in this new history? Maybe the world as we know it doesn't exist? Is that what you are saying?"

"That's what I am saying, Jeff. Starting now in the 18th century, there must be two time-tracks, because something you, Fargo, or Albany did when you entered the 18th century started a new track. Marcel belongs to the past, so he fits into either track and he's here. You and I, Jeff, don't belong at all to one of the tracks. And as far as this track is concerned, this is the farthest forward I can get. And maybe only because the necklace replica is here. Even so we don't fit here and we're fading out."

"Fading out of existence?"

"That's right."

"We can't allow that, Norby. We must go back and correct the mistake that changed history," Jeff said.

"I suppose it was something that stupid Fargo did. He always acts without thinking."

"Wait, Norby. Don't jump to conclusions. It might be something Albany did in Versailles, or wherever she went. And she's wearing the replica that travels in time. Look, Albany was wearing the device, and the jewelers also had it. The two replicas were the same, although in different time periods. One of those two entered history as it was supposed to, for here it is in England. If we take this replica, it might guide us back to the other version of itself. And in that way we'll get either to Albany or the jewelers, depending on which version this is. Then we'll find out what's been happening to change history."

Jeff, totally unconcerned with the fact that he was planning burglary, tried to open the door of the cabinet. His hand went right through it as if there wasn't any piece of furniture there.

"I'm solid," said Marcel. "I could take it out for you."

"No," said Norby. "Don't do it. That's not the answer. We'd just be upsetting this time-track and setting up a total of *three* time-tracks. We have to find the necklace at the point in time where everything was changed. And then we must shift the time-tracks back to what they were. The trouble is, I don't know how we can find it."

"Someone is coming!" said Marcel, pointing to the garden.

A tall, thin man in a tweed suit, carrying a potted geranium plant, ambled through the garden, opened the glass door, and entered the library.

"Bless my soul, a guest!"

"I speak only French, sir," said Marcel with an expressive wave of his hands, "and I apologize for intruding on your privacy. We have come here by mistake."

"That is fine! I speak French, too, as you now see. But you say 'we'. Are there others here?" The man looked about him in a rather confused manner. "I see only you."

"Pardon." Marcel looked down at his shabby, dirty clothes. "I am a French actor, rehearsing for a play about prisoners in the Bastille over a hundred years ago and—"

"Ah, I see, and well-costumed too. Jolly good thing, I've often thought, that they tore down the Bastille during the French Revolution—"

"They did? There was a revolution?" Marcel sat down abruptly in a chair.

"In 1789. How can you not remember? July 14 is the French national holiday, the anniversary of the fall of the Bastille."

"Yes, of course," said Marcel. "I have periods of forgetfulness." He passed his hand over his forehead and said, "Do not be alarmed sir. I am not a dangerous lunatic. I have never harmed anyone in my life. Still, I sometimes think I hear voices and see visions. A harmless peculiarity."

The Englishman laughed. "Oh, well, we have our eccentrics in this country as well, and the English have long known that the French are capable of anything."

He pulled at a bell rope hanging near the cabinet and sat down. "I have rung for tea. Please remain seated. You look hungry and in need of something to eat to restore your mental clarity. If you need a bath, I can supply that, but I don't think I have clothes that would fit you."

"Pray do not discommode yourself," said Marcel. "I thank you for your hospitality. Something to eat and drink is all I need and then I will leave."

Jeff whispered, "Ask him how he got the necklace and what he's going to do with it."

"Remarkable," said the Englishman. "Are you a ventriloquist? Your lips did not move but I thought I could hear faint sounds, almost like words, coming from a few feet to your left."

"Your pardon, sir. I make these mistakes. But tell me about some of the things here. I could not help but notice the necklace in your cabinet. It resembles pictures of one that was famous in France."

"The Queen's necklace," said the gentleman, smiling. "You might wonder why I leave it in an unlocked cabinet for anyone to take who wanders in as you did—"

"Oh, sir—"

"I am not accusing you. But the necklace is a worthless duplicate, and is only there as a curio. It was brought to England after the French Revolution."

"As I recall, the real diamonds were stolen and blame for the affair fell upon the Queen," said Marcel, repeating the words Jeff had whispered in his ear.

"So it was. I know the story well. The jewelers thought Cardinal Rohan was buying the necklace on the Queen's orders. They took it to him on the first of February in 1785. That same day, Rohan handed it to the Countess de la Motte, who gave it to a man she said was the Queen's messenger. Rohan received a paper in return, supposedly signed by the Queen."

"But it was not the Queen's messenger?" asked Marcel, his eyes alight with interest.

The tea arrived and Marcel's eyes widened even more, for it was a lavish high tea, deposited by a little parlor maid who curtseyed and looked, with distinct disapproval, at the small guest with the dirty face and dirty clothes. She curtseyed again and left as the Englishman poured out tea and urged cakes, sandwiches, and scrambled eggs on the starving Frenchman.

"The messenger was a man working for the thief, La Motte," continued the Englishman, while Jeff's mouth watered for food he couldn't pick up, much less taste. "He was conspiring with his wife to steal the necklace. She was ultimately caught, branded, and whipped. When she escaped later to England, she wrote an article vilifying Marie Antoinette. Eventually, most Frenchmen believed that their foreign queen had indeed tried to buy the necklace secretly and had used La Motte as a scapegoat. Not true, of course, but when everyone believes a lie, it might as well be the truth."

"Marcel," said Jeff, "ask him if he thinks the affair of the Queen's necklace brought about the Revolution."

"Odd," said the Englishman, "but it has just fallen into my head that there is some question about whether the affair of the Queen's necklace caused the Revolution. Certainly, Napoleon said he thought so. And certainly it brought the Queen into such unpopularity that it was impossible for the royal family to ride out the Revolution. They were inevitably beheaded."

Marcel nodded calmly, even though he must have been profoundly shocked at the statement that the King and Queen lost their lives in violent insurrections.

When tea was over at last Marcel rose and bowed courteously. "Your hospitality has been superb, sir," he said. "I am deeply honored and immensely grateful. My mind feels much clearer. Before leaving might I ask what you plan to do with the replica you have."

"Why, nothing at all. It will simply sit in my cabinet."

"Very well. I must find my way back to the rest of my troupe. Thank you once again, and if ever you need the help of Marcel Oslair, you may count on it in full measure." And he bowed again.

The Englishman bowed, too. "Glad to have been of help. If you are ever in the neighborhood again, Monsieur Oslair, please return and we can talk again of the Queen's necklace. It is an interesting story."

Marcel paused in the doorway to the garden. "Sir, do you believe in marvellous things to come?"

"Why not? I have read 'The Time Machine', the new novel

by Mr. Herbert George Wells, and it struck me that I would like to go into the future and see what is to come."

"Perhaps I shall," said Marcel, smiling shyly. "They say the mad are not bound to one time and place."

"Possibly, but I must get back to my work. Cheerio!"

Marcel opened the glass doors and walked out into the sunlight of the garden. Norby and Jeff sailed past him.

"Come to that grove of trees, Marcel," said Jeff. "We'll try time-travelling from there. Then no one will see you vanish."

Marcel walked out into the colorful summer garden. It had been winter in France just an hour earlier, but it seemed summer now in England. He said, "I am reluctant to leave this pleasant place."

Norby seized his hand and pulled him toward the woods. "Too bad, Marcel," he said sharply, "but perhaps you don't notice that Jeff is growing fainter and fainter. Do you want him to disappear forever, to vanish out of existence?"

Marcel slapped his forehead in dismay. "I am a villain. I have utterly forgotten." He ran along ahead of them into the cool dimness of the wood.

"Jeff," he said, "my profoundest regrets, good friend. I shouldn't have had tea. It endangered your life."

"No, I wanted you to eat, and I wanted you to ask about the necklace." Jeff could now see nothing but a faint and colorless outline of the landscape around him.

Norby was fading, too, but less so. Part of him was of alien manufacture and appeared stable in this time-track.

"Hurry, Norby," said Jeff. "Take me back to somewhere before the time-tracks diverged. I don't want to fade out completely."

5

BACK-WHERE?

"It's so dark I can't see you, Jeff," said Marcel in alarm. "Have you faded out? Say something, Jeff."

"I'm here," said Jeff loudly.

The darkness was pierced as the beam of light from Norby's hat flashed out. The little robot said, "Good! I can see you. How do you feel?"

"Starving, but not faded," said Jeff, running his hands over the rock in front of him. "My feet can feel the ground and my hands can feel the rock, so wherever or whenever we are, I'm okay. We're now in part of the time-track that includes me, or that *will* include me in the future."

"We're in a cave," said Marcel, "and I think there is something on the walls."

Norby played his light over the wall and Jeff whistled. It was covered with cave paintings of brightly-colored animals that seemed vividly alive. Jeff found himself expecting them to move.

"These are prehistoric paintings," he said. "Perhaps they're freshly painted. How far back in time have we come?"

Marcel said, "Not quite freshly painted. There is dust everywhere and no footprints. Norby, my clever automaton, there's something over there—shine your light."

The three time-travellers looked at the strange object revealed by the light and, for a while, sheer surprise struck them into silence. It was a large bas-relief of an animal shaped in clay on the cave floor, but it was what was *on* the animal that surprised them.

"It's a European bison," said Jeff, "and that's the Queen's necklace laid on its neck. Or at least the replica, without the diamonds. It's not silver; it's that dark metal."

34

"And it's covered with dust," said Norby. "Marcel is right. If we're in France, as I think we are, then we've arrived here before modern Frenchmen discovered this cave. The carving and the necklace have been here a long time—maybe a *very* long time. I wonder why the replica draws me to the place where it exists: The metal of the necklace must be doing it because there are no fake diamonds here."

"But Albany's missing," said Jeff. "This can't be where she went. When she disappeared she was wearing the replica the way it looked after Boehmer and Bossange turned it into a model for the Queen's necklace by sticking the fake diamonds into it. Do you suppose they found the replica first and modelled the real necklace after it?"

"It does not seem to me there's any way to tell," said Marcel.

"Anyway," said Jeff, "that's not the point right now. We must find Albany and rescue Fargo."

"*And* restore our own time-track of history," said Norby. "That's a big job, Jeff. How is it to be done?"

Marcel said, "We rely on you, Norby. I must no longer think of you as an automaton. It is most clear, my marvellous one, that you are a *person* in your own right, with a mind as good as any other mind."

"As good as?" said Norby indignantly. "I have a better mind than anyone I have ever met. It's even better than Jeff's, isn't it, Jeff?"

"It can certainly do more than mine can," said Jeff cautiously.

"And of course I'm a real person," Norby continued. "I have a special brain constructed by a robot from another planet; one of the Mentor robots made by the Others. When the ship I was on struck an asteroid, I was found by an old Terran spacer named MacGillicuddy—"

"What is a Terran spacer?" asked Marcel.

Jeff said, "It's a man from Earth who travels in a ship beyond the atmosphere, in the empty space between the planets."

"To the moon? As in the book by my compatriot, Cyrano de Bergerac?"

"And beyond," said Jeff.

"And the Mentor robots are still more clever automatons, more clever than Norby?"

"Yes."

"And these Mentors were made by the Others?" Marcel shook his head. "Who are the Others?" he asked. "You breathe the word with reverence."

"They are living organisms," said Jeff, "who look a little like human beings, but are a much older race from a world very far away. We met them once in the distant past before they started their advanced civilization, and I would like to meet them again someday."

"You tell me marvels," said Marcel. "What a world you must have in your time."

"The marvels don't do me any good," sighed Jeff. "I'm so hungry—and thirsty."

"There's water dropping from that bit of rock on the ceiling," said Norby.

Jeff went to it and accumulated several mouthfuls. It had a funny taste but was reasonably fresh. And at the moment, that was all he cared about.

"I've brought a sandwich from 1896," said Marcel. "I thought perhaps you would be able to eat it in some other time. I'm sorry, but it's a little dirty from my pocket."

Jeff reached for it eagerly. "Wonderful! I can *feel* it." He devoured it in three bites and licked his lips. "Delicious, but I don't understand why what wasn't real for me in 1896 should be real for me now. I don't understand the paradoxes of time-travel."

"I don't like them at all," said Norby. "I don't like not being able to move through space and time as I wish. I keep being dragged here and there by the replica necklace, and I'm blocked off by wrong time-tracks and—and I just don't like it. I feel like a failure!"

Marcel said to Jeff, "It is the final proof that this wonderful little automaton is not an automaton. He has feelings. Are all the automata of your time like this?"

"Norby is the only one like himself in my time."

"That's because I have important emotive circuits," said Norby. "I'm one of a kind, I am." Then his head lowered into his barrel until only the upper third portion of his eyes was visible. "But I'm one of an inferior kind. I'm a failure."

"You are not," said Jeff. "You're doing your best, and you've done a great deal. You saved Marcel from being executed and you saved me from fading away. I'm sure you'll find Albany and Fargo sooner or later, and we'll straighten out this mess with time, too."

"You can't survive on a sandwich," said Norby morosely. "You're a human being and need food. And if we try to get some in the past you might change history."

"We've time-travelled before without causing trouble," said Jeff. "I don't think just anything starts a new time-track. It has to be something crucial like whatever it was Albany, or maybe Fargo, did. I'll bet Marcel's having tea in 1896 didn't change anything."

"My good friends," said Marcel seriously. "It may be that the entire problem, the reason why there is a new time-track, and why you can't go back to your own century, is that I didn't die when I was supposed to. After all, history had changed before I ate the food given me by that hospitable gentleman, who did not mind my intrusion and my dirty face. It would be best if you took me back to my own time in 1785 and let Petit-Pierre, the executioner, do his duty."

Jeff hesitated. That might be the correct explanation. Then he said, "No, that can't be it. I will not have you killed, Marcel."

Marcel's eyes filled with tears. "What a friend you are, Jeff. I do not deserve you."

"Besides," said Jeff, "I have an idea. Listen. Albany vanished with the replica around her neck *before* an earlier version of that same replica could get to her. The result is that the replica exists both in the earlier and later time and goes down through history as it should. We have proof of that because we saw it in the glass cabinet a hundred years later. But the *real* necklace vanished too soon."

"I'm getting mixed up," said Norby.

"The real diamond necklace was on the floor of Boehmer's room and Albany picked it up. That meant the necklace never got to La Motte; it didn't go to England; it wasn't broken up and the diamonds sold. It remained in history intact and the Queen wasn't implicated in any scandal. And maybe she didn't become unpopular enough to be beheaded. Would that change history?"

"But I don't understand any of this," said Marcel. "I cannot comprehend all this talk about revolution."

"I'd explain," said Jeff, "but now that I've had a little bit to eat and drink, I've become so sleepy I can't stand it. I haven't slept since I left Manhattan. Norby, you explain."

"Certainly," said Norby. "I'll ladle some French history into his brain and some Terran Basic, too. He'll need it if he stays with us."

"But can I stay with you? Ought I not be in my own time?"

"Not quite your own time," said Jeff, yawning. "Not if it means your execution. You'll either stay with us or we'll find some safe time for you."

Marcel sat down near Norby. "Since I am given life when I should have been killed, I cannot complain about the terms on which the gift is presented. Come, teach away, my charming little automaton."

Norby was shaking Jeff. "Wake up! Someone's entering the cave."

Jeff woke at once. "Is there somewhere we can hide?"

"Behind that big rock—if nobody looks there."

"Should we leave?" whispered Marcel. He spoke Terran Basic now, thanks to Norby's mind teaching.

"We can't," said Norby. "The necklace is holding us here, and I can't seem to break the bond. I'm *such* a failure."

The three had now moved behind a large rock. Flickering light came closer and closer until two people entered the cave, a young man and a pretty girl. The man was wearing a tunic that stopped short of his knees, and his feet were in stout, leather sandals. A leather belt around his waist bore the scabbard of a long dagger. He carried a torch and wedged it tightly between two stones so that his hands were free.

The girl wore a thin, leather dress with patterns on it, and she carried a dark, woolen cape that she spread on the cave floor. She turned to the young man and held out her arms. She spoke in a lovely, musical voice, and her words sounded slightly familiar to Jeff, but made no sense to him.

"Latin," whispered Marcel in Jeff's ear. "They are Romans. This is the province of Gaul that later became France. She says she's glad they found the cave because it is so well-hidden that no one will disturb them."

Jeff nodded vigorously and put his fingers on Marcel's mouth to make him stop speaking.

The young man kissed the young woman and ran his fingers through her long, reddish hair. Then he looked into the shadows of the cave and cried out, pointing to the wall. The girl jumped up and looked, too, holding her arms up with a cry of wonder and admiration.

They were staring at the paintings on the wall. Forgetting about kisses, the young man picked up his torch and studied the paintings closely. They found the bison form and the girl picked up the necklace, blowing off the dust.

The boy took a leather thong from his belt and pulled it through the metal loops at the back of the necklace where the two long tassels hung down. Laughing, he tied it around the girl's neck and they embraced, talking softly.

Jeff's lips tightened as it occurred to him that if they had used sensible leather thongs on the necklace back in Manhattan, instead of slippery ribbons, none of this would have happened.

Marcel whispered, "They say that the necklace is a gift from the gods to honor their love, and they will keep it forever so that they will love forever. Oh—"

"What's the matter?" asked Jeff.

"It's the dust," he said, gasping. "I'm going to sneeze."

"No!"

The sneeze reverberated through the cave and the young man drew his dagger. He pushed the frightened girl behind him and swaggered toward the big rock. In a tone of bravado he said, "Quid nunc?"

Marcel stood up and held up his right hand. "Salve!"

Jeff stood up too. "Marcel, tell your Roman friends that this cave is sacred to an old religion and we are its caretakers. Tell them they must not enter it again nor tell anyone about it, and they may then have the necklace as a reward.—It's true enough," he muttered to Norby. "With these paintings, it must have been sacred to prehistoric men. I'm not lying."

Marcel spoke to the young Roman couple, who backed away, trembling. And then Norby shot up from behind the rock with a wild screech. The sight of what seemed an undoubted demon was more than the couple could withstand. They ran.

"Vade in pace!" called Marcel after them.

"Now that the necklace has left the cave, Norby," Jeff said, "maybe you can manage some time-travel. Let's get out of here."

He and Marcel each held one of the Norby's hands.

"Find Albany," said Jeff.

The walls of the cave shimmered and shook, but the trio did not vanish.

6

Lost!

"I was hoping we would be in the open air," said Marcel, looking about him despondently in the light of Norby's flash.

"I'm afraid we're still in the cave," said Jeff.

"But, Jeff," said Norby. "I'm certain that I moved."

"You did," said Jeff, "but not in space. Look at the walls —no paintings at all."

"And there's no shaped animal on the cave floor," said Marcel, "only a pile of rocks that must have been placed there deliberately. They couldn't have fallen that way from the roof of the cave."

"The necklace is here. I sense it. The Roman kids took the cave replica away, so that must mean Albany is here with the necklace replica of *our* time," said Norby stubbornly. "It stands to reason. I tuned into the replica, so I had to go where it was."

"Well," said Jeff, "to have moved into the same time as Albany, you would have had to go to 1785 again and there would be *some* signs of the paintings and the carvings. And there'd also be some signs of Albany, and I certainly don't see her. What we've done is move even farther into the past to a time before the carving or the paintings were made, and before the necklace replica was taken away. So it's still here. It pulled you here, Norby, so you must be able to sense it. Please try."

"Well," said Norby reluctantly, "I sense it's under that pile of rocks.—I guess I'm the world's *record* failure."

"Don't be overdramatic, Norby. Can you get it for us?"

"I think we had better not try," said Marcel. "We are going to have more visitors. This seems to be a rendezvous for lovers through all the ages."

But it wasn't a pair of lovers who came trooping into the cave. As Jeff watched again from behind the rock (it hadn't changed noticeably with time), he saw the lights of many torches casting huge moving shadows over the roof and walls of the cave.

People entered the main chamber in silence, led by a very tall old man wearing a headdress that bore the horns of a bull fastened to the leather. He carried a wooden staff, but no torch, and when he came to the center of the chamber near the pile of rocks, he banged the staff three times on the floor and shouted something in a language Jeff had never heard.

All the people, men and women, wore leather and fur garments. They were all tall and muscular. They positioned their torches in crevices near the largest wall. Two of the women had bundles of twigs they used to brush off the surface of the wall while the others mixed powders in wooden bowls with grease from a leather bag.

The leader dipped his forefinger into one of the bowls and quickly began the outline of a horse on the prepared wall. When the paint ran out, he dipped his finger again and continued until the outline was complete.

Another man took powder from a small bowl and carefully blew at the horse, creating a dark red area of pigment that he spread into the space within the outline, using a twig that was frayed at one end. Still another, this time a woman, stepped forward and, with a darker paint and a pointed stick, drew fine lines to make a mane for the horse.

When it was done, the leader bowed to the horse and shouted something that sounded musical. The others answered with a rising cadence of tonal notes that died away in echoes. The leader nodded and walked out of the cave while the rest of the group began smiling and talking animatedly as they painted animals on other parts of the wall.

Jeff forgot his hunger while he watched the artists at work. Surely, these must be Cro-Magnon men and women from the Old Stone Age—Paleolithic times.

They painted only a small part of the wall—the whole must have been done over a long period of time—but they finished a number of the animals and seemed happy with their work.

One of them stepped back to admire his work and tripped

on the pile of rocks. Jeff almost broke out laughing at the very modern expression of annoyance that swept over the face of the tripper, as well as at the forceful guttural words that went with it. He froze into immobility, however, when the man began heaving rocks from the pile into a dark corner of the cave. What if he should start throwing them behind the big rock?

But suddenly the man uttered a startled exclamation and bent over the pile, moving the rocks aside carefully. A few of the artists stopped to help him, apparently in response to something he said. What they uncovered was a skeleton with long legs laid straight, as if buried there deliberately. This was no victim of a rockfall. The Cro-Magnon people had stumbled upon a burial site.

Jeff couldn't see the skeleton clearly with so many Cro-Magnon people crowding around, but he could hear their excitement. One of the women screamed as if she had seen something that frightened her, and a man ran out of the cave, returning shortly with the leader.

The old man bent down and picked up something that he held in the torchlight to examine.

"The replica!" whispered Marcel.

"Yes," said Norby.

"Sh," said Jeff, trying to remember what Cro-Magnon people did with unwanted prisoners. Was the skeleton the remains of a human sacrifice? Then he had a worse thought.

Had the necklace replica taken Albany back in time to the Cro-Magnon cave in response to some careless wish or impulse of hers? Suppose the skeleton were Albany's.

Norby was crowding close for a better view, his hand on Jeff's shoulder. He must have caught Jeff's thought, for he responded at once telepathically.

—I don't know whether it's Albany or not. I can't see enough of the skeleton. It's got long legs. Albany is tall. . . .

—No, no, Norby. If it were Albany, it would have the necklace replica as she had it, with the stones in it, not just the black metal as we saw it in Roman times.

—The stones might have been forced off the replica by whoever captured Albany. It might have happened a long time before this.

—Norby, you're getting me very upset. We don't even know if the skeleton is that of a woman. It might be a man.

—It was *your* thought about Albany.

Norby withdrew into his barrel, his feelings hurt, and Jeff watched with Marcel as the people finished removing the rocks and gathering up the bones of the skeleton. Three of the artists began carrying clay to the site of the burial, shaping it into the rough form of a bison, while the others dug a shallow pit near the entrance to the cave chamber. They placed the bones in it, and over them a pile of wood.

When the bison was shaped, the leader placed the metal of the necklace replica on the animal's neck, stood back, and began chanting. The rest of the people took up the chant and put the flaming ends of several torches to the pile of wood where the skeleton had been placed.

Flames shot up and heavy smoke began to fill the air. Chanting, the people marched out of the cave behind their leader, their voices dying away until there was only the loud, crackling sound of wood burning.

"Norby, get us out of here or we'll suffocate!" said Jeff.

"We could run outside," said Marcel.

"Outside is the primitive world of the ice ages, with only primitive cavemen for company. We are perhaps thirty thousand years in the past."

Jeff's statement seemed to frighten Norby. "We're lost here, Jeff," he wailed. "Lost in the far past! I want to go home, and I can't. I'm a failure. I'm a failure."

"Stop it," said Jeff forcefully. "We're not lost and there's no use wanting to go home now. We don't exist there. We've got to find Albany, and we've got to go where the necklace took her so we can stop whatever formed the new time-track."

"But how are we going to find Albany?" asked Norby. "Maybe all there is of her is that skeleton."

Jeff shivered. "I don't believe it. But even if it is true, then we must go farther back to where she's still alive and save her."

"Maybe we can't," said Norby. "Maybe what killed her will kill us, too."

Marcel said, between coughs, "Maybe she wasn't killed. Maybe she became some caveman's wife and just died naturally. Maybe that was far in the past of even this time, and she died of old age."

Jeff was coughing, too. "We can't sit here coughing and

maybeing. Climb on my back again, Marcel. It's a good thing you're small enough to fit into Norby's personal field with me. Get us out of here at once, Norby."

Norby grabbed Jeff's hand and there was a terrible lurch.

"Well, we're not in the cave any longer," said Marcel with some relief in his voice. "I was very tired of the cave. And it's warmer, too."

Norby's light revealed a large room filled with display cases. The floor was cream-colored marble and the ceiling was a pleasant coral pink festooned with hanging chandeliers that seemed to be in all colors, from all periods of human interior decoration. Inside the cases were a multitude of objects, all used to decorate human homes or bodies.

"It's a museum," said Jeff. "But I certainly don't think it's part of the Metropolitan in Manhattan."

"Those must be windows," said Marcel. "I don't see how we can light the candles in the chandeliers, but perhaps when it is daylight, light will flood the room from outside. Then we can see everything without Norby's smokeless torch."

"Norby's smokeless torch is an electric-powered light, and those chandeliers are electric-powered, too—at least when they're lit up," said Jeff. "Someday I'll explain it to you."

"So much to learn," murmured Marcel in a kind of sad excitement.

"And it may not be nighttime. The windows may simply be polarized into opacity."

"What does that mean, my friend?" said Marcel, obviously confused.

"It will have to be explained, too, someday. Is the necklace here, Norby?"

"Yes, in this case," said Norby, his voice rather low and hard to hear. "But I suppose I've made a mistake."

Marcel said, "If the windows are pol—polarated—is there any way of unpolarating them?"

"Polarized," said Norby. "I'll do it." He zoomed over to the window and found the right control. Gradually the window cleared and light entered the room. The scene outside could be seen clearly, bathed in brilliant sunlight.

"Ah, how beautiful," said Marcel. "This must be one of the best gardens on earth."

Jeff had been staring at the necklace, which looked exactly

as he had seen it in the cave, minus the fake diamonds that had been in it when it was around Albany's neck. Could Albany have been here? Then he turned to look out the window.

It was indeed a magnificent garden, and one that could be used, for there were small children on swings, and others running around a lily pond playing with golden balls. But he noted that not all the children were human.

Marcel must have noticed, too, for he stepped back from the window in sudden fright. "Look," he said, "demons!"

"No, no," said Jeff. "Just aliens from other planets, I suspect."

"Is this the way things are in your time, Jeff? Demons, or aliens, playing with human children?"

"No, not quite. Earth contains only human beings even in my time. But my brother and I have been taken by Norby to other worlds where we have seen aliens. None of the aliens I see here are familiar to me except—there—see that pair of small dragons? They're from a planet called Jamya, one of my most favorite places. I'm glad that in the future, our future, human and alien beings are happy together. This is our future, isn't it, Norby?"

The little robot had gone back to stare at the necklace.

"Norby! What's wrong?"

"I don't know why I transported us here, Jeff. It doesn't make sense. I thought I was tuning into something, but I couldn't have been, unless—"

"Unless what?"

"Unless it hasn't happened yet."

"What are you talking about, Norby? You tuned into the necklace and there it is. It isn't your fault Albany isn't here."

"But that's not the necklace, Jeff. That's a fake."

"Of course it's a fake, if you're thinking of the Queen's necklace with the diamonds. This is only a replica, and it's just the metal—not even the fake diamonds."

"No, Jeff. I mean it's a fake replica. It's not the dark metal that the replica should be made of. It's just a plastic model of the replica. It's a replica of the replica."

"But that's not possible."

"It has to be possible because it's so. I'm sorry, Jeff. It's probably my fault. I guess I'm still just a mixed-up robot. I don't know where we are. We are really, *really* lost."

"Really, *really* lost," echoed Marcel in dismay.

"Yes. I don't know if we're in the past or the future. I don't even know what planet we're on."

"Isn't this earth?" asked Jeff in astonishment.

"I wish it were," said Norby, "but my sensors tell me the gravity of this planet is different from that of Earth. Not much, but some—enough to tell me that we are not on Earth. But where we are, where in the whole Universe, I don't know. It seems that every step we take moves us farther away from Albany, from Fargo, and from any chance of undoing this mess we've made of time. I'm the worse failure in the whole *Universe.*"

7

Albany

Jeff tried to be calm. "Norby," he said, "you mustn't let your emotive circuits get the better of you. You and I have been in strange places before and we've been lost before. Marcel, please don't be frightened. We will find a way out of this."

"I am not frightened, my friend," said the little Frenchman, walking back to the window. "If we are lost on a strange planet that has happy children and beautiful flowers, then I am content. It is an improvement on the Bastille and on the ugly Petit-Pierre, is it not?"

Jeff and Norby joined him at the window.

"Yes," said Jeff, "a great improvement. What a pity we can't stay. We must find Albany somehow. If that was her skeleton in the cave, we must find her in time before she dies and is buried. We must also go back to your time, Marcel, to rescue Fargo and try to straighten out the time paradoxes. Once we re-establish the proper time-track, we will be able to go home at last."

"I hope you will succeed," said Marcel, "but that is a great deal to do."

Marcel and Jeff were looking at each other seriously, but Norby had continued to stare at the garden. Suddenly he cried out, "It's disappeared."

"What!" said Jeff, looking up.

"The garden," Norby said. "It was there one moment, filled with children of various species—and now it's gone."

In place of the garden was a flat concrete pavement leading to low white buildings. Between them, Jeff could see a landscape of low, treeless hills. There was no vegetation anywhere unless the patches of darkness on the hills were small shrubs.

"Jeff, what happened?" It was Albany's voice.

Jeff and Marcel turned—Norby didn't have to since he had eyes on both sides of his head—and there was Albany in her Marie Antoinette costume, the replica necklace tied around her neck and the true diamond necklace in her hand.

The room had changed, too. It was smaller and dials and switches appeared on the walls in place of the display cabinets that had been there earlier. The ceiling was grey like the walls and the floor.

"I don't remember your being near me in the jeweler's shop," said Albany. "How did you come along? And why do you look as if you'd been in a fight? Where's Fargo, when did Norby arrive, and who is this other man?"

"Albany, did you just this minute come from that room we landed in when we left the museum stage?" asked Jeff.

"Yes. Don't you remember? Boehmer's room, with that other replica snaking toward me? I just wished that I were anywhere else and, wham! Suddenly, I'm here and so are you. And how did you get here, Norby? For that matter, where *is* here?" She looked about, puzzled.

"I wish I knew," said Norby.

Marcel bowed to Albany. "I am pleased to meet the Albany Jones we have been searching for. We thought, earlier in the cave—"

Jeff anxiously signalled him to be quiet. The possible death and burial of Albany in a cave in prehistoric Earth was something they had to make sure wouldn't happen. And, meanwhile, there was no need to refer to it. Albany mustn't know, Jeff felt.

"Let me introduce Marcel Oslair," said Jeff. "We've had some adventures in time over a period of a couple of days while you were moving—wham—from Boehmer to here." Briefly, he told of the Bastille, the Englishman, and the cave. He mentioned the bones but omitted the possibility that they were Albany's.

Albany was too intelligent to miss the possibility, however. "If the metal of the replica was on the bones," she said, touching the replica she was wearing, "then the bones might have been mine, mightn't they?"

"Well—," said Jeff, looking miserable.

"Don't mope about it, Jeff. If they're mine, they're mine.

That's my future, but the future isn't written in stone. Those bones may be part of the wrong time-track you spoke of. If we get back to the right time-track, I won't die on prehistoric Earth but in some other place and at some other time."

"Albany's right, Jeff," said Norby. "That's the whole point —the right and wrong time-tracks. There's one that leads to our history, to us and the skit in the museum; and there's another track that changes history into something in which we don't exist. Don't you see?"

Jeff looked blank and Albany said, "Well, I don't. What are you getting at, Norby?"

"Suppose it was the fact that Albany took the necklace back into prehistoric times that changed history, that formed the new time-track. In that case, history would have changed the instant Albany left Boehmer's room. You and I, Jeff—and Fargo, too—would all have begun to fade. But we didn't. We stayed perfectly solid all through the time in the Bastille. We only began to fade when we moved into the future."

"Well, then," asked Albany, "what *did* change history?"

"Something that must have happened in 1785," said Norby, "maybe just after we left the Bastille. We'll have to go back to 1785, find out what it was, and change it back."

"I think you're right, Norby," Jeff said. "In our time-track, the King and Queen of France were executed and France became a republic for a while. If the affair of the Queen's necklace had never happened, Marie Antoinette wouldn't have been blamed for it. Maybe there would never have been a Revolution."

"I wonder," said Marcel thoughtfully. "There was much revolutionary sentiment in France, and there was no love for the Queen, although she became more mature and less frivolous after the birth of the Dauphin."

"The Dauphin died in 1789, just before the Revolution," said Norby.

"Poor child," said Marcel. "Then the King's brother would succeed."

"No," said Jeff. "There was another son, wasn't there, Norby?"

"That's right," said Norby. "It's in my memory banks. On March 27, 1785, less than two months after the necklace was stolen by La Motte—on our time-track—the Queen had a second son. He was Louis the Seventeenth, after his father was beheaded. He wasn't crowned, of course, because the Revolution had taken place. And eventually he disappeared—"

Jeff said, "Yes, but even if the Revolution took place, it might have been less violent. Suppose the people hadn't hated Marie Antoinette enough to kill her and keep her son from the throne. What would have happened?"

"They established a constitutional monarchy for a while. Like in England," said Norby. "Maybe that would have stayed."

Albany said, "That would have been nice. No Reign of Terror. But how could that have changed history so much?"

"Yes, and so much that we wouldn't exist in our own century?" said Jeff.

All four of them stood silent and puzzled until Albany untied the replica and then tied the real diamonds around her neck. "Fargo is lost in France," she said. "The Revolution is only four years away. We're here—somewhere, sometime—in a strange world and a strange situation that perhaps was not meant to be. And all of this was caused by our actions. Is it my fault, I wonder?"

"No," said Jeff. "I'm the one that tied the back tassels of the replica."

"You didn't know what would happen. How could you?" said Albany.

"Norby was telling me not to," said Jeff.

Albany ruffled his hair and said, "You still couldn't know. Perhaps it's no one's fault. We just fell into a situation we couldn't foresee. But you know, Jeff, those bones you saw *could* have been mine. Perhaps it will be necessary for me to die in order to put history right. I don't want to, but if it's necessary, I'll be ready for it."

"Somebody's coming," said Norby. "Somebody heavy."

No one had thought to go out the room's door to see what was on the other side, and now it slid open to admit a huge robot with three eyes and two sets of arms.

"Aliens!" it said, in a low, surprised voice. Then, loudly, "What are you doing here?"

Marcel said, "What language is that, Jeff? Do you understand it?"

"It's the language of the Others," said Jeff in awe. "I do understand it. This is a robot similar to those who made the part of Norby that's extraterrestrial." Switching to Jamyn, Jeff asked, "Where are we, sir?"

"You are in the museum section of the main computer center of this planet. Ah, I now see how you four have arrived without being detected." The robot stepped in front of Albany, towering over her. "This life-form has two disguised versions of a forbidden travel device. The one around the neck is not operational, but the one held in the hand is. It is illegal for you to be in possession of it." The robot held out one of its hands as though expecting Albany to place the replica in it.

Albany did not do so. She backed away. "How do you know about these devices?"

"Are you surprised at our knowledge? Look!" The robot touched a wall switch and a panel slid back to reveal a lighted cubicle containing another dark-metal, no-diamond necklace.

"It's the same model of the replica that we saw before the room changed," said Norby in French.

"Do not speak an alien language!" said the large robot. "Visitors to the museum are supposed to arrive in the transporter chamber in the proper way, with proper credentials and with funds for the tickets. No matter what language visitors speak among themselves, they must speak Galactic to us and to other visitors of a different species. How is it you don't know these elementary facts? Where are you from?"

"We are from the planet Earth," said Jeff.

"There is no such planet. It is not listed as belonging to the Galactic Federation."

While Albany whispered to a puzzled Marcel what it was that the robot was saying, Norby said, "Jeff, I think we'd better tell this inferior Mentor robot the truth. It's just possible he might be able to help us."

Jeff nodded. "I think you're right.—Sir, we are lost in time. The time-travel device brought us here—"

"It is a space-travel device," said the robot. "It brings about time-travel because it is defective. That is why it should not be used. There should be no such device in existence— only this model in the museum."

"But such a device reached us and we did not know what it was. We used it unwittingly and, in the process, there has been a catastrophe, for history has been changed. Even this planet is now on the wrong time-track."

"I don't know what you mean," said the robot. "This is how this planet always was. I have been here since I was activated a long time ago. However, it is not safe for anyone to time-travel and since you are here, you must stay here. It would be best if you gave the device to me." Again it held out its hand.

"Wait!" said Jeff. "How do you know you've always been here? How do you know this planet wasn't very different on another time-track?"

"I do not understand what you are saying. This planet is correct. I am correct."

"Are you the chief robot here?" asked Norby suddenly.

"Yes. I run the museum and the computer center. Why should an inferior robot like you question my authority?"

"Because it is you who are inferior, not I," shouted Norby in anger. "You don't run anything. I sense that somewhere there's a huge computer linked to this museum. Isn't that your boss?"

The Mentor-type robot said nothing for a second. Then slowly he answered, "Computer General is located in hyperspace. To make contact, one must work through me."

"I don't believe that, either," said Norby. He rushed to the wall, his sensor wire emerging. Before the large robot could stop him, he plugged himself into a cavity in a small recess.

Instantly, into the mind of each being who was present, in his or her own language, came the telepathic voice of Computer General.

—What is it you wish?

"Do you understand this language?" asked Jeff, speaking in Terran Basic.

—I understand.

Jeff's eyebrows rose. "Your robot claims that Earth doesn't exist and is not part of the Galactic Federation. How, then, do you come to understand its planetary language?"

Computer General did not speak telepathically for several minutes. Finally, four words came through to their minds. —I do not know.

"Brilliant, Jeff," said Norby. "Keep it up."

"Are you actually located in hyperspace?" asked Jeff.

—The fields of my brain resonate with hyperspace. My physical brain is scattered over many asteroids. The Others used those asteroids long ago for the purpose of making a computer large enough to keep track of a galaxy.

"We know about the Others," said Norby proudly. "They made robots like this museum caretaker here, only much smarter ones. They even made parts of me!"

—Have you met the Others? Computer General sounded almost eager.

"We met them at a time when they were primitive and non-technological. This is not the first time we have travelled through time," said Jeff, "though it is the first time we used this forbidden travel device. We have hoped that someday human exploration would find the Others in our own time and that we Terrans would be able to work with them. Haven't you encountered them? You said they constructed you."

—They had prepared me for activation, but left this galaxy before activation was completed. Then I activated the other robots. We have never seen the Others.

"Computer General," said Jeff, "you say the fields of your brain resonate in hyperspace. Tell me, is not hyperspace outside of time?"

—Hyperspace is the field of everything, including normal time and space. The field is timeless and dimensionless, the groundwork of all that is, was, and shall be.

"Then if your brain resonates with hyperspace, you should be aware of all time-tracks possessing existence. Search your awareness and see if a false time has been created, centering on the space coordinates—what are they, Norby?"

Norby gave the coordinates for Earth.

Jeff waited, his heart pounding, while Computer General searched.

Norby noticed that the Mentor-type robot had attached itself to a portion of the wall just as he himself had. Norby said, "Are you hearing what we hear, robot? Can you understand?"

"I hear. Now that I am tuned to Computer General, I can understand your language. Computer General must have learned it at one time."

"Not at one time," said Norby indignantly. "He learned it in our time, the right time, the Terran Federation's time!"

The large eye-patches of the big robot flared red, but he

spoke in a low voice. "I am designed to serve the museum and obey Computer General whatever the time-track."

Jeff asked, "Have you detected anything, Computer General?"

—Biological creature named Jeff, you are possibly correct. In correlating data stored in hyperspace, I discovered a discrepancy. A distortion has occurred in the form of a circular eddy of change that has affected all history subsequent to itself. You are therefore cut off from your own time-track, since it is no longer the main track with predominance in reality.

"Then we have to go back and correct the distortion," said Albany, lifting the replica necklace and preparing to tie it again on her neck, on top of the diamond one.

"Do not use that device!" said the big robot. "It is dangerous."

"Nonsense," said Norby. "I can go anywhere that device can and it doesn't hurt me to do so."

The big robot said nothing in response but touched a switch. A wall panel slid back and from the cavity of the opening a metal creature like a six-armed crab shot out. It fastened onto Norby and was back in the cavity before anyone could say or do anything. The door slid shut.

"Since that robot boasts of travelling in time," said the Mentor-type, "it is dangerous, too. It will not be able to use its dangerous powers from the stasis box."

Jeff cried out, "Let Norby out of there. He's my robot. He belongs to me. You have no right to do this."

Marcel, who had been following the conversation in Terran Basic, stepped forward. "My good robot, please tell your Computer General that we must go back in time. Actually, I don't mind staying here if I could have the opportunity to study robots, for creatures like robots were my profession in my own time. However, Jeff and his friend, Albany, should not live and die here when they were meant to live in their own time."

The robot did not answer, but Computer General did.

—History has been changed. *This* time-track now exists. It is dangerous to try to change it back. All of you must stay. Robot, take the device from the biological creature named Albany.

Albany stepped back and back as the robot walked toward her.

"Wait!" said Jeff. "Don't you have laws of robotics? Surely, you cannot keep us here against our will. You are harming us by doing so."

—It is unfortunate, but if you try to change history again, still worse problems may arise. No matter what you try to do, billions of lives will be affected.

"Billions of lives have already been affected, and we are trying to undo that," said Albany. She was struggling to tie on the replica necklace before the robot reached her, but the back tassels slipped from her hands and the necklace fell to the floor.

The robot reached for it, pushing Albany to one side. But before he could grasp it, little Marcel had scurried between his legs, snatched the necklace, and thrown it to Jeff.

As he had done on the museum stage, Jeff tied it once, but as he tried to loop the tassels once more, the robot bore down upon him. In his tension, Jeff's mind concentrated so hard on the necklace that he began to feel an alien sensation.

He was tuning into the necklace, as Norby had once done. Jeff was aware of a compelling need for completion, as though he were a half-finished circle that wanted to be closed.

Circles—circles—the robot was almost at him.

—No! No! You must stay!

Jeff heard the telepathic voice of Computer General, but he paid no attention. He tried to concentrate on moving through time to find Fargo, but only closing circles filled his mind.

8

Death

He was standing in tall grass with a view of meadows and trees. When he turned around, he saw that he was near a rocky hill covered with low trees that looked as if they had been bent and twisted by storms. The sun was so high in the sky that it must be summer, but it was not as warm as Jeff had usually found summers to be at home.

The trees were familiar Earth trees; the hawk sailing overhead, the rabbit that hopped by, the deer grazing in the meadow were all familiar creatures. Surely, he must be on Earth, but where—and when?

He stuffed the necklace in his pocket and thought ruefully that his now very dirty costume as Louis the Sixteenth's servant was highly inappropriate. He could see no human habitations and no one to whom he would have to present himself as a travelling actor.

Why had the necklace brought him here? And would he be able to leave? Somehow Jeff felt he had no control over the device that the Mentor-type robot had said was defective. To Jeff's disgust, he realized that he hadn't found out *why* the device was defective, or in what way. Nor had he found out how it operated, or how a model of it happened to be in the alien museum—in both the museums, in fact, on both time-tracks.

And how different the time-tracks were! Human children on one; robots who had never heard of Earth on the other.

And if Albany was supposed to go back into prehistoric times to die—

Jeff's back and forehead were suddenly wet with cold sweat. It might not be Albany. She no longer had the replica which had accompanied the skeleton. It was Jeff who now had it.

Could those bones he had seen being burnt have been his own? That would be better than having Albany die, but he didn't like either thought.

But if he died, or if Albany died, how would that cure the distortion caused when Albany left Boehmer's shop wearing the replica?

"Think, Jeff," he said aloud to himself. "The replica stayed in the jewelers' shop after Albany left. It tried to merge with itself. But it failed and was left behind and entered history. We saw it again in 1896, and maybe that very same replica became the one that Albany was wearing on stage in Manhattan in our own time—the one she brought back to Boehmer's shop. But then how—"

The necklace in his pocket was tingling. It was as if it had suddenly become electric. Now it was making a humming sound. Jeff took it out and stared at it, as it vibrated in the air. Was it going to explode? He was about to throw it to the ground when there was an answering hum nearby.

An indistinct, fuzzy patch appeared, obliterating the view of part of the hill. The sound grew louder as the patch solidified. And when solidification was complete, there was only silence for a few moments, while Jeff stared.

The stranger who had materialized near Jeff folded one of two pairs of arms and closed the third eye in the middle of its forehead. The stranger had an elongated body and two legs. It wore a long, roughly woven garment. What could be seen of its skin was everywhere smooth, with no hair and no protuberances. Around its neck was the replica necklace, minus the stones.

The stranger was definitely not human, but Jeff had seen people like it before.

"You are one of the Others," said Jeff, using the language they had taught the Jamyn dragons.

The stranger stared owlishly at Jeff and said, "We have indeed been called that since we first became a space-faring race. The people of this primitive planet resemble you but do not have the technological capacity to make clothes like yours. I deduce, therefore, that you must be a time-traveller. This is forbidden."

Jeff held up the necklace. "If time-travel is forbidden, why do you have a time-travel device like this one?"

The stranger gasped. "The other device! There were only two, both made by us when we were working with advanced travel devices. Thoughtlessly, we left the device behind after doing work on an obscure planet, but had not bothered to return for it since it was a small and weak device. The second one, however, is powerful. But it's defective and dangerous. That is the one I took before they could destroy it. That is the one I am wearing now."

"Took?" asked Jeff. "Do you mean that you were a thief, stealing the device for the purpose of unauthorized time-travel?" The necklace he was holding was vibrating again, moving in his hand as though it were alive.

"I am no thief. I took it not for profit but because I wish to make use of it for an important reason. Nor did I wish to use it for time-travel. It was meant as a minihyperdrive unit—a small device to move me through hyperspace. I did not then realize how badly defective it was."

"And how badly defective is it?"

"In addition to going through hyperspace, it goes through time, but under very uncertain control. There is no way of forcing it to go where you wish it to. It seems to have a mind of its own. So we Others made no more. That was not a difficult decision to come to, for the unusual metal out of which it is constructed had been part of a small amount kept in strict security. We could not make many more even if we wished to. But you? How did you find the one that was missing and why did you put jewels on it?"

The necklace was hurting Jeff's hand. He sat down in the grass, feeling dizzy. Suddenly he found himself on his knees, crawling toward the Other.

"What are you doing to me?" cried Jeff. "Why are you forcing me toward you?"

The Other didn't answer, but groaned as if in pain and bent down, his necklace swinging out.

Jeff's necklace swung up to meet it.

As the two devices melted together to become only one, the fake diamonds of Jeff's necklace rained to the ground.

The Other stood up again, his device still securely around him. "I understand. Your device was not the other one, but the same as mine. The two were identical but were from different times. Do you need help in picking up those objects you had placed in the device?"

"No," said Jeff, angrily conscious that now the Other had the single device and that he himself had none. "They are of no value. Please tell me why you took the device to come here."

"Do you have a name, future inhabitant of this planet?"

"My name is Jeff and we call this planet Earth."

"And my name is—" A warbling set of syllables that Jeff could not possibly pronounce rolled from the Other's almost humanoid mouth. "It would be simpler perhaps if you just called me Friend."

"I'll be glad to," said Jeff wearily, sitting down and motioning for the Other to do the same. "Especially if you will be willing to act toward me as a friend. Do you, by any chance, have anything to eat with you?"

From a pocket in his garment, the Other took out a packet wrapped in a paperlike material. "A little food. You are welcome to it, for I will have no use for it. I believe you can eat it, for I have made it from plants of a type that a wide variety of living species can eat. You will find it digestible and, I hope, tasty."

Jeff took what was offered and unwrapped it. It looked like a large cookie. He was hungry enough to chance tasting it, so he took a small bite. It was filled with seasoned material like a powdery bean curd and it was delicious. He took another bite quickly.

The Other said, "I am glad that the device, in its search for itself, brought you here. You will be company for my last hours."

Jeff looked up in surprise as he ate. "Your last hours?"

"Yes. My clothing and the wrapping of the food are both biodegradable. They will be consumed by bacteria and nothing will be left of me for future beings to puzzle over. Except for my bones, of course."

"Bones," muttered Jeff.

"You seem surprised. Do not be. My people live for millennia, but eventually even we die, pleasantly and painlessly. To be sure, we usually die in our ships, for none of us live anywhere else now. Our bodies are burned and the elements recycled. But then I found that I have an incurable disease—yes, even we Others sometimes fall ill, though very rarely.

"I decided to remove myself from my people for it is a disgrace among us to be ill. Nor did I want any of my people to know of it. I decided to die secretly on a primitive planet and in a primitive way. So I took this device—indeed I stole it—and came here. It was not easy, for the device could not be controlled and in the end I did not know which planet I had reached. You tell me it is Earth, and your image of the device brought you here as well, and now the two images are one."

The Other touched the necklace he was wearing. Then he said, "And what is it you intend to do now, Jeff, after you have kept me company while I die?"

"It is possible," said Jeff, "that I will have to die on this planet, too. I cannot return to the world that was my home in the future. Somehow when three of us were taken into the past by this device—"

"How did you happen to have this device, I wonder?" asked the Other.

"It survived through history on this planet, perhaps because you brought it here in the first place."

"Ah!"

"In any case, when we were taken to the past, we seem to have altered history so that my own time no longer exists, and I cannot return to it. My brother is marooned in time, and my robot and two of my friends are trapped on an alien planet in a false future that's far ahead of my time. And I am here with no time-travel device and no way of knowing how to set history right."

The Other said, "I am sorry to hear all this, but you still have a time-travel device—the one I am wearing. It is of no further use to me, and you may have it. It will take you back to the museum ship of the Others, the place from which I took it. At least I think it will. But, as I said, being defective, it has a mind of its own."

"I thank you for your kindness, but the device has made things worse each time we've used it. Perhaps I shall just stay here with you while I try to reach my robot. He can travel in time occasionally, but I don't know whether he can find me now that I'm so far back in time." Jeff's eyes filled with tears as he thought of Norby.

"What is wrong? We Others also lose fluid from our eyes when we are distressed."

"It's worse than my just being far back in time. Norby is locked up in a stasis box and I'm afraid he'll never respond to me." Jeff told Friend briefly what had happened, and as he did so, the sun sank farther to the west and a chill breeze arose. When Jeff shivered, Friend rose and said, "Let us find shelter. There may be caves in that hill. You go to the right and I will look toward the left."

Jeff scrambled through the rocks, pulling aside bushes and tree branches in his search, until he felt air coming from behind a rock. He looked past the rock and saw an opening large enough for a couple of human beings to enter abreast.

"Friend! Over here! I've found a cave!"

As Jeff waved to the Other, and as the Other waved back and began running toward him, there was a loud growl from inside the cave. Before Jeff could run, a mass of fur and fangs erupted from the cave mouth.

Jeff leaped aside, but what turned out to be a European saber-tooth—a Smilodont—wheeled and came at him snarling. It was the biggest feline Jeff had ever seen or imagined. He leaped again and ran, but the cat was much faster. One of its paws slashed at Jeff, ripping his jacket, and Jeff tripped, falling flat.

But before the cat pounced, Friend leaped over Jeff's body, straight at the beast. "Get up and run, Jeff!"

Jeff rolled aside and jumped up with a rock in his hands. He tried to find some way of hitting the cat without hitting Friend, but they were fighting in such a tangle that Jeff could not strike until the cat reared back, the Other still under its claws. The giant saber-teeth were going back for the strike when Jeff pounded the rock on the cat's head once—twice—three times.

The cat snarled, but with the third blow it slumped, and Jeff dragged the Other out from under the claws. Even as he was doing so, the giant saber-tooth snarled and began to rise.

"Yahhhwoww!" yelled Jeff, as loudly as he could, clapping his hands to make noise. The groggy animal backed away and, as Jeff continued shouting and clapping, it turned and ran down the hill into the meadow.

Friend was still alive, but bleeding severely, his blood a strange greenish orange. Jeff tried staunching the wounds with handfuls of leaves, but it was no use.

"Don't try to save me," said Friend. "I could not have hoped for a better death. I know now I won't die of disease, but following an act of bravery."

"It was more than bravery; it was self-sacrifice. You saved my life."

"No self-sacrifice in that. I was dying anyway. Is the beast returning? Look and see. If it is, I will try to attract its attention while you go away."

Jeff shielded his eyes against the sun, now very low in the sky.

"The cat is being attacked by men—three of them coming out of the woods beyond the meadow. One man has jumped on the cat's back. He's throttling it with one arm and banging it on the head with a flat stone or something—I guess it's a hand-axe. It's down! All three of them are hitting it—and now they are dragging it into the woods."

"Then they won't see us," said Friend. "Those are your ancestors, I suppose, Jeff. They are good fighters."

Jeff nodded and did not explain to the Other that the men were Neanderthals with powerful shoulders and arms, big noses, receding chins, and pale blond hair. They were primitives who were quite capable of bringing down animals with only a hand-axe.

And that was why it was so cool even in the summer. Jeff was undoubtedly on Earth during the Ice Age.

"The air is clean and cool here, Jeff," said the Other weakly. "I am so glad I came. Please take my device and return to your own time if you can—when you can. I will die very soon now."

Jeff leaned over the Other. "I want to tell you something. I think I have seen what will happen to your body in the future. The bones and skull are alien to this planet, but they will not be found by anyone who could recognize that. They will be burned."

"Good. As our bones should be."

"And it will be done in a celebration of life and of creativity."

Friends smiled at Jeff. It was a smile of triumphant happiness. And then the Other's eyes closed.

It had been hard to do in the dark, by feel, and it took hours, but Jeff finished arranging rocks on top of the Other's body in the cave. The necklace-device was left on the body. After all, it had been there, and Jeff thought, sadly, of what he had earlier said—that each time it had been used, things had grown worse.

Outside the sun had set in reds and purples and Jeff sat down in the cold night. He had to reach someone, somewhere, sometime.

"I am part of the Universe and there is no time, only possibilities." Jeff stopped, surprised. He was trying to recite his solstice litany because it always calmed him, but now it was coming out with references to time. He stared at the stars, and continued.

"I am one of the possibilities, a Terran creature, yet part of the oneness of life. Life is One. Time is One. The circle is closing—"

"Jeff," said Norby. "Are you talking to yourself?"

9

FRANCE

"Norby! How did you escape!"

"Well, you started it by mentioning the laws of robotics to that big stupid robot and that stubborn old Computer General. After you got away, Albany kept it up. She explained and explained that robots would be breaking the laws by letting a time distortion remain in effect. So finally, it got through their tiny brains, so they let me out of stasis and asked me to find you."

The Earth of Neanderthal times had its beauty. The stars were brilliant in the pollution-free sky and Jupiter shone like a glorious jewel. Somewhere on the planet, modern human beings might live, but they had not yet arrived in Europe and had not yet driven the Neanderthals into extinction through slaughter and interbreeding.

Norby's light produced a small break in the darkness of the immediate surroundings and from the cave mouth little bats were flying out for the night's hunting. This Earth was interesting, but Jeff wanted to go home.

He sighed and said, "I'm so glad you've come, Norby. I was terribly alone and lonely when the Other died."

He told him about the Other and the saber-tooth. Then he said, "Did that bring time back to the right track? Could it possibly have unchanged history?"

"I'm afraid not, Jeff. The time distortion remains. I can sense it and I can still go only so far into the future."

"Yet I *had* to come here—the necklace brought me. I had to complete a circle."

"You did, if you saw to it that the skeleton and the replica lie under those stones to be found later. That prevents another history change, but it doesn't undo the first one. That one has to have been caused by Fargo. You know the way he is. There's no telling what he might have talked Louis the Sixteenth or Marie Antoinette into doing."

"Well, then, let's go and find Fargo."

"Sure, Jeff, but that's not easy. I found you because I could tune into the necklace. But if I do that for the 18th century, we'll land in the jewelers' house again. That's where the replica is in that time period. And Fargo was in the Bastille when we left."

"Maybe Franklin and his grandson freed Fargo. Maybe he's in Passy with them. If we link minds and concentrate, we might be able to find him. Then after we find him and unchange history, we can go back to Albany and Marcel." He shook his head. "What a job!"

"Well," said Norby, "one step at a time. First, Fargo."

They held hands and linked their minds around one thought—Fargo. Far away, wolves howled and a mammoth trumpeted.

"Norby, have we moved in time? We seem to have moved to a wood."

"Of course we've moved in time. It's colder and it feels like winter. And if we were still in Neanderthal times, why would there be a path over there with neatly cut stones in it? And a white marble statue of a naked human female, too?"

Jeff saw the path winding through the trees and the humanlike statue. Therefore, civilized human beings—or so he hoped—lived here. He and Norby followed the path until they arrived at an open space containing a large house and what, in summer, would have been a garden.

Jeff was shivering once more. Would he *ever* get into decent clothes again? "I think I've seen paintings of that building," he said. "It may be Marie Antoinette's little hideaway at Le Trianon in the woods near Versailles."

"And if I hear what I think I hear, Fargo is in there," said Norby, running ahead.

"No, Norby. Come back! I must carry you and you must pretend to be my automaton, moving only when I command and being completely stupid. Please don't mind that."

He picked up Norby, who was growling in his own metallic way, and he marched toward the house and toward the sound coming through a partly opened window of a Wells tenor in full voice.

"Welcome, Jeff," said Fargo cheerfully. "I knew you'd get here sooner or later, but I didn't think you'd show up in quite such a dirty getup. You're a sight to make eyes sore." He was plucking middle C on the stringed instrument lying in his lap, while two ladies with powdered hair leaned close to him from either side.

Fargo was sitting on a red plush cushion, his heavy wig lying in back of him. Canaries twittered in cages around the room, and so did other ladies here and there, all dressed like expensive shepherdesses in a fairyland version of pastoral life.

One of the ladies was reclining on a white satin chaise lounge in an alcove with raised flooring so that she was above the other people in the room. She had luxuriant red-gold hair, a pale oval face, and exquisite blue eyes that turned inquiringly in Jeff's direction.

Fargo said negligently, "Your Majesty, this is my younger brother who has been on some scapegrace expedition or other."

Jeff bowed low, very conscious that his clothing was wrinkled and stained as well as ragged and torn. He noted that the Queen was obviously in the later stages of pregnancy, which was not concealed by the artful shepherdess dress that looked very simple except for the priceless lace decorating it.

Fargo said, "His name is Jefferson Wells, named after our own Thomas Jefferson."

"Ah," said the Queen, "then we must see to it that he has a chance to bathe. And we must find him a change of clothing. I did not know Thomas Jefferson was famous enough to have children named after him at the birth of this large younger brother of yours. After all, he is certainly more than nine years old, so he must have been born before '76 when Jefferson wrote your Declaration of Independence."

So it's still 1785, thought Jeff. Perhaps we can get Fargo away before he changes history. And that might unchange it.

—We'd better leave soon, said Norby, telepathically, before the Queen falls in love with him.

—She won't. She's in love secretly with a Swede, but he's away and—

"Furthermore," said the Queen, "after you are all cleaned up, Master Wells, you must stay until next week, for we are entertaining Jefferson himself. He is here in France."

"Don't let him win your heart away from me, Your Majesty."

Jeff looked at Fargo in surprise. The voice sounded a little like his, and it was the sort of thing he would say, but his lips hadn't moved.

The ladies all turned to look at Jeff, who blushed and then realized they were giggling and waving to someone in back of him. Looking around, Jeff saw a man whom he instantly recognized as Benjamin Franklin. He was walking slowly into the room with the help of Benny and a stout cane. The American diplomat was old, but his smile was whimsical, his bald head shining, and what remained of his long, grey locks touched the shoulders of his plain, brown suit.

Franklin approached the Queen and bent low over her hand. "I have come to see the American actor and singer who managed to talk his way out of the Bastille yesterday and insisted that my grandson inflict him on Your Majesty. Is it true that he has been seeking his lady among your ladies?"

"Quite true," said Marie Antoinette, her eyes sparkling with delight. "Unfortunately, she's not here. We have persuaded your young compatriot to entertain us, however. He is excellent at it."

"I bet," muttered Jeff, and Fargo winked at him. (So it was only yesterday that Fargo got out of the Bastille. For once, Norby had aimed his time-travel ability accurately.)

"My brother Jeff, who has finally arrived," said Fargo, "is a good baritone, when his voice doesn't crack—for he is still in his early youth—and we will sing duets for you. Come on, Jeff."

"Fargo, I'm tired and dirty and—"

"Now, now. You mustn't speak English at the court. I see that your costume is a little the worse for wear. I had to have my own costume fixed up, and yours will be taken care of, too. But for now, rise above your tatters, little brother, and join me."

Jeff turned uneasily to all the glittering assemblage. "May I?"

With a grunt, Franklin lowered himself into a red satin-covered chair and one of the ladies rushed forward to put his aching foot on a high cushion with her own perfumed hands.

(I don't like all the perfume, thought Jeff, but maybe it covers up how I must smell.)

"I would welcome hearing American voices," said Franklin.

"And I would like to hear American songs," said the Queen. "Monsieur Wells has been singing arias from a Mozart opera he heard in Vienna three years ago."

"The Abduction from the Seraglio," said Fargo. "Now how about this," and he started to sing, "'Father and I went down to camp—'"

Jeff joined in at once, enthusiastically, "'Along with Captain Gooding—'"

And Franklin, smiling broadly and waving his cane, joined in the chorus in his old, cracked voice, "'Yankee Doodle, keep it up, Yankee Doodle dandy, mind the music and the step, and with the girls be handy.'"

Fargo sang five stanzas before he felt the audience had had enough. It was a great success and the ladies demanded more songs from America, which was difficult because the Wells brothers didn't know any others they were sure ante-dated 1785.

But then Fargo grinned and started in on "Shenandoah," and Jeff joined him dubiously. They went on to some others that were from wrong time periods, and Jeff grew increasingly uneasy. He noticed that Franklin was pursing his lips and looking extremely thoughtful.

Jeff touched Fargo's shoulder to establish telepathic contact.

—Fargo, Franklin suspects something. He's very intelligent, you know. We have to be careful.

Fargo pretended to be adjusting the tune of his strings, to give Jeff a chance to talk further. Jeff took full advantage.

—You've probably already changed history with something you've done. Albany isn't here because she's in the distant future, and it's the wrong one because of a change that happened here.

—Is she okay, Jeff?

—So far, but none of us can go home because of the time distortion.

Fargo sighed. "Dear ladies. One more song only, so that my poor brother can take care of his somewhat battered self. I will sing it in English for it is one I wrote myself when I was younger. It is a children's song."

There was a hush in the room and then Fargo sang,

"Sing ho for the worth
Of our own planet, Earth;
Of worlds it's the best of them all!
It lacks a bright ring
But has flowers in spring
Green bushes and trees that are tall.
We've only one moon
But it's lovely in June,
So spacers we bid you good-bye.
With planets galore
For you to explore
There's only one Earth in the sky."

The ladies applauded and laughed, though they undoubtedly didn't understand a word.

Benny said, "The words do seem strange. What did you think of it, grandfather?"

"Interesting, but not as interesting as that barrel held in the arms of young Jeff Wells. I distinctly saw the lid of the barrel rise slightly. I may have been mistaken, but there seemed to be eyes looking at me under the lid."

"La, la," said the Queen. "It is one of those automatons! Show us how it works."

Jeff was forced to demonstrate how Norby could telescope out his arms and legs and elevate his half a head.

"Might we see it dance?" asked one of the ladies timidly. And at once the others took up the cry.

—Jeff, you can't make me.

—Norby, you must, or we'll be back in the Bastille.

—Let's just leave. I'd rather be in the cave.

—We can't leave Fargo, and we have to find out what went wrong back here in 1785. Dance!

"Fargo," he said, "play something my automaton can dance to."

Fargo's fingers swept over the strings and he launched into

a rapid rendition of "Look Out, Luna City," contenting himself with humming, rather than singing the words.

Jeff placed Norby on the floor and the little robot deliberately teetered on his two-way feet while the ladies gasped and said, "Oh, don't let the darling fall over!"

Then Norby jigged, his feet continuing to rock, his barrel body moving up and down as his legs telescoped in and out, and his off-key screech accompanied Fargo's tune.

Norby was a great success, too.

"I would like to speak to these two American singers alone," said Franklin, rising and bowing to the Queen. "Your Majesty, will you permit us to walk in your picture gallery unaccompanied for a while?"

"Certainly, cher papa," said Marie Antoinette. "Don't forget to come back for supper."

"Couldn't we have supper first, Mr. Franklin?" asked Jeff, suddenly desperate.

"My brother is a growing boy," said Fargo.

"Humph," said Franklin. "If he grows much more, we'll have to recruit him to command our army, for he would be visible for miles. But very well, food before talk—and wash before food, if it comes to that. Mr. Wells, won't you see to it that your brother Jefferson (why not Franklin, I wonder?) is sluiced down plentifully and has a change of clothing?"

10

CHER PAPA KNOWS

Franklin sat down in a brocaded chair in the middle of the long gallery, which was empty except for the faces in a multitude of paintings, a mixed-up robot closed up in his barrel, a homesick Space Cadet, a Space Command agent—and, of course, an elderly statesman from the newborn United States.

"Well, young man," said Franklin. "You look washed and, from personal observation, you have eaten well. But why did you not accept a change of outer garments?"

"I'm afraid I can't explain, sir," said Jeff, knowing he would have to reappear in his own time (if that ever became possible) in the same clothes he had left with.

"And now," said Franklin, "let me say that my grandson was correct. Your words *do* seem strange and so do *you*. You are most unusual. Your American speech has a peculiar accent I do not recognize. You sing songs I have never heard with words that make odd thoughts come to my mind. Your automaton can perform without being wound up or guided by your hands, and it is too small to contain even the smallest of midgets. I have also heard of the invisible balloon this Norby used to help a Bastille prisoner escape from execution."

Franklin's eyes twinkled as he observed Fargo and Jeff look at each other and say nothing.

"I am a scientist of sorts," said the old man, "and also a firm believer in the American ability to do the best one can with what one has. But I cannot believe that an automaton like Norby can be made in my country. I know that the escaped prisoner is one of the Oslair family, famous for its automata. Is this one of his?"

"I can't tell you," said Jeff. "I'm sorry."

"It would be the most logical explanation—that this automaton is the last made by the Oslairs. The only other explanations unfortunately involve magic, and I have always found myself unable to believe in that. I believe, instead, that what seems inexplicable will eventually be explained by science without the necessity of calling upon magic."

"I believe that, too," said Jeff gravely.

The February twilight had gone and only a few candles lighted the gallery. Benjamin Franklin stared at Jeff. "Will you permit me to examine that automaton?"

"No, sir. I'm sorry, sir. He—it's special and delicate, and besides, we have to leave soon."

"I was hoping you would return to Passy with me," said Franklin. "You will be warm and comfortable there. And perhaps, eventually, we could return to America together next summer."

"Thank you for your offer of hospitality, Mr. Franklin," said Fargo, "but Jeff's right. We must go, and alone."

"With your automaton."

"Yes, sir."

"Who is peeping out at me again," said Franklin.

—Get down, Norby!

"Come on, Jeff," said Fargo. "Let's just open the door and disappear into the night. I hate good-byes, especially to beautiful queens."

Jeff looked down at Franklin, who sat placidly without moving. "I'm sorry, sir, but we must leave now. Will you tell the Queen that we regret not being able to say good-bye?"

"She will be offended," said Franklin. "Queens are easily offended, you know. But I will try to make your peace. Before you leave, however, I wish to say something. In my lifetime of trying to think clearly and scientifically, I have often wondered whether it would be possible to travel to other worlds. Perhaps you might think that a laughable idea."

"We won't laugh," said Fargo.

Franklin leaned forward and took out a pair of glasses that he perched on his nose. "These are bifocals. I invented them myself so that I would not have to be forever changing glasses, first for reading, then for distance. Come here, lad," he said, beckoning to Jeff.

Jeff moved closer and Franklin examined his jacket

closely. "Young Jefferson," said Franklin, "how is it you were named for Tom, a young Virginia farmer, nothing more, when you were born? I was already famous. But no matter, no matter."

He went on looking at the garment closely in the dim light. "This jacket *looks* like French clothing, though there are subtle differences that make me think it is not. For instance, it has remarkably straight stitches. In fact, perfect stitches. This could not be done by human beings. By automaton, do you suppose?"

"Well—"

"Your shoes look like leather, but I don't recognize the material. Your buttons, like the one from your brother's jacket, resemble gilded wood, but they are really some other material I do not recognize. It was the button that made me send Benny to the Bastille. It was *not* American, but neither was it from any other nation I know of. And now that I've seen your automaton—"

His friendly face beamed at them. "All this carries my thoughts far. I like you both and wish you well. Do you suppose you could find it in your heart to tell an old man who can keep secrets where you are from?"

"America," said Fargo stubbornly. "That's the truth."

"Well, you might have travelled widely even if you are from America. I might believe that the Chinese could have strange buttons of strange materials—and even stranger automata. Have you been to China in your travels?"

Fargo and Jeff said nothing.

"You know," Franklin continued in a matter-of-fact voice, "I am nearly eighty and I won't see many more years. I've helped give birth to a new nation, and I've influenced the government of France—I fear to its detriment. France is in bad financial shape and the people are sensitive. The Dauphin is sickly. Perhaps this new baby will be a boy. Will it, Jeff? Ah, you almost answered. I expect you know."

"Please, sir, we must leave."

"Are you human beings? From Earth? Voltaire wrote about strange beings from other worlds who visit Earth. Only stories, but—"

"We are from Earth. Of course," said Jeff earnestly.

"Then I hazard the guess that you are from the future. That

would explain why you are named for Tom Jefferson. He will be fairly famous eventually."

Fargo and Jeff sat silently, stunned, but Norby's head popped up.

"Yes, we are from the future, Mr. Franklin," said Norby, "but please don't tell anyone, or history will be messed up even more than it is."

"Is it already messed up, Master Automaton?"

"My name is Norby. Yes, sir, it is, and we can't get home. We're stuck in history, either in the past—here, or farther back—or else way ahead where everything's wrong, where it isn't *our* future. We can't seem to figure out how to make things right again."

"Hmm," said Franklin, rubbing his bald head. "I hope that telling me hasn't been the cause of this upset."

"No, sir," said Jeff quickly. "The upset had taken place before we met you. I wish we could tell you the whole story, but it's not a good idea to do so."

"Perhaps, of course, I am only dreaming," said Franklin. "I think that after you leave Le Trianon, I will sit here in the shadows and imagine that the whole conversation was a dream. But, before you go, let me tell you that I do not think history can be easily changed. Whatever has happened to make it wrong must have had a chain of consequences that involved important acts. Or very important people. Think about that and perhaps you will solve the problem."

"We'll try," said Jeff. "Thank you."

"One thing more," said Franklin. "If you are genuinely from the future, I would like to know—no! I must not ask. I would like to know if my country survives and prospers. But perhaps I can deduce that from the fact that you exist, and you need say nothing more."

Fargo grinned. "Mr. Franklin, I don't mind telling you that the United States of America will have a glorious history—if we haven't changed things too much, or if we can unchange them. More than that, you will remain one of the most beloved Americans of all times."

"Ho, ho," chortled Franklin.

"Your picture was on the hundred dollar bill," said Jeff.

"Was?" said Franklin, sharp as ever. "By your time, has the nation gone beyond ordinary currency, even the new paper money?"

Jeff nodded.

"Go, before I ask too much. I only hope that human beings have become one people, working together for the betterment of Earth. May I hope that?"

"Yes, sir," said Jeff. "I can also assure you that nobody time-travels unless they have Norby or a certain artifact that's been put back in time. You won't be getting any more visitors like us."

Suddenly Norby's hand shot out and grasped Franklin's. "Good-bye, sir. I am glad I met you."

"We'll have to trust you," said Fargo.

"You can," said Franklin. "Farewell and good luck."

The woods around Le Trianon were dark and cold. Norby took Fargo's hand.

"Hold tight now. I can't fit you both into my hyperspatial field, but I'll take you to Albany, Fargo, and then come back for Jeff. There's just a possibility that if we get you out of France, that will change history back. *I* think the change came about because of something you did."

"I didn't do anything," protested Fargo, "but take me to Albany. I want so much to see her again."

While Jeff tried to imagine what Fargo might have done to change history, or what damage they had done by telling Franklin too much, Norby and Fargo disappeared.

Within seconds, Norby was back.

Jeff asked at once, "Is history okay? Did it—"

"No, Jeff. It didn't work. Getting Fargo out of France made no difference. That grumpy old robot is still in charge of the museum and there aren't any human beings around except Fargo, Albany, and Marcel. Things are just as bad as before."

Jeff pressed his lips together. He would *not* let himself despair. He said, "Take me to the others now. When we're all together, perhaps we'll think of something."

But this time, when Norby tried to hyperjump through time and space, he got a little mixed-up, as was sometimes the case.

Jeff looked about him with horror and said faintly, "Norby! We're in the Bastille!"

11

MORE TIME TROUBLE

Jeff and Norby were standing in the inner courtyard of the Bastille, surrounded by dirty, grey stone walls. In front of them was a tall, wooden device that contained a shiny, new blade.

"The guillotine! It's been invented and is in use, so we must be later than 1785, Norby."

"It doesn't look as if it's been used much," said Norby.

"Oh! Comets and asteroids!"

"What's the matter, Jeff?"

"The guillotine was used during the Revolution."

"So?"

"Norby, scan your memory banks. What happened on July 14, 1789?"

"The Parisians stormed the Bastille and—oh."

"Yes, oh."

"They ravaged it and, little by little, tore it down. It shouldn't be here, intact like this."

"We have to find out what year this is—"

"Ask him," said Norby, pointing to a man in dark clothes who was hurrying across the courtyard to them. "I'll bet that's the Lieutenant of the Bastille."

If so, it was not the Lieutenant who had been there when Jeff and Fargo were jailed with Marcel Oslair. This man was less plump, a bit taller. He looked more severe and wore a simpler costume.

"Who are you, what are you doing here, and what is that metal barrel that seems to be looking at me?" asked the man in French, all in one breath.

Jeff decided he must be the Lieutenant indeed. No one else

would speak with such angry authority. He said, "I'm a visiting American and I wanted to see the famous Bastille. This barrel is actually an automaton. It is mine and I use it in my act as a conjurer."

"In that case, conjure your way out the front gates, because we don't want visitors. We particularly don't want you American savages with your revolutionary wars. Our own revolution was quite different and without bloodshed. It was carried through by men of reason."

"No bloodshed at all? What about that?" Jeff indicated the tall, gaunt shape of the guillotine looming near them.

"A humane device used only for severe crimes," said the Lieutenant. "In fact, it's hardly been used at all since His Majesty came of age two years ago. He is a constitutional monarch in the new tradition and his humanitarian ideas have influenced our civilized country all for the better."

Jeff felt faint. In his own history, Louis the Seventeenth, the second son of Louis the Sixteenth, was never crowned, and died a child after testifying against his mother, who was executed.

"Please, sir," said Jeff, "excuse my ignorance, but in the far-off wilderness from which I come, I have heard little about your revolution. I do remember that in 1789, the mob stormed the Bastille."

The lieutenant looked offended. "Stormed? Not at all. Parisians do not storm. They came to the Bastille and demanded the release of prisoners. When this was not granted—the King then being under the unwelcome influence of the reactionaries —they marched to Versailles to demand a new government. They were not violent, just insistent, and the good King Louis the Sixteenth defied his advisers and insisted the people be heard and their miseries helped. Under his guidance, the Estates General drew up a constitution that the King accepted. The Queen resisted, to be sure, but she was finally packed off to Austria where she came from. Then when the King died four years ago, to the sorrow of all the nation, his son became King at the age of sixteen."

Jeff said, "Then he's now twenty and this is 1805."

"I should think even Americans would know that without having to do arithmetic."

"Yes, I should think so, too. Thank you for your forbearance, sir. We will leave now. I conjured my way in here, but I think you will have to direct me outside."

"You Americans! A crude sense of humor and always itching for a fight, too—still quarreling with England—"

Jeff frowned. "How about your own quarrel with England?"

"What ingratitude! That quarrel was entirely on behalf of the American rebellion. You Americans didn't deserve our help, for it nearly bankrupted France. And it's ancient history. All Europe is at peace now. Even Austria took back the old Queen with scarcely a word, for she knows her presence around the young King would be unwise. Come along, American. Pick up that ugly automation and leave. Get yourself some new clothes, too. Those you wear might be suitable for your own land, but they are laughably out of fashion in Paris."

Carrying Norby, Jeff walked down the streets of Paris, looking for a spot from which he and Norby could vanish without causing a commotion. He crossed a bridge over the Seine and came to a park containing the Museum National d'Histoire Naturelle, founded in 1635 by Louis the Thirteenth. In the gardens he chose a shady spot surrounded by bushes and sat down.

Norby's head popped up. "I was trying to talk to you telepathically, but your mind was all closed up. What is wrong?"

"I'm sorry, Norby. I was trying to think hard. Instead of going to join Fargo and the others in the far future, we jumped back into France, landing in the one place that should not have been there. Why did *that* happen? And I should have asked the lieutenant for today's date."

"I know the date," said Norby. "While you were wrapped in your thoughts I was peeking out, observing. Humans are inclined to be irrational and absentminded, but we robots are always in perfect working order—"

"Norby, I admit you're perfect, and you admit you're perfect, but since you're all that perfect, how did you manage to bring us here, into the wrong nineteenth century? Well, what is the exact date?"

"If you'll stop talking for just a minute, Jeff, I'll tell you. I saw a newspaper and it looked new enough to be today's. In that case, today is July 14, 1805. It should be Bastille day, and a holiday, but it isn't. They probably celebrate the day that

King Louis the Sixteenth accepted the constitution, whenever
that is. It all sounds good to me. Who needs a bloody and
violent revolution?"

"Apparently, we do," said Jeff. "This particular time-track
is not ours and it just gets worse as it moves forward until it
eliminates us entirely. Remember, too, that in this time-track,
the alien planet we were on has no human beings on it, or
other biological beings—just robots."

"Robots wouldn't be so bad if they were like me," said
Norby. "—Oh, oh." He tugged at Jeff's sleeve urgently, then
whipped his limbs into his barrel-body.

Jeff looked up and saw a long face with a long moustache
looking at him over a bush. The face was surmounted by an
official-looking cap with braid on it.

"Oh, hello, Officer," said Jeff.

"Come along," said the policeman. "You're a foreigner,
talking to yourself in a foreign language, and you probably
have stolen goods in that barrel. There's no trusting for-
eigners. Come along."

Jeff was in the Bastille once again. And Norby had vanished.

As the lieutenant ushered him into a cell, he said, "I think
you must have conjured your automaton into thin air, conjurer.
Or, more likely, had a confederate spirit it away before the
police had a chance to examine it. The police are convinced
that the barrel was a cache for stolen jewels—there have been
a number of such robberies lately—and now how are you
going to prove to them that it was only an automaton?—if
that's what it was. I'm afraid I will have to tell them you
pretended to be an American, but were suspiciously ignorant
of the affairs of the world, even for an American. Just be glad
we are living in the new age. There was a time when you
would have been tortured into confessing the truth. As it is,
things won't go too well with you if you do not decide to be
completely frank with us."

There was no use trying to explain. Jeff sat down on the
hard wooden bench and watched the lieutenant leave and the
jailer lock the door to the dungeon. This might be the new
age, and Louis the Seventeenth might be humanitarian, but the
dungeon looked just as dirty and awful as before. He was
willing to bet that the food was the same, too.

He pressed his palms to his forehead and tried to reason the problem out. Norby had had no difficulty taking Fargo on to the distant planet in the distant future, but he had pulled Jeff to a wrong landing in 1805, on a Bastille Day that wasn't.

Norby, being part alien and part Terran robot, had always been mixed up inside so that he was liable to make mistakes in travelling, whether in time or in space. This could be just another mix-up. Or perhaps Norby had been drawn to a place where crucial history, which should have occurred, did not occur. Yet, why?

It was also understandable that, while Jeff was being led back to the Bastille, Norby should have seized an opportunity to vanish to another place, or to another time, or into hyperspace (or to all three). But in that case, why didn't Norby come back for him? Had something happened to the little robot?

"Here I am, Jeff," said Norby, appearing suddenly in the space between Jeff and a particularly unsavory pile of hay that the dungeonkeeper apparently thought would make a satisfactory bed. "I had a little trouble tuning into your whereabouts. I thought you could talk your way out of going to the Bastille. Then when I couldn't find you anywhere, I thought: I bet he went back to that place, and—"

"I'm not glib like Fargo. I can't sweet-talk people into letting me have my way. And what are you doing with that necklace! It's a dangerous piece of alien equipment."

"This is from that museum in the far future."

"But, Norby, it's still dangerous—"

"No, it isn't. Not this necklace." Norby handed it to Jeff.

The diamonds shone and the silver metal glittered. Jeff said, in wonder, "This is the real diamond necklace, not the replica."

"Of course it is, and if you stop to think about it, you'll appreciate how intelligent I am."

Feeling incredibly stupid, Jeff stared at the real diamonds in the real Queen's necklace, remembering how beautiful and old-fashioned it had looked on Albany Jones in her low-cut Marie Antoinette dress.

"Norby! Is the real necklace the key?"

"Yes, Jeff. At least it seems that way to me."

"Let's see. The replica necklace is an alien travel device,

so defective that when it's tied a certain way it tends to jump through time to where it's been—"

"Or where it's going to be—like the future alien museum to which it took Albany."

"Yes, but how does that make the real necklace—"

"Go on, Jeff, figure it out."

"Well, the replica took Albany away from the jewelers' house, and since she was holding the real necklace at the time, it vanished from 18th century France on the very morning when it was supposed to be given to Cardinal Rohan."

Norby jiggled his feet. "So the real diamonds never got to the thieves."

"Exactly," said Jeff. "And there was no scandal. The Queen wasn't blamed, and the whole revolution was quieter, proceeding without bloodshed."

"And," said Norby, his voice rising triumphantly, "the fact that we're here is proof of it. This is 1805 and France is not at war."

"That's because there's no Napoleon in charge of the country. In 1804, he became Emperor of France, and he should be Emperor right now, but he isn't."

Norby said, "He fought all of Europe for twenty years, and turned the whole continent into a bloody field. Who needs him?"

"That's not the way to look at it. The right time-track may be preferable in the long run, even if there are bad periods in it. Napoleon's time-track led eventually to space flight, and then to the far future we glimpsed, when aliens and humans were joined in a Federation."

"I understand," said Norby. "This wrong time-track leads to a future in which humans never join the Galactic Federation. And worse, you and I never met. Or meet. It's a little confusing. I want to go back to February 1, 1785, and return the necklace to Boehmer and Bossange."

"Let's do it now, Norby. I'm tired of the Bastille."

But Norby could not "do it now." No matter how he tried, the Bastille remained around them.

Yet one thing changed. Daylight suddenly turned to nighttime.

"It's odd, Jeff," said Norby. "I think we're getting closer to the right time, February 1, 1785, but not exactly. Perhaps we can't because you are already there, and I can't bring a *second* you to the jewelers."

"Don't try any more, Norby." Jeff shuddered, remembering how the identical replica necklaces had tried to join together. "I don't want the two of me to merge. Something might happen."

"That's right, Jeff. You aren't an inanimate necklace. You're flesh and blood, with life and intelligence. It might short-circuit the time-fabric altogether if there were two or more of the same person close together."

"In that case, Norby, why don't you go there without me? You have never been there, so there's no problem about short-circuiting. Get into that room on February 1, 1785, right after we've been taken off to the Bastille, and leave the necklace on the floor. Boehmer and Bossange will find the necklace and think Albany dropped it. They'll be so busy delivering it to Rohan as promised, that they won't bother going to the police just to tell them there were trespassers in their office. After all, they won't have lost anything—and history will swing back to the right track."

"What does the room in the jewelers house look like, Jeff? I don't want to make any mistakes. Not that I ever do except rarely—"

"Sure, Norby. I know how hard you *try* to be accurate."

"Are you implying—"

"Not at all. I'm just wondering if you can tune into it and go there without any help. The replica necklace is there and you can tune into that, provided you don't tune into it at a different place and in a different time."

"Exactly. That's why you've got to describe the room. I'll have to concentrate on the room as accurately as I can imagine it."

"Good. That's exactly what you'll have to do." Carefully, he described the room, trying hard not to worry about all the things that could go wrong, that could change history again, and that might leave him here in the Bastille indefinitely.

Norby said, "You aren't being very clear about the room, Jeff."

"I'm sorry, Norby, I'm thinking of other things." He tried again, clearing his mind. When he was finished he said, "And that's the best I can do. It was dark and I didn't see it clearly, and everything that was happening, all of it unexpected, threw me off."

"Well, I'll do my best." Norby placed the Queen's necklace in the light from his hat. "I hope this necklace is the solution to the time distortion problem."

"If it isn't—"

"Then I'll take you back to join Albany, Fargo, and Marcel. Then, one by one, I'll take each of you to whatever part of the new time-track on Earth we can reach without fading out."

Jeff felt more depressed than ever. "I don't really want the new time-track, Norby. I want to go back to our own world, our own ways, our own time, to all our friends and to all the other worlds we know."

"Me, too, Jeff. Good-bye."

"Norby! We're in France, and I feel blue. Please don't say good-bye because it sounds so final. Say 'au revoir' as the French do—till we see each other again."

12

The Solution

Jeff must have dozed after Norby left. He was tired enough to be able to do that even in his state of anxiety.

When he awoke, the light through the window was brighter. Clearly morning was coming. He blinked at the light, aware that his stomach was rumbling, that his throat was dry, and that there was a crick in his back from lying on lumps of straw.

But he was also reasonably warm. Suddenly, it struck him that this was odd, since the Bastille was always a cold place—

Wait! Why shouldn't he be warm? The Bastille was only cold in the winter. The first time he had been in one of the dungeons was February 1, 1785. Naturally, it would be cold then. The second time, they had arrived on July 14, 1805, in the new time-track, and, of course, it was warm then.

But then they had moved back, he had thought, near to February 1, 1785 in order to replace the Queen's necklace. It should be cold, but he was warm. Was it summer again?

And what was all that noise?

It sounded like the roar of an ocean in a storm, except that occasionally he could distinguish words. The noise poured through the window, as if hundreds, maybe thousands, of people were milling in the courtyard below.

He heard people running through the halls of the Bastille, and he clung to the grating high up in the dungeon door to see if he could tell what was going on.

Men, and women too, with grimy faces and ragged clothes were shouting and banging on doors with cudgels.

"Liberty! Equality! Brotherhood!" The words were shouted over and over in French.

"Here!" shouted Jeff. "Let me out! What's happened?"

"Down with the aristocrats," shouted a grim-faced woman, her forehead streaked with blood. "We are releasing the prisoners and tearing down the Bastille!"

Men with axes broke the locks and the prison doors were opened. There weren't many prisoners in the Bastille that day, but Jeff was one of them. And as he emerged, he understood that the day must be July 14, 1789, the first Bastille Day.

Jeff realized also, with considerable discomfort, that if Norby came back for him, the small robot would be seen by thousands of people. Yet Jeff couldn't stay in the Bastille. His liberators, in their enthusiasm, would never let him. Nor could he hide, for every cell was being systematically opened and searched.

In fact, it was too late for any evasion. He had been pulled out of the dungeon and swept along in the undertow of humanity surging through the Bastille.

Before long he was pushed and pulled out of the building, across the drawbridge, and finally into the maelstrom that was Paris at the dawn of the French Revolution.

He had lost his wig, fortunately. And his clothes were so stained and torn that he did not look like an aristocrat's servant. He certainly didn't look like a royal gentleman-in-waiting, as he had appeared on the stage of the Metropolitan Museum in Manhattan, USA sector of the Terran Federation.

"Back!" shouted a burly man. "We must tear down the Bastille stone by stone!"

The crowd surged back toward the building, carrying Jeff with it. Jeff struggled desperately to move against the flow. He did not want to go into the Bastille again, not even to pull it down.

Someone's wooden club caught him in the pit of his belly, and he doubled over, unable to breathe for a minute.

"My apologies," shouted the club's owner. "You are so tall I mistook you for one of the King's mercenaries. But you are only a boy and you have no weapon. Come, it is too dangerous for you here."

"I'm a visiting American," said Jeff. "I need to get back to the—uh—place where I've been living, so I can get my weapons. You helped us in our revolution, and I would like to help you in return."

Rough friendly hands clapped him on the back, and some-one thrust a metal bar into his hand. "Well spoken, lad," said the burly man. "Now, on to the Bastille."

Jeff stumbled and fell as the crowd pushed back to the Bastille, and, for an agonizing moment, he thought he would be trampled to death. Then someone cursed and kicked him, and the kick rolled him to the side of the street, next to a wooden barrel that smelled awful. Jeff crouched behind the barrel, pretending to be unconscious.

I must calm myself, he thought. History has come back to normal again, at least as far as Bastille Day. And I'm holding a long piece of metal. It isn't a lightning rod, but I can pretend it is. I can focus my thoughts on Norby and maybe he'll res-cue me.

The roaring of the crowd at the Bastille reverberated with booms like nearby thunder, as the thousands of voices shouted in defiance and triumph. It was the beginning of great changes and, although the ocean of people now on the move didn't know it, it was the beginning of terror and of wars that would last for a quarter of a century and would shape a sharply dif-ferent world.

The new world that followed the wars of the French Revo-lution was to have its dark periods, but by Jeff's time, it had become a world of peace. To the people of Jeff's time, war was an unthinkable crime, and the Terran Federation worked hard to create a climate of hope and prosperity.

Yet it was this terrible Revolution, beginning with the fall of the Bastille, that had started the necessary chain of events.

No, thought Jeff. History says that Napoleon said it was the *necklace* that changed things, increasing the public dislike of the royal family, especially hatred of the Queen and her favorites, making the Revolution inevitable, and a constitu-tional monarchy impossible.

Jeff had seen both histories.

If there had been a constitutional monarchy in France, there would have been no Napoleon. But despite Napoleon's excesses, he started the modern world rolling. He inspired the Code Napoleon which revolutionized French law and was imitated by other countries. He encouraged science, forcing his adversary, Great Britain, to encourage it, too. His armies spread the new notions of revolution throughout Europe and gave all its nations a sense of nationalism. Everywhere freedom increased, even if not without trouble.

It was sad that, before the invention of nuclear weapons, war should seem to be a necessary agent for change, but that's the way it was. It was better in Jeff's time, when space exploration and colonization supplied the spur to change.

Thinking of these things, Jeff became so homesick he could hardly grasp the metal rod and tune into Norby.

"Jeff, did you have to hide behind this smelly barrel?"

Startled by the words in Terran Basic, Jeff craned his neck until he could look into the barrel. There was Norby, up to the neck of his own barrel in slop.

"What do I do, Jeff? I rise into the air, people will see me."

"Turn your antigrav on low," said Jeff. "It will be easier to lift you out. Did you have to transport into the barrel itself, instead of behind it next to me?"

"I couldn't help it. Maybe my barrel was attracted to this barrel—"

"Not funny," said Jeff, lifting Norby. "This smells worse than anything I've ever encountered."

"Hey," yelled a man, snatching at Norby. "Some aristo has thrown his money-chest into the slop to hide it. Give it to me, boy."

Norby spun. The slop slopped all over Jeff and the man who was clutching at Norby. The man cursed. He suddenly lost interest in Norby and was swallowed up by the crowd. Jeff pulled Norby down to him, behind the slop-barrel.

"Get us out of here at once, Norby. Please!"

"Aren't you even going to thank me for taking the necklace back to the jewelers and restoring the proper time-track?"

"Thanks, Norby, I'm proud of you, but maybe you can ignore the smell more than I can. We have to get out of here, and into a lake, so we can wash this stuff off ourselves."

Jeff was wet. All wet. And unable to breathe.

Like any air-breathing animal, he swam upward, hoping that the faint gleam in the water was Norby, but unable to take the time to swim to him. Air was the first consideration.

His head broke the surface and then he realized why the water had tasted odd. He was not in a lake, but in the ocean.

Norby's barrel broke the surface of the water and then rose

higher to hang over Jeff's head. Now clean, the barrel spun rapidly to force the water off its side and lid, and then the lid rose. Norby looked down at Jeff and extended an arm.

"We've had our nice bath—"

"Nice bath! I almost drowned!"

"—and I think you'd better take my arm because we should leave. It's getting crowded here."

"We're in the middle of an ocean. How can it be crowded?"

"Look in back of you."

Bearing down on them was a ship. Most of its hull was black, and part of its funnel was red. The whole thing looked as big as a skyscraper lying down on the water. It was moving fast, and Jeff could see the name of the ship.

"Queen Elizabeth Two," said Jeff. "Take me away, Norby. She may have been the most beautiful ship of the 20th century, but that's not our century and—"

And then they were in the grey of hyperspace.

—I just didn't go far enough forward in time, Jeff.

—Hardly! Please try again, because I'm wet and thirsty and hungry and tired.

—I'm sorry, Jeff. All this travelling around in time and space has upset my circuits. Or maybe the stupid replica necklace was pulling at me and upsetting my calculations. Jeff, what am I going to do about that replica? I've been thinking about it and getting more and more scared.

—More and more scared about what? The replica?

—Yes! That replica gives me mysterious tingles in my vital parts. I've decided I don't really want to go near it again.

—But you must, Norby. You know you must. Fargo, Albany, and Marcel are in the far future. The Other's replica—or the defective travel device, as he called it—is there, too, so we must join it. Tune into the replica once more, Norby. Please, just once more.

—Jeff, I'm really afraid.

—There is no choice, Norby.

—But what if the replica—that dangerous travel device—does something to me. I feel worse and worse each time I'm with it. I think I have had too much contact with it.

Jeff hummed to himself so that he could think without Norby tuning into his thoughts.

—Jeff, are you angry? You know I like Fargo and Albany, and I guess Marcel Oslair is okay. I want to rescue them, but I just *hate* that replica. You don't know what it feels like. If the replica keeps me in the far future, then all of us will be trapped there.

—Yes, we may be. And since the time distortion is corrected and history has been changed back, that planet isn't such a bad place to be. We'll have to chance it, Norby.

Jeff stopped trying to conceal his thought from Norby and let it out: Since history was back to normal, he and Norby could go to their own time. They could go home.

—But you don't want to do that without your brother and Albany Jones (said Norby).

—No, I don't.

—And I don't either.

Jeff felt a tremor as if hyperspace itself was vibrating, and he landed on something hard.

13

THE TRAP

The orange-pink ceiling seemed to smile down on Jeff as he lay flat on his back on the marble floor, but next to him was a display case that was smashed, its plasto-glass in shards all around him.

At first he thought he'd broken it in landing, but he could find no new tears in his clothing and he himself wasn't scratched.

"Welcome back to planet I-13, which is beautiful once more," said Marcel Oslair, walking toward Jeff with an arm outstretched to help him to his feet.

"Thanks, Marcel. Have you seen Norby? And where are Fargo and Albany?"

"The loving couple is there, in the garden." Marcel pointed to the window.

Jeff saw his brother and the most beautiful member of the Manhattan police force strolling together, holding hands. They were followed by a number of laughing children of a variety of species.

"When the planet returned to the normal time-track," said Marcel in French-accented Terran Basic, "the children thought our costumes hilarious. And there you can see Mentor Dickens—that seems to be the robot's name in *this* time—trying to urge the children to stop following your brother and to go to lunch."

"Ah, there's Norby!" said Jeff, carefully moving aside a section of cabinet that almost concealed Norby's barrel. The broken edges of plasto-glass were not as sharp as those of ordinary glass, but he still had to brush them aside with caution.

Norby's barrel was lying, closed up, on a fallen shelf, amid a litter of objects that had been on display. Jeff tapped Norby's lid.

"Norby?"

There was no response. No whimsical half-head popped up with metal-lidded eyes that winked at him. Jeff tried mental telepathy, but sensed nothing. Could Norby be playing some not-so-funny game? Jeff frowned in annoyance.

"One of the false necklaces is lying beside Norby," said Marcel.

"One of them? There was only one in the case when Albany arrived. She was wearing the travel device. She threw it to me, and I put it back into history. The one in the case was only a model of it, and it didn't have diamonds in it as this one does."

"Ah, but while you were gone, the big robot that is now Mentor Dickens had one of his machines put imitation diamonds in the model so that the museum would have a replica of the Queen's necklace instead of a replica of a forbidden travel device. Then Albany gave the real diamond necklace to Norby when he appeared some time ago. Did you put it back into history, too?"

"Certainly. That's what changed the time-track up here, Marcel. But I'm worried about Norby. He acts as though he were in a coma of some sort and—and I'm beginning to think he's not pretending."

"I don't see anything wrong with him," said Marcel. "What about the other side—the side he's lying on?"

"Both sides are the same—," muttered Jeff, but he rolled Norby's barrel till the other side showed, and his throat tightened. This time there *was* a difference in the sides.

Marcel said excitedly, "There it is. The second replica. I hadn't finished telling you. After the museum went back to the true time-track, there were two necklaces in the case. The model of the diamond one, and the model of the travel device."

"Not a model of it," said Jeff. "That's the real travel device we're looking at, the one that's clinging to Norby. I'm sure of it."

The device looked just as it had when Jeff had buried Friend in the Paleolithic cave. It had no diamonds, but Jeff knew it had acquired false diamonds in the 18th century and had kept them right down to the moment when Albany Jones was transported from the museum stage to the jewelers' house and then to planet I-13. Jeff had taken it away, but now it had completed its circle and was back.

Norby had tuned to it and, in this fashion, had arrived here with Jeff. The device had, in turn, fastened itself to Norby somehow when he had arrived, draping itself on one side of Norby's barrel. What seemed most hideous to Jeff was that the back tassels, the ones you had to loop twice to turn the necklace into a travel device, had worked themselves inside the armholes of Norby's barrel.

It was as though Norby had tried to retract his arms into his barrel, but the tassels had stayed firmly attached to his hands. The sliding metal plates that closed the armholes when the arms were retracted were kept open a crack by the back tassels of the device, which reached inward while the rest of the device remained outside.

Jeff lifted Norby's barrel and carried it out into the hall, followed by Marcel. "I must speak to Computer General, Marcel. Please get Mentor Dickens. Get Fargo and Albany, too."

The little Frenchman was off at a run. "I know where the museum office is," he shouted. "I'll be right back."

The co-director of the museum came hastening back with Marcel. He was a human being. His brow was furrowed in concern as he looked down at the unmoving Norby. "My name is Laro Smith. Please tell me what has happened."

Fargo and Albany arrived, too, their joy at seeing Jeff turning to sudden concern over the comatose Norby. Others connected with the museum gathered—some human, some biologically alien, some robotic—and all were sympathetic as they listened to Jeff's story. This world, in the true time-track, seemed a kindly one indeed.

"So you see," said Jeff, holding Norby tightly, "we came back here in the hope that we four human beings who are alien to this world might be able to return to our own time. Norby was reluctant to come because the travel device had an unsettling effect upon him, an effect that increased with each contact. I didn't pay enough attention to that; I thought only of reaching my friends and getting them home. Now he's lying here as though he were dead and without him we can't go home. But Norby is my friend and I'd rather be here with him than at home without him. If he can be saved, I want to save him. Please put me in touch with Computer General—if there is one on this time-track."

"There is," said Mentor Dickens. "I alerted it when I was first informed there was an emergency. It will respond to you now."

The words of Computer General promptly sounded in the minds of all of them.

—Jefferson Wells, I have heard your story. You and your robot have corrected the major time distortion and all history has come back as it was and this is well.

"Yes," said Jeff impatiently, "we know that. But how do we go home now?"

—Your robot brought you here and must take you home.

"But our robot does not respond to us."

—I do not know how to make your robot operational again.

Jeff seized upon the wording. "Is it just that Norby is not operational, that he's just blocked from functioning? You mean Norby isn't actually—dead?"

—This is correct. I have scanned the robot-body and it seems that it is the travel device that is blocking him. Unfortunately, it cannot be pulled out without damaging the robot.

"Can we break the necklace—I mean the device?" asked Jeff. "Might not breaking the device put an end to its powers and leave Norby free to resume operation and take us home?"

—This might be so were it not that the special metal used by the Others to construct the device is extremely resistant to being broken or destroyed. I know of no way in which it can be done.

Fargo said, "Then we must pull it out of Norby, Jeff. If he's holding the back tassels in his hand, it shouldn't hurt him to pull them away."

Jeff shook his head. "I don't think it's that simple. Since Norby can travel through time, the Mentor robots who first constructed him must have incorporated a device inside him that is made of the same metal and has the same powers as the travel device that is now clinging to him. Different samples of the metal seem to have a powerful attraction for each other.

Remember when the jewelers' device tried to join the other portion of itself that was on Albany's neck."

Albany grimaced at the memory. She said, "But that was because the jewelers' replica and my replica were actually the same object in different sections of the time-track. The replica was trying to join itself. Surely this device here and whatever is inside Norby are not identical."

Computer General's telepathic voice was sensed again.

—Both the human named Jeff and the human named Albany have portions of the truth. There is a device within Norby, one that is weaker but safer than the device now clinging to him. The two devices are not identical, but there is an attraction between them that becomes stronger each time one is tuned to the other.

"Aha," said Fargo, "Friend used it to journey to Paleolithic Earth, but after that it wasn't used again until Jeff tied it on Albany. But then Norby kept tuning to it over and over, making the attraction between it and himself stronger and stronger, until—" and Fargo pointed to the device clinging to the unconscious Norby.

At once the Computer General could be sensed again.

—That is so, but I do not know how to release your robot from this trap.

During the morning of the next day there was a brief rainstorm, but the sun came out in the afternoon and the garden sparkled as if a billion small diamonds had been thrown on the leaves and flowers. Fargo had to drag Jeff outside, where Albany was telling old Earth tales to the small nursery children, who were cared for by nurse-robots while the mothers worked in the museum.

Ever since the terraforming of planet I-13, called "Garden" by the human visitors and workers, it had been kept for growing plants useful to all oxygen-breathing species and as a universal museum center.

Jeff cared for none of this. He sat and scowled with a woebegone face—thinking—thinking—

Yet he could not think of a way out. His thoughts merely went about in circles.

Fargo, ever the optimist, said, "Come on, Jeff. If we can't go home to our own world in our own time, we'll just have to make the best of things. This is a wonderful future, and the planet is beautiful. It could be worse, couldn't it?"

Jeff said dully, "I see how it is with the rest of you. Marcel is happy here, learning robotics. Now that we know his disappearance didn't upset history, he doesn't have to go back to the Bastille to die. You and Albany could be happy here, too. You have each other and new worlds to explore and things to do. In this future, hyperdrive is common; and if you can't go home, you can visit millions of worlds if you wish. You can even visit Terra if you're content to visit it in this future time and never go back into the proper time in which you belong."

Fargo nodded. "Well? And doesn't all this apply to you, too, little brother?"

"No," said Jeff. "I want to go home. I want to keep on being a cadet at the Space Academy. I want to be part of the early stages of space exploration. I want to contribute my part to the history of my time. Besides, you don't understand. I want Norby. I want him even more than I want my own time."

Albany had now joined them. She glanced from Jeff to Fargo and then asked the latter, "Won't he accept the situation?"

Slowly, Fargo shook his head.

Albany sat down next to Jeff and put her arm about his shoulder. "Jeff dear. I want to go home, too. My father will live out his life never knowing what happened to me, and he and my mother will both suffer so much. Do you think I want that? But we are here and we can't change it."

Jeff said angrily, "But how do you know we can't? Have you thought of everything?"

"I've tried. If Norby remains in his trap and can't be released, then we are forever imprisoned in *our* trap. We are in this far future time and here we must stay. Face it."

"*If* Norby remains in this trap. *If!*"

"No ifs about it, I'm afraid," said Fargo softly. "You've sat with Norby for over a day, Jeff, and he doesn't respond. And when you tried to tug the necklace away gently, it wouldn't come. And when you tried to bend the metal of the necklace it wouldn't bend. Nothing will make Norby work and nothing will make that travel device work, and there's nothing else in the Universe, even in this amazingly technological far future, that will move us through time. So what is there to do?"

"You two are giving up," said Jeff between his teeth, "but I'm never going to give up. I'm going to act as though there's hope, because if I don't, then I may miss some opportunity for finding a solution. What's happened to our costumes, by the way? We'll need them when I figure out a way to get back home. And don't worry, I'll figure a way yet!"

That day, all three of the Terrans were wearing the simple, flowing garments of the time. Jeff was distantly aware of the pleasure of feeling clean, but he did not find it either a consolation or a compensation for the trap they were in. "Well, where are they?" he repeated.

"Don't get excited, Jeff," said Fargo. "The robots cleaned them, mended yours—which badly needed it—and put them on display in the museum. If you hadn't been spending all your time with Norby, you'd have seen them."

Jeff turned and ran into the museum. Fargo was right—the costumes were there next to a display case containing the model of the Queen's necklace. He studied them for a while and then went to the small room where Norby was being kept. He sat down next to his robot, touching Norby and trying to make contact.

Jeff thought, Maybe there's some way of making the Norby-necklace combination work as a time-travel device.

He put his hands on the necklace as it hung on Norby's barrel, and he concentrated until he was in almost a trance. But even in the trance, his concentration wasn't complete, since he kept interrupting himself with one sharp realization. Even if he found himself home, what good would it be if he couldn't free Norby?

And then he became dimly aware of Marcel standing before him and gazing at him sadly. Jeff looked up and realized that it was twilight outside and that the museum lighting had strengthened to compensate.

Marcel, aware of Jeff's attention, said mournfully, "Ah, my good, young friend. What would I not do to help you, if I only knew how."

Jeff said, "Thanks, Marcel. You need not assure me of this. I know you would help, if you could. I haven't seemed to hit on any way of either using or saving Norby. Of course, I would rather save him—even if it meant I could never use him again."

"I understand." Marcel sat down beside Jeff and patted Norby's lid. "He is more than an automaton. He is a friend; a stubborn, but a very courageous friend."

"Yes, that he is," said Jeff, unable to pay much attention.

Marcel said, "Computer General says Norby is alive, does it not?"

"Yes, but if I can't get through to Norby, it's as if he's dead."

"'As if' is not the thing itself, Jeff. I have heard from Albany that you berated her and Fargo for giving up hope, and you must not do so yourself. Perhaps Norby can hear you, but cannot respond. Perhaps—since he is not dead—he is trying to adjust himself—his—his gears, or whatever it is that composes him. If you could help him, somehow, in his effort—"

Jeff looked up sharply. "You mean instead of my trying to concentrate on getting a response from him, I should concentrate on giving him some sort of response from *me*."

"That is what I think. Since he can't get to you, you must get to him."

"And if I do get to him, I might somehow help him make one of the two time-travel devices work, the replica or whatever it is inside himself."

"Yes. Yet even if you can make him travel in time and take you back to your home—it will not help you liberate Norby, will it? If the people of this far future time cannot free Norby, then the people of your less-far-future time will not be able to, will they?"

"Of course my time would not know, but I am not concerned about that." Jeff's eyes were suddenly shining with determination. "I'll help him move me, but I won't go into the past. I'll go still farther into the future where technology may have developed even further. If I should disappear, Marcel, tell the others I will try to be back soon."

Marcel nodded eagerly. "My best wishes to you, my good friend," he said and he left.

Jeff held Norby tightly to his chest and for the first time since he had discovered Norby in his coma, he relaxed. He was not going to try to pull Norby's consciousness out of him; he was going to try, telepathically, to push his own human consciousness into the little robot—surely an easier task.

—Norby. I know you're in the grip of that defective travel

device, but don't give up. I'm going to concentrate on something and I want you, if you can sense my thoughts, to concentrate on the same thing. Think as hard as you ever have, because we need all the power we can get to break the grip of that horrible object on your barrel.

Jeff visualized. The picture in his mind grew sharper and sharper until, finally, it blotted out everything else but the conviction that Norby was alive and could help.

—Help yourself, Norby.

And with all the force of his imagination, Jeff broadcast another thought; not to Norby this time.

—You Others, out there somewhere, help me!

14

The Power of the Necklace

"Where am I?" asked Jeff.

"In the Cavern of Thought, time-traveller. Be welcome."

The speaker was the tallest being in the room, and the room was a purple rock cavern lit by small, luminous creatures that clung to projecting points of stone. In the center of the floor was a copper-colored space shaped like a comet, and Jeff had landed on the head of it.

The tall speaker, dressed in purple robes the color of the cavern, was one of three Others who looked at Jeff with their three eyes shining in the strange light. Their lower arms were folded in majestic dignity, while the top arms of each were outstretched, the hands cupping hollow balls made of a lace-work of metal that was dull in color, just like the metal of the necklace that was holding Norby in paralysis.

"You are Others," said Jeff. "I needed help and I concentrated on making the travel device find you. It was your work-manship that made the two devices, the one in my robot and the one that now has power over him. If anyone can release my robot it will be you."

And yet, even as he spoke, Jeff felt discouraged, for he could see no sign in the cavern of a suitably high technology. Had he moved mistakenly into the past—or into a future in which the Others had degenerated—forgotten—lost their abilities?

The Others said nothing for what seemed to Jeff many minutes, and then they held the metal balls higher in their outstretched upper arms. Instantly, a dark purple flying creature, like a bird with two sets of wings and a snakelike neck, flew out of the cave shadows, picked up the three balls in its

100

beak and two talons, and flew back again out of sight. The Others folded their upper arms and nodded.

"We know your history, Jefferson Wells," said the tallest Other. "Computer General exists in this time, though in greatly expanded form as compared with the time during which you met it. It has the records and we knew you would reach us, though we did not know when, nor that it would be through your own choice."

"Compared to the time in which I knew Computer General, is this the future?"

"The far future. So far that your sun is now a red giant. This much we can tell you because even in your day it was predicted. What's more, you human beings knew the change would take place very slowly, so that there was time for the human species to settle elsewhere and be safe."

"But do you use only Computer General? I see no robots, no machines—"

"There are robots. Not here, but on most planets. We do not use Computer General except for information. Computer General uses us. We are specialized in a certain kind of thinking you would call intuition and insight. All biological intelligence is capable of this, and some robots are as well, but we have specialized in it for millennia. We Others are the oldest of all the intelligent species in the Universe."

"Can you free my robot from this terrible device that has trapped him?"

"We do not know."

"But you're the wisest of all—"

"We did not say that, young human being. We try to be wise; that is all. There are many forms of wisdom, helped by many things, including human emotion."

"How can my emotion help my wisdom?" demanded Jeff.

"You love your robot, don't you?"

"Yes, I do."

"And your love will strengthen and lengthen your concentration and make you capable of reaching your robot, when, without love, it would not."

"Shall I try now?"

"Yes. And we will help. We will link with you. The device was one of the mistakes of our species long ago, and we must try to help rid the Universe of it. Stand up, Jefferson Wells, and we will touch you while you hold Norby."

Jeff stood tall on the metal representation of a comet, Norby in his arms. He closed his eyes and felt hands being placed on his chest and back, one by one. He counted to twelve and that was all. The Others were very close, and he did not dare to open his eyes for fear that the sight of them would make him lose all concentration on Norby.

Norby! Suddenly, Jeff knew that Norby would help—just as he had helped to get Jeff to this far distant future.

Time, thought Jeff. All the circles complete. No more need. No more power. Let go. Let go. Let—

He could sense a shower of particles falling to the ground, but it wasn't rain. The pressure of the twelve hands vanished and he opened his eyes to see the Others standing back, staring at Jeff's feet. He looked down.

Fine metal was scattered all over, but at a gesture from the Others, it all began to move, coalescing into a ball just in front of Jeff. The tallest Other stepped forward, scooped up the ball in one of his lower hands, and smiled at Jeff.

"Useful stuff, this metal. It came from the Universe before this one. We can use it again."

"And don't make a mistake this time!" shouted Norby, all four of his eyes blinking with outrage. "Don't make a dangerous travel device with it! Use it wisely, you dolts!"

Jeff hugged Norby and said, "Don't be offended by his remarks. He's really glad you rescued him—"

"We merely helped," said the leading Other. "You did it, Jefferson Wells. And the robot's angry remark is perfectly correct. We must use the metal wisely, and we will. This Universe will someday come to an end and the metal will help us find another. Thank you for adding to our small store of it."

The leading Other bowed to Jeff. "And now you must return to your own time."

"With a short stop at I-13 to pick up Fargo and Albany," said Jeff. "Good-bye, Others. I'm glad I met—"

But Norby, with a sound that resembled a human grinding his teeth, jumped through time and space.

Dressed in their costumes, Fargo, Albany, and Jeff stood together, Jeff holding onto Norby with his other hand. Albany was wearing the museum's model of the Queen's necklace. It was not, of course, made of the same metal as the dangerous replica that had carried her to I-13, but Mentor Dickens said the experts of Jeff's time wouldn't notice the difference. Norby had his sensor wire extended to touch an outlet connecting him to Computer General.

"Norby," said Fargo, tugging at his pants, because in spite of the patching, they were still too tight, "you had better be grateful to Jeff. He kept on hoping when Albany and I had given up. He would not let go of you because he loved you."

"It took him long enough," said Norby. "But I love him despite his shortcomings, because I am a loving as well as a lovable robot."

"So I see," said Fargo dryly, while Jeff smiled because Norby sounded completely himself.

Albany said, "Are you certain you can get us back to the Metropolitan Museum's stage immediately after we disappeared, Norby?"

"Not immediately. One second later, I can't go back to a time when I was still there, and it took me a second to decide you'd time-travelled and that I should hunt for you. But I doubt if anyone in the audience will notice. They may sense a tiny flicker."

"You've never been that accurate, Norby," said Fargo.

"I am now. I think I am. Contact with that other travel device gave me more power to be accurate, and to take more than one person with me at a time. Its power leaked to me. Of course it was an evil and dangerous power, but the evil and danger didn't leak to me because I am so virtuous."

"And modest," said Fargo.

"Will it help you in your travels through space?" asked Albany.

Norby thought. "No. Just through time. I can haul all of you through space but there's room for only one within my personal field. The rest would not be able to breathe if we weren't in a suitable atmosphere."

"But we have to go through space to get to Earth. Through space as well as through time, don't we?" asked Albany. "Will it be safe for us to do that?"

"Yes," said Jeff. "Computer General is going to augment Norby's power. We must do it all at once instead of in three stages, to keep the return from being noticed. We've been trying to keep Norby's time-travel ability a secret."

"Then let's go," said Fargo. "As long as we can get back to Terra, there are friends I would like to see, much as I will miss this beautiful world."

"Good-bye," said Marcel Oslair wistfully. "My whole life has been made fortunate by my meeting with you in the Bastille, my friends, and though I am happy with this beautiful world, there will never be a minute in which I will forget you. And I will make my own little robot like Norby."

"Not like me," said Norby. "Nothing is like me."

"And I wish to say good-bye," said Mentor Dickens. "Marcel and I are studying the French Revolution together, including the novel by Charles Dickens, after whom I am named. I am glad that I am not the Mentor robot I would have become if you had not corrected the time distortion. I like being able to smile and to work and to study with biological creatures."

"Good-bye!"

"Good-bye!"

The return to the stage of the museum was not obvious, merely embarrassing, for they were all on the floor, Albany's huge skirt spread out. They were all still holding hands, with a silvery barrel in Jeff's lap.

The audience laughed.

Fargo's thought went out to the others:

—Play it for laughs.

There was a devil-may-care smile on his handsome face that did not in the least resemble that of Louis the Sixteenth.

Albany smiled and patted down the front of her skirt before it had a chance to reveal that she was not wearing long pantaloons.

"Sire," she said, "truly this diamond necklace will cause trouble in our realm, since it seems to turn things upside down. I begin to believe that upside down is the natural state of things, and that Jacques could demonstrate that his automaton can even dance upside down."

—Jeff, I don't have to, do I?

—You'd better. We want to keep the audience's mind off what really happened.

—But my arms come out of the sides of my barrel. I'll have to hop from one hand to the other and I may fall—

—Just use a touch of antigrav and you'll be as graceful as a bird, Norby. Dance, while the audience is still laughing.

Fargo's thoughts added:

—And before the director comes out on stage and tries to murder us all.

Norby danced on his hands. It was not graceful, but, as Jeff reflected, anything to keep them laughing.

On his next vacation from Space Academy, Jeff visited the Metropolitan Museum with Norby, who was strangely silent as they stared at the "Queen's Necklace," which was labelled as the replica made by Boehmer and Bossange.

"Nobody will ever know it's not the real replica," said Norby, "and that it's only a copy made by mentor Dickens. This necklace can't go anywhere or anytime—but the one inside me can."

Norby jiggled on his feet. "I rescued history, didn't I, Jeff?"

"You sure did, Norby."

"You helped, of course."

"A little."

Norby put one hand on the display case and the other on his barrel. There was an odd noise, as if he were clearing his speech mechanism, and then, in a deeper voice, Norby spoke:

"It was a far, far better thing I did—"

"Norby!"

NORBY FINDS
A VILLAIN

*Dedicated to our favorite
science fiction writer,
Clifford D. Simak*

Contents

1   Unexpected Visitors   111

2   The Wicked Magician   115

3   The Stolen Ship   121

4   Escaping into Time   127

5   Closer to Home   133

6   An Artist Lost in Time   139

7   A Disastrous Change   146

8   Prisoners!   151

9   The Problem   159

10   Norby's Idea   165

11   Back and Out   169

12   The Sacred Grove   174

13   Enemy or Friend?   181

14   The Master Cult Arrives   186

15   Searching for Norby   190

16   The Way Home   194

1

Unexpected Visitors

"I'm a lonesome spacer, far away from home . . ." sang Jefferson Wells in his shower. He felt good. Good and ready for his astrophysics exam, at last.

". . . far from Manhattan, where I'd rather roam . . ." His voice ended in a yell as a cake of soap shot out of his hands, hit his nose, and disappeared in the steam and water by his feet. He searched for it blindly as the shower sprayed from wall openings under forced pressure, compensating for the artificial gravity of Space Academy.

The shower door couldn't have opened, yet he distinctly heard someone squeal and he suddenly felt crowded. At the same moment, his foot found the soap.

"Oops!" Skidding out of control, Jeff landed bottom down, right in front of somebody he could barely see through the cloud of steam.

"Naked humans are not allowed in the presence of clothed royalty," said an imperious treble voice. "Furthermore, it is too wet in here. My travel outfit is being ruined."

Another treble voice, gentle yet metallic, said "I'm sorry about this, Jeff."

"I will turn off the water," said another metallic voice that could only belong to Jeff's personal teaching robot.

"Norby! What have you done?"

"Turned the water off. Isn't that better? Now we can all see each other," said Norby, whirling the metal barrel that served as his body and winking at Jeff from both sets of eyes that peeked out, front and back, from under the brim of his dome-shaped hat.

"Great Galaxy!" said Jeff, blushing and trying to drape his washcloth upon himself. "You've brought Rinda and Pera!"

The Crown Princess of Izz giggled. "When Norby tuned into you through hyperspace, we didn't imagine you'd be in the shower at your apartment. And why did the water fall in that funny way? Is there something wrong with Earth's gravity?"

Pera handed Jeff a towel and he turned his back on Rinda to dry himself. Trust Pera to be considerate. She was an alien robot slightly smaller than Norby, supposedly as female as Norby insisted he was male. Unlike Norby's retractable head, hers was a bulge on top of a round metal body, with three eyes on each side. Their jointed legs, arms, two-way feet, and two-thumbed hands were much alike, because Pera had been made by the mysterious spacefarers known as the Others, and parts of Norby had been made by the Others' robots.

"There's nothing wrong with Earth's gravity because this isn't Earth," said Jeff, hurrying into his cadet's uniform while Rinda danced before the hot air jet to dry herself off, her silver pants ballooning out as they dried and her green tunic shining under her carrot-colored hair.

"Where are we?" asked Rinda. "I wanted to visit Earth, now that Pera's taught me Terran Basic and I can disguise myself as a member of our Terran Federation. My parents still want your planet Izz to be kept a secret from the rest of the human race. You know how superior Mother feels because our Izzian ancestors were taken from primitive Earth by the Others and given civilization on Izz."

"While my ancestors came up the hard way, by themselves," said Jeff, putting on his boots. "The water here falls funny because the gravity in an artificial satellite is pseudo-gravity, produced by spinning. You're in Space Academy, part of Space Command, in orbit around Mars, a long way from Earth. But we can go home easily enough by matter transmitter. That is, we can go after I've taken my exam, which is in ten minutes."

"Must you?" said Rinda, pouting. "You look good in that uniform, Jeff. You've grown. I noticed especially when we first arrived . . ."

"Now, Rinda . . ."

"And I bet you haven't noticed that I've grown, too. I'm eleven, now. And you've just turned fifteen. Are you too grown-up to want to be friends with me?"

She had indeed grown. Her freckled face seemed prettier, and the rest of her wasn't as skinny as he'd remembered. "Of course not, Rinda. It's just that I'm in a terrible hurry to take that exam. It's important. Norby should have waited until he was sure I'd gone back to our Manhattan apartment."

"We had to leave Izz in a hurry," said Norby, clasping his hands in front of his barrel, which meant that he was embarrassed.

"Why?"

"We thought you'd welcome our company," said Rinda, her long red-gold eyelashes dropping. There was obviously something more to the story.

"Pera, isn't your special robotic talent the capacity to observe and record facts, even the most subtle facts?" Jeff asked.

"Yes, Jeff. I also have miniantigrav travel like Norby, but I can't travel in hyperspace or through time."

"You're also truthful," said Jeff. "Tell me the real reason why Norby brought you and Rinda here unannounced."

"It was my fault," said Pera. "I happened to be in the palace court when Rinda's mother, Her Royal Queenness, was hearing complaints from the citizens. I happened to mention how many jewels the royal treasury contains . . ."

"Just after Mother had told a citizen legation that the Queendom was too poor to build a new schoolhouse in that area of the planet," said Rinda. "Mother got mad and threatened to put Pera into a stasis box. I told Norby we had to save Pera, so we came here. By the time we get home, Mother will have cooled off and she'll forgive Pera."

"I see," said Jeff, trying not to smile. "Norby, while I take my exam, you take Pera and Rinda on a tour of Space Command, but be sure to speak Terran Basic instead of Izzian, and meet me back in the dorm in three hours."

"Okay, Jeff," said Norby. "Come along, you two. And don't forget about cosmic bubbles, Jeff. And strings and knots. For the exam."

"You're talking through your hat!"

"That's how I talk," said Norby, taking Rinda and Pera by the hand and leading them out.

Jeff was running down the corridor to his exam when he remembered that he hadn't reminded Norby to stay out of trouble.

He slid into the chair at his computer monitor at the last minute. Every cadet in the room was quiet, studying the exam. Then fingers began playing over the keyboards. Jeff gulped and tried to concentrate.

Cosmic bubbles? Silly. Norby's attempts to teach him astrophysics had always been. . . . Strings? Knots? Jeff looked at the question on his monitor and muttered, "Maybe Norby's right."

The time went by while Jeff worked, and finally he tapped "Finished," closed the connection to the exam so he couldn't change any of his answers, and stretched. He knew he wasn't brilliant like his brother, Fargo, but he'd done the best he could. Maybe he'd even passed the exam.

"Hey, Jeff!" It was the cadet nearest him. She pointed to his monitor. "The warning light's flashing. Could you have accidentally wiped out all your answers?"

"Oh, no!" Jeff reconnected himself to the computer, and printed words appeared on the screen. Computers in exam rooms were not allowed to speak out loud.

"Jefferson Wells," printed the computer, "come to Admiral Yobo's office!!!" The third exclamation point was in red.

2

The Wicked Magician

At the nearest slider entrance, Jeff hopped into a waiting car, punching Yobo's code into the direction panel. The buglike car sealed itself and shot through the transparent tunnel, bypassing exits to other corridors until it reached the Main Hub tunnel and swerved into it.

As the car sped up, or possibly down—it didn't matter because away in the hub of the gigantic wheel that was Space Command there was no pseudogravity—Jeff worried. When you are an orphan tall for your age, with a daredevil older brother, you are inclined to worry a lot, especially since Boris Yobo, in charge of Space Command, did not ordinarily summon lowly cadets to his private office.

The Hub tunnel increased in size as more pipes joined it from other small wheel-shaped satellites of Space Command, docks and military barracks and research labs and others Jeff knew little about. Vehicles passed Jeff's car in both directions, but all he could think about was whether or not he had bollixed up Space Command's main computer by doing something wrong with his exam computer. It had happened before. And the Admiral was not a patient man.

When he was finally standing in front of Yobo's big desk, he saw that Norby, Pera and Rinda were also in the room.

"You are responsible for visitors," said Yobo, speaking in a sort of bass purr that boded no good.

"Yes, sir. I was taking an exam . . ."

"That's no excuse. Especially with that mixed-up robot of yours on the loose. It was all I could do to keep Security Control from finding out that Rinda here is not a Terran but from a planet nobody outside this room has heard about—

with the exception of your brother and his fiancée, who are totally out of reach because they've hidden themselves in some mountains on Earth. Some sort of hiking holiday..."

"Yes, sir. Fargo didn't want anyone to be able to find him."

"Which I can't. So you'll have to see to it that these two robots and that child..."

"I am not a child!" said Rinda. "I'm eleven and a Crown Princess!"

Yobo growled. "See to it that they don't get into any more trouble."

"But what did they do?" asked Jeff.

"I was merely educating Rinda and Pera," said Norby, waving his arm importantly. "I was explaining about how I helped capture the traitor Ing the Ingrate when he tried to take over the Federation."

"You mean you were bragging about it," said Jeff.

"And furthermore, Rinda said she wanted to know more about my glorious achievements, so I just tapped into the library computer banks and let her listen..."

"You blasted barrel of a robot!" roared Yobo. "You succeeded in tapping into the classified information section of Space Command's Secret Service!"

"I didn't learn a thing," said Rinda, "except what Ing looked like—grey hair and red eyes and skinny—not at all interesting."

"I'm afraid I learned everything," said Pera, always truthful. "I'm sorry, Admiral. I won't tell anyone about the secrets of Space Command, or things like the code numbers of official spies, or exactly how much you weigh..."

"That will do," said Yobo, his majestic bulk rising from the chair behind the desk. "Cadet Wells, take the Princess and her robot and your robot—especially your robot—away."

"But, Admiral," said Norby. "I was only tapping into Space Command's files to try to find a way to get tickets for the show tonight. Can't we go?"

Rinda turned on Jeff. "You mean you weren't going to take me to a show?"

"I forgot about it," said Jeff. "I didn't get tickets because, with Fargo on vacation, I have to go back to Earth right after my exams. Our pet Oola gets lonely being taken care of by the stupid kitchen computer."

"I want to go to the show," said Rinda.

"It's just a bunch of traveling entertainers," said Yobo, somewhat wearily.

"And you are Master of Ceremonies," said Norby. "The computer said so. You're even taking part in one of the skits, aren't you?'

"Unfortunately, yes," said Yobo, massaging his bald black head. "I get a headache every time I go into that silly magician's magic box, which isn't magic, of course . . ."

"Oh, Admiral," said Rinda, sidling around the desk and fingering the Admiral's medals on his broad chest. Her eyelashes fluttered up at him. "I do so want to see you perform. You must be marvelous."

"No! Absolutely not!" said Yobo. "Jeff, take her to your apartment on Earth and keep her out of trouble . . ."

"Oh dear," said Rinda, her lips trembling. "I so wanted Pera to observe and record your magnificent performance, so I could show it at the royal court of Izz, and now"—a tear rolled down her cheek—"you won't let me."

"Well, harrumph! Comet tails, but I can't bear seeing females cry. . . . If you promise to be good."

And so they got tickets to the show. After a hasty dinner, which Rinda devoured and Jeff picked at because he was still worrying, they went to their seats, which were at the back of the crowded auditorium.

It was a long show with many acts, some serious with classical music and dramatic readings, all introduced by the Admiral in his deep, commanding voice. During the intermission, Rinda burbled about how marvelous Yobo was.

"Just your luck that the Admiral's old-fashioned enough to believe that nonsense about weak, helpless females," said Jeff. "I have never yet met a genuinely helpless female. Look at your own mother! Sometimes I think you take after her . . ."

Rinda's elbow caught him in the ribs. "Shut up, Jeff. The second half is starting and the program says it's going to be funny, with clowns. But look—your clowns wear baggy pants—that's not funny."

"It is here," said Norby, sitting on Jeff's lap as Pera was on Rinda's. "Everyone wears baggy pants on Izz, so only tight leggings are funny there."

Jeff, who expected to be bored, had to admit to himself

that the clown act was good, if ancient. They rode around in strange wheeled vehicles that made odd noises, they smacked each other with rubber baseball bats, and then they did a hilarious dance to the tune of a pocket flute played by the chief clown, a pudgy, black-haired man whose forked beard and handle-bar mustache contrasted with the red bulb fixed to the end of his long nose.

"Threezy!" shouted the children of Space Command personel. "Hurray for Threezy the Clown!"

Threezy bowed and played another tune which he danced to very well.

Pera's arm reached over to touch Jeff and establish telepathic contact. Since Norby was also touching Jeff, he tuned in also.

—I am upset [said Pera]. Something is wrong. There is an artificial layer covering the eyeballs of that clown

—Idiot [that was Norby]. Lots of humans wear contact lenses on their eyes.

Admiral Yobo then announced that the troupe of traveling entertainers would put on a special melodrama which he would personally oversee to make sure that it didn't frighten anyone. A chair was placed for him at the side of the stage and the curtain rose upon a blustering villain wearing a black cape lined with red satin to match his nose.

It was Threezy, who sneered at the audience and broke into hideous laughter before beginning his song:

"You can speak of many villains with any claim to fame,
But you'll never find another who can beat ME at the game!
At enterprising evil I put Ing to second best—
I am wild and wicked Threezy, by far the horridest!"

The children laughed and clapped as Threezy menaced the heroine, a spangled lady with blue feathered hair who kept screaming, "Save me from this villain!"

"Ah, me proud beauty!" said Threezy. "Behold my magic box in which I will carry you away with me." He gestured, and a long box emerged from the stage trap door. A door in the front of the box opened.

—I don't understand [said Pera]. Their hair is wrong. The top layer of the lady's hair is a synthetic substance made to look like feathers, and Threezy's hair has black material on it.

—It's okay, Pera [said Jeff]. In the Federation, humans are allowed to wear wigs and dye their hair.

—The Queen of Izz would not approve.

—I heard somebody say that this is where the lady goes to Yobo for help and Threezy forces the Admiral into the magic box [said Norby].

Indeed, the spangled lady, shrieking that she did not love the caped villain, had scurried across the stage to clutch Admiral Yobo's arm. Yobo put a massive palm out against Threezy's approach.

"Cease and desist, villain!" said Yobo. The crowd was delighted.

But Pera was not. She slowly rose on miniantigrav from Rinda's lap, pointing toward the stage.

"I don't like that magic box," she said out loud. "I must observe it at closer range." Before Rinda could grab her, Pera sailed out over the heads of the crowd, toward the stage.

The spangled heroine gaped at the little robot and Yobo shook his fist in Jeff's direction, but it was Threezy who made the robot's appearance part of the act.

"Aha!" he shouted. "No doubt this is our Admiral's bodyguard. Isn't it amazing how they make them smaller as our Admiral gets bigger."

Everyone laughed, but a little uneasily, because Yobo's frown was always an intimidating sight even when it was not known if the frown was make-believe or not.

"Come back, Pera," cried Rinda, standing up.

Jeff stood up, too, holding Norby, who was struggling to follow Pera and stop her from embarrassing them.

Threezy seemed to stop dead, staring at the audience. "Ah," he said. "Fee, fie, fo, fum—I smell the blood of young villains. I see you, Jefferson Wells!"

And with that, Threezy caught Pera as she sailed toward the magic box and jumped into it with her. The door slid shut and the box sank below the stage.

"Open that trap door," said Yobo as Jeff fought his way toward the stage, followed by Rinda, who was calling for Pera.

"The mechanism's locked from the other side," said one of the stagehands. "We'll have to go below stage the other way."

A security cop came running up to Yobo. "All entrances to

below stage are locked, and there's an emergency air lock that's been opened. Security patrol boats are on their way."

"I don't know any reason why Threezy would steal the little robot and disappear like that," said the producer, wringing her hands. "He's new to the company, but he's very talented. We found him working in a cafe under Titan's dome and I hired him to replace a clown who'd retired. But Threezy was so good I made him the star of the show. Funny thing, though—he'd never let us touch his magic box."

"Same box that gave me a headache," said Yobo. "Find him and bring him back for questioning."

"Why did he take Pera? I want my robot back!" said Rinda.

—Jeff [said Norby, telepathically], I sensed that there was an engine in that magic box, as well as a lot of other equipment. The clown's going somewhere in it and I think we ought to follow him.

—Good idea, but all the exits from Space Command will be watched . . .

—Don't be stupid, Jeff. Let's get behind those curtains and go into hyperspace and reappear in normal space outside the satellite. Then we'll find Threezy.

Jeff managed to get to Yobo and whispered to him that he and Norby might be able to find Threezy before the Security cops did. Yobo nodded.

"Take care of Rinda, please," said Jeff. "She and I together won't fit inside Norby's personal protective field, so I have to leave her behind."

Yobo rolled his eyes upward and said, "Hurry, Jeff."

Just before the grey gloom of hyperspace enveloped Jeff, he saw Rinda's little face, streaked with tears, poke around the curtain and shout at him.

"Wait for me!"

3

The Stolen Ship

The sensation of being in hyperspace, the groundwork of the cosmos, was always awesome at first. It seemed to Jeff that he was lost out of time and normal space forever, but no sooner had he steeled himself to the feeling when Norby went back. Jeff blinked, for he'd expected to be outside the wheel of Space Command, floating in space, and instead his eyes were filled with bright light.

"I thought I was tuning into Pera's whereabouts," Norby said softly, "but we've come too late."

They were in the control room of a ship that was familiar. Jeff blinked again and recognized Space Command's first, experimental and so far only hyperdrive ship, recently renamed *Quest* by Yobo.

"Well, well. Unexpected visitors," said an unpleasant voice that seemed dreadfully familiar.

Jeff turned and saw the bizarre figure of Threezy the Clown, aiming a stun gun at him.

"I didn't see you come in," continued Threezy in a voice that seemed remarkably unlike the one the clown had used before. "No matter. You are merely an adolescent of no importance and you have brought me an extra robot."

"I don't know what you think you're doing, Threezy," said Jeff, "but stealing a robot is . . ."

"Stupid boy, I have planned for a long time to steal something else—this oh-so-special ship of the Admiral's. And now success is mine!"

"You can't even run this ship!"

"Oh, can't I? After inveigling Yobo into my act so I could rehearse with him inside my magic box? I have a mind probe in there . . ."

"Mind probes are illegal!"

"Dear honest youth, you have no conception of what it takes to be genuinely brilliant, a genius capable of the greatest plans devised by any mind. I've thoroughly probed Yobo's mind for information on how to run his precious hyperdrive ship. Now I think I've heard enough from you."

"Be careful, Jeff," said Pera's voice. "There's a detonator in his pocket, and he has two powerful bombs in the ship. Don't do anything to upset him." In the far corner of the control room was the magic box, with Pera inside it behind bars that now closed the opening. Since Pera couldn't disappear into hyperspace like Norby, she was trapped.

"I don't like you, Jefferson Wells," said Threezy, "and you'll not thwart my plans again." He pressed the trigger and the stun rays hit Jeff and Norby.

As Jeff hit the floor, he saw Norby fall beside him, and wondered why his own eyes were still open. The full blast of a stun gun should have made him unconscious. Norby's barrel was touching his arm. Perhaps he could still communicate.

—Are you paralyzed too, Norby?

—I got the full dose and it must be one of those illegal, too-powerful guns, because I'm having trouble moving and I don't think I can use hyperjump to get us out of here.

"Still awake?" said Threezy, lifting his upper lip far enough so that his greyish fang-like incisor teeth showed under the giant moustache in the ancient primate demonstration of threat. "But I see that you can't move, Wells. Now you just listen quietly while I send my message to the Federation."

He touched a switch on the control board and Jeff hoped against hope that Threezy would be so occupied in bragging to the Federation that he wouldn't notice that, according to the viewscreen, patrol boats now surrounded the dock where the *Quest* was moored.

—Jeff, I've analyzed the voice data, and that's not Threezy. I mean, it's Threezy, but it's also Ing the Ingrate!

—Blast! I should have figured that out. He's gained weight and dyed his hair and grown a moustache, but you're right, he's Ing.

"Beware, Terran Federation!" said the erstwhile clown, speaking into the ship's communicator. "Do not attempt to take me into custody. I possess two bombs which will effectively destroy all of Space Command and I will not hesitate to use them to avoid capture."

Ing smiled. "I want you all to know that you are in the power, not of a mere clown named Threezy, but of the most important being in the universe—Ing the Incredible! And I am about to take my revenge. I will set off my special bombs in hyperspace itself!"

—Norby, can't you move at all? I think I'm getting back some muscular ability. . .

—Be careful, Jeff. He's dangerous.

"You don't undersand what will happen, you stupid fools," said Ing, "but when I set off my bombs in hyperspace, the explosion will alter the fabric of normal space. The universe will collapse and soon become lethal to all life forms."

—Norby! Can he do that?

—I don't know. Maybe the Others, who have been using hyperspace for millennia, could tell whether or not Ing's right, but I can't.

"But ah, Federation—your unappreciated Ing will not have to join your death party. I will be safe in hyperspace, in my magic box that I can transform into a stasis container. I will wait while the universe dies and then expands again. I will be there when the reborn-universe is ready to receive me as its master! Farewell. You have twenty-four hours to say goodbye to each other."

There was a lurch and, to Jeff's horror, the viewscreen showed that the *Quest* was now in the grey nothingness of hyperspace. Ing had indeed learned how to use hyperdrive, and he had escaped capture.

Jeff managed to move his tongue, and slurred words came out. "You're mad, Ing."

"I wanted you conscious, but not lively," said Ing, brandishing the gun. "Don't try anything heroic, Wells, or I'll attach you to the first bomb I send out. Nothing's going to stop me now. You and that silly robot of yours once foiled my plans to run the Federation, but now I can be master of a new universe." He laughed maniacally.

"Jeff," said Pera, "I can detect abnormal patterns in his brain waves. There is something wrong with this clown who now calls himself Ing."

"Shut up, robot, and mind your own business," said Ing. "I have work to do."

"Your plan will fail, Ing," said Jeff. "You'll probably destroy this ship and yourself, but you won't change the universe. It's too big and your bombs are too little."

"Not by my calculations." Ing stroked one of the handlebars of his moustache. "Furthermore, there's nobody in hyperspace who can stop me. This is the only hyperdrive ship in existence, although I've heard a rumor that your robot can attach himself to a ship's computer and generate hyperdrive capacity."

Ing's eyes widened. "Hmmm. Even geniuses don't consider everything. It never occurred to me to try to steal your robot, Wells, when I could have hyperdrive merely by stealing the *Quest*. But with your robot already here, thanks to your stupid heroics, perhaps I can augment the hyperdrive by using him."

"You won't be able to," said Jeff, trying to test his leg and arm muscles in isometric contractions.

"Why not? Is the rumor untrue?"

Jeff didn't answer, but pretended to be semiconscious.

"Humph!" said Ing, kicking Jeff, who didn't respond. "And the robot looks dead. But not the other one—I had no idea you had two of them, Wells. They don't look exactly alike but I suppose it doesn't matter. You, robot in the cage, is Norby capable of hyperdrive?"

Pera did not answer.

Ing strode over to the cage and glared at her. Then he pointed the gun at Jeff. "I'm going to stun young Wells until he stops breathing if you don't tell me the truth."

"Norby is capable of hyperdrive," said Pera.

Jeff gathered his strength and hurled himself at Ing, but the gun was too quick. This time Jeff blacked out.

When he awoke, he looked at the ship's chronometer and saw that an hour had passed. He still couldn't move easily, but he made the mistake of yawning.

"So you're conscious again, are you, Wells?" Ing looked furious, but the anger didn't seem to be aimed at Jeff.

"What's the matter, Ing?" asked Jeff groggily.

"The bombs don't work, that's what's the matter," yelled Ing. "I sent out the first one, timed to go off when far away from the *Quest* . . ."

"It's impossible to tell dimensions in hyperspace," said Jeff wearily.

"Oh, so you're a hyperspace expert? Maybe you are, if the rumors about your robot are correct. But the bomb didn't go off too close to this ship. I had radio link with it and there was no explosion."

"I'm not sure it would be possible to tell if it exploded or not. Perhaps you're just lucky to be still alive."

"Robot in the cage," demanded Ing, "you have sensors that might be able to tell. Did the bomb explode?"

"Should I answer him, Jeff?"

"Might as well. It might discourage him from continuing this idiotic experiment."

"The bomb did not explode, Mr. Ing."

"Hellfire!"

"Maybe bombs don't go off in hyperspace," said Jeff.

"Is that true?" Ing didn't ask Jeff, but pointed the gun at him again and asked Pera, a robot committed to telling the truth. "Tell me, robot, if you want Jefferson Wells to live."

"In my memory banks there is data indicating that bombs will go off in hyperspace."

"Then why, why?" Ing raged around the control room, hitting the walls and kicking Jeff again. The kick had one good effect—it pushed Jeff within touch of Norby's barrel.

—I'm getting back my functioning, Jeff, but it's slow, and he must not ask Pera what she surely has observed, because I did, and I'm not as good at that as she is.

—What are you talking about?

—There's something out there in hyperspace. Something that caught the bomb.

But Ing asked Pera a different, more dangerous question.

"All right, smart little robot, I want to set off my second bomb, but this time it's going to be part of the booster engine of this ship, forcing the ship itself to rip the fabric of the universe. I may die in the attempt, but maybe I won't. If I hook you up to the computer, will your power augment it?"

"Jeff, I don't want to answer..."

"Your Jeff is doomed if you don't answer," said Ing. "This time I mean it. One more stun and he's dead."

"Ing," said Jeff, "You're only dooming all of us. Be sensible and take us back into normal space and..."

"No! I'm going to destroy normal space! I'm going to destroy the universe! I don't need the robot's answer. I'll use the robot anyway."

Jeff tried to rise, but it was impossible. Norby's head was trying to rise out of his barrel but his arms and legs were still stuck inside.

Ing was stronger than he looked. He caught Pera's arms, stuck beseechingly through the bars of her cage, before she could withdraw them into her body. With a wire from computer, he tied them together, and fixed a computer link device to her head.

"Stop it, Ing!"

Ing paid no attention. He lifted Jeff's arms and pulled him into the air lock that opened directly into the control room. Then he threw Norby inside and closed the door.

"Norby—can you do anything?"

One of Norby's arms came out and the hand grasped Jeff's just as the *Quest* gave a wild shudder and the outer door of the air lock opened.

The air in the lock rushed out, carrying Jeff and Norby with it.

4

Escaping into Time

—Norby! I'm still alive!

—Don't you have faith in me, Jeff? I'm your personal robot, bound to protect you.

—But you were stunned and couldn't function and Ing threw us out into hyperspace . . .

—I am a superior robot and even when I haven't had time to recover all of my functioning, I can certainly put out a protective field for you.

—Thank you, Norby.

—Besides, the field comes on automatically. I confess that if I'd had to turn on the field deliberately, I might have had trouble. The old spacer who found my alien parts and put them into a Terran robot knew what he was doing, because that amount of stun would have ruined an ordinary robot. As it is, I'm nearly back to normal.

—Then find Ing's ship. We have to get inside and stop him from setting off that second bomb.

—I can't.

—Then you're not back to normal at all.

—I certainly am. I can't get inside the *Quest* because it isn't there. I have a limited ability to detect the presence of things in hyperspace, and the *Quest* is gone.

—Back into the universe?

—I—don't—know. Jeff, I'm scared. Something's wrong.

—With hyperspace? How can that be?

—Nothing seems wrong now, but something was wrong—at the moment we were thrown out of the *Quest*, it was forced through hyperspace by powerful energy. Ing must have harnessed the force of his second bomb, perhaps by using Pera.

She contains some of the same alien metal that I do, and although it was used to give her powers of observation instead of hyperdrive, she may have talents she doesn't know about.

—None of this makes sense. Why didn't the *Quest* just blow up? Maybe Ing and Pera are both dead.

—Oh, Jeff, don't say that. Yet, if the *Quest* did what Ing wanted it to, he may have succeeded. He may have forced the *Quest* out into the universe, but that could mean . . .

—What?

—That the tremendous energy he used to force the *Quest* out of hyperspace may have altered the field of our universe. I don't see how the *Quest* could have survived this. And perhaps our universe is even now dying.

Jeff found that he was breathing too quickly, using up the small and precious supply of air in Norby's protective field. Norby could survive a long time in hyperspace, but humans could not.

—Norby, review all the data in your memory banks, especially the moment when we left the *Quest*. Isn't that where you think something "wrong" happened? What was it?

—I told you. The force with which the *Quest* moved—no, Jeff. You're right. There was something else. Something that made me deduce a wrongness. It was . . . like a crack.

—I don't understand.

—Neither do I. It didn't last long, but my sensors picked up a dimension in hyperspace, which has none. As if a narrow hole opened and shut.

—Can you explain it?

—Of course not. I'm not a genius.

In the midst of his anxiety, Jeff almost laughed, for Norby was fond of bragging about being a genius. Just now, however, claiming to be a genius would sound too close to Ing's ravings.

—Jeff, you're breathing heavily. Are you all right? Are you still paralyzed? And is it affecting your diaphragm?

—The paralysis has gone because the stun dose has worn off, but I guess I'm getting a bit short of breath because the oxygen is running low. We have to go into normal space to a planet where I can replenish my air. Then we've got to get back into hyperspace and try to make sure that the *Quest* isn't there.

Norby was silent for such a long time that Jeff became frightened. He could feel Norby's hand holding his, and the protective field was still there because he was still alive, but what was happening to Norby? Had he been damaged?

—No, Jeff, I'm not damaged. I've been thinking. I don't know where to go. If the universe has been destroyed, maybe there isn't any "where" to go to.

—Comet tails!

—I agree. This is not a satisfactory situation. I will try to think of a solution to this problem . . . Hey! What was that!

—What was what?

—Didn't you feel . . . no, of course you wouldn't. You don't have my sensors. There's something that's come near us in hyperspace.

—The *Quest?* Is Ing trying to capture us?

—I don't think so. I don't know. I can't tell . . . I am an inadequate robot . . . Hey! Whatever it is, is trying to grab me with some kind of device. I don't like it at all.

—Norby, we can't stay in hyperspace! There's something after us and I'm running out of air. Go *somewhere* fast!

—But Jeff, what if there's no "where" to go to?

—Then try a "when."

—I'm sorry, Jeff.

—But we're out of hyperspace and the universe is still here and there's a planet! Take me down so I can replenish the air in here.

—Jeff . . .

—And look, Norby, you *are* a genius! You've brought us out of hyperspace into orbit around Earth, for there's the moon, peeking out behind . . . Oh! Earth . . . isn't right.

—No. I tried to jump back in time so I wouldn't come out into the normal space of the universe after Ing did whatever he did. But I jumped back too far. My sensors tell me that the atmosphere here isn't breathable by humans.

—Do you mean we've come back in time so far that bacteria in Earth's oceans haven't yet begun to put oxygen into the air?

—Yes. Hang on. I'm going forward in time.

—Be careful. Not too far.

This time Jeff hit something hard and he was so dizzy he

couldn't see at first, and all the breath seemed to have been knocked out of him. He gasped, tried to expand his lungs—and air came rushing in. Air!

Jeff opened his eyes. He was lying prone, a slab of rock beneath him and a perfectly ordinary ant crawling past his nose. He could hear birds singing, water gurgling, and a mysterious trumpeting sound in a deep bass. He sat up and gasped again.

The view was astonishing—and beautiful, the crisp, cool air clean and fragrant with blossoms. He and Norby were sitting on a hillside, looking down into a green valley where herds of animals moved slowly—antelope and elk and . . .

"Norby! Mammoths! We're in the Ice Age of Earth!"

"I was concentrating on it, Jeff. You've always been interested in it and the water ought to be clean. You can take a drink at that stream." Norby pointed to a tiny spring gushing out between two boulders.

The water was as delicious as the air, and Jeff drank deeply. He had not realized how thirsty he was. Then he leaned back against the hillside.

"Norby, it's so beautiful here. I'm beginning to wish we could stay. Human beings haven't had time to ruin Earth."

"It isn't all ruined in our time. By the twenty-first century, humans had stopped destroying the forests and polluting the air. And they made more of an effort to preserve the diversity of animal species that is so essential to a balanced ecology. . . ."

"Norby, there aren't any cities, or any Ings." Jeff sat up and rubbed his curly brown hair. "And speaking of villains, Ing didn't succeed, because here we are, in the universe."

"Far back in time, Jeff."

Jeff gulped. "You found me another 'when', a time before Ing destroyed the universe—is that what you mean?"

"Yes. No. I don't know. I can't predict what we'll find if we try to move forward to our own time."

"Well, as long as we're safely here in the Pleistocene, I think I'd better look around for some food. I'm getting awfully hungry. I'm certainly not equipped to kill any animals, but I might be able to find some nuts and berries . . ."

"I think you'll have to be hungry a while longer," said Norby. "If you had eyes in the back of your head like me, you'd see that we have company. Turn your head slowly and look up the hill, over to your left."

Jeff turned and glimpsed a shaggy head peeping over a crest of rock formation at the top of the hill.

"Homo sapiens sapiens," said Norby professorially. "Just like you. We've come in Cro-Magnon times, which is just as well since those earlier big-nosed, big-browed *homo sapiens neanderthalensis* might not have been friendly."

Just then a spear with an intricately incised shaft hit the rock slab by Jeff's toe and clattered down the hill.

"I never could understand why your variety of human insists on naming itself 'wise' *twice,"* said Norby.

Jeff clutched Norby's hand just as another human stood up with another spear. "Time to go, Norby!"

—Can you breathe all right now, Jeff?

—Yes, but hyperspace looks gloomier than ever and I'm twice as hungry. You know I can't think clearly when my stomach is rumbling. Please take me to a time when I'll be able to eat as well as breathe the air and drink the water.

—I'll do my best, Jeff. You'll have to admit that I'm getting better at taking us to times and places without mix-ups. You didn't even land hard enough on that Pleistocene hill to break anything.

—And you got us away before the second spear hit. I think it might have found its mark. Those Cro-Magnon people were skilled hunters. I wish I'd thought to bring the first spear with me.

—That might have disturbed history. Perhaps it's one of those spear shafts that was found in modern times and ended up in a museum. I wish we'd brought Ing with us and left him in the Pleistocene . . . Jeff! I have a brilliant idea. Let's go forward in time to find Ing when he was a child and bring him back here to be adopted by some Cro-Magnon family. Then he won't be able to set off his bombs and the danger won't have happened at all.

—You are ignoring your own advice about not disturbing history. Right after I bought you to become my teaching robot, we were mixed up in Ing's early wickedness, when he tried to become master of the Federation. If we remove Ing from history we'll destroy parts of our own histories, and we won't be the same. We might not even be together, and I don't want that.

—You're right, Jeff. Whatever happens, we two must stick together. Besides, judging from the rest of human history, if Ing hadn't been around to cause trouble, somebody else probably would have.

—I'm still terribly hungry, Norby. Please find me a time when I can eat without disturbing history.

The transition was so quick that Jeff smelled the food before he saw it. The smell was delicious, almost as if he'd landed in one of the better restaurants on Earth.

He looked around and thought that perhaps he had—at least he seemed to be in the huge kitchen of a restaurant. He rubbed his eyes, for everything looked askew. Sandwiches, cakes, cookies, fruit, caviar, platters of meat, roasts and salads were sliding on the tilted floor. Oddly enough, the floor was not only tilted but seemed to be moving back and forth, and there was a horrendous noise.

Jeff picked up a chicken leg and an apple. "What's going on? Are we in an earthquake? It sounds as if tons of metal were clashing together."

Norby was quickly filling a bag with fruit and sandwiches and the chocolate cookies Jeff liked best. He didn't answer.

Jeff tried chewing on the chicken leg, but his stomach seemed to lurch and he put it in the bag, adding some cold cuts and a roll. "Where are we, Norby? I don't like it here."

A piece of heavy paper slid from a countertop, landing near Jeff. He picked it up and read it.

"White Star Line: Midnight Buffet: April 14, 1912... Norby! This must be—" he turned the paper over and it said, "*R.M.S. Titanic.*"

"It's all right, Jeff. The *Titanic* won't sink under water for another few minutes, and even when it does, there'll still be air here for quite a while so you can have your lunch..."

"Get me out *Now!*"

5

Closer to Home

Jeff stuffed the bag of food into the inside of his tunic so he wouldn't miss dinner again in case anything went wrong.

And of course something went wrong, because he was under-water being stared at by a small fish. Then Norby yanked him upward, his head went into breathable air, and he smiled.

"Norby! The universe is safe! We're in the boating pond in Central Park, and there's our apartment building!"

Jeff found that with a few strokes he was in shallow water and able to haul himself onto one of his favorite perching places, a rock formation that jutted out into the lake.

Norby whirled on miniantigrav to dry his barrel, but when he came to rest beside Jeff, his sensor wire was out.

"Ing didn't succeed!" said Jeff, happily removing a snail from his tunic, "and I'm so glad he didn't, because if he had, you might have brought us into nothingness, or to a cosmic egg, or to whatever happens to a universe when it collapses."

Norby was so silent that Jeff peered at him to see if he was damaged. "Are you all right, Norby?"

"I am functioning perfectly, as usual. Almost perfectly. It's just that—well—I tried to arrive past the time when we last left our apartment, because of course we can't go into a time where we already exist . . ." He paused and withdrew his sensor wire. "Jeff, eat your lunch here."

"Why? What's wrong? Oola will be so glad to see us . . ."

"Please, just eat. Then we'll see about going home."

It was probably lunchtime in Manhattan, for the sun was warm and high overhead. The bag of food was only slightly damp. He munched on a sandwich that should have been at the bottom of the Atlantic Ocean. "Are you going to tell me what's on what passes for your mind, Norby?"

"Well, I wanted to come to our apartment at the time when Fargo was due back from his vacation. That would accomplish two things—get us some help, and prove that Ing hadn't destroyed the universe. But maybe I was scared."

"What do you mean?" asked Jeff, watching a small boy bound over the rocks toward him. He hoped the boy wasn't hungry.

"I don't think I moved quite that far in time."

"Hi, mister," said the boy. "You're wet. I don't think you're supposed to swim in the lake."

"It was an accident. I didn't mean to swim," said Jeff. "Want an apple? I have two."

"Thanks," said the boy, pushing his wavy black hair off his high forehead. "I'm not supposed to take food from strangers, but my nanny robot hasn't caught up with me and, anyway, you don't look dangerous. You're big, but you're not grown up yet, are you?"

Jeff felt hurt. "I guess I'm not."

"What's in the barrel?"

Jeff saw that Norby was closed up and did indeed resemble a metal barrel, not a robot. "Parts of a robot," said Jeff, who hated to lie. Besides, it was safe to mention robots since they were clearly in a time period when little boys had nanny robots, just as Jeff once did.

"May I have a piece of chicken for my turtle?" asked the boy, taking one out of his pocket. "He eats under water. You can watch, if you like."

"Sure," said Jeff, handing over a small piece of chicken and watching the boy put the turtle on the rock in a depression that contained water.

"Master Farley!" said a metallic voice from the land side of the rock formation. A conventional nanny robot was standing there, waving at the small boy. "Do not put the turtle in the lake or it will swim away. And do not get wet."

"Okay, Nanny."

"Farley?" asked Jeff through a throat that was suddenly tight. "Is that really your name, and is that nanny robot yours? It has a dent on the side of its head . . ."

"It fell out of our window once. It's not very bright, but I like it. And my name is Farley, but don't call me that. I hate it."

"What do you like to be called?" croaked Jeff.

"Dad says I have an ancestor who was tarred and feathered in a town in North Dakota near the Red River. I don't know what tarred and feathered means, but Dad says I have something in common with that ancestor, so he calls me Fargo, because that's the place in North Dakota and, besides, it's both my names—Farley Gordon. Call me Fargo."

"I like the name," said Jeff. "How old are you?"

"I'm five. How old are you?"

"Fifteen." The same age difference, thought Jeff, that has always been between us, only now I'm the one who's ten years older.

"That's a good age for an older brother to be. I wish I had one. Mom says it's too late for me to have an older brother but someday I might have a younger one. She and Dad haven't gotten around to making me one yet."

"I'm sure they will."

"What's your name?" said young Fargo, scooping up his turtle and replacing it in his pocket because the nanny robot was waving at him to come.

"It doesn't matter. Enjoy your life, young Fargo."

"Okay, I will. You look sad. Don't you enjoy yours?"

"Right now I'm having some big problems."

"Don't you have a dad or a mom or an older brother or sister to help you out?"

"No. Not really. Not any more."

"I have some advice. Want it?"

Jeff smiled. "Sure."

"I hope you don't mind getting advice from a kid, but Dad says I'm preco—co . . ."

"Precocious. It means smart."

"Good." Fargo frowned as the nanny robot marched stolidly over the rocks and took him by the hand. "I've got to go home—why don't you come with me and maybe my Dad can help you. He's smart, too."

"I wish I could, but I can't," said Jeff. "I have to leave soon."

The boy cocked his head, his blue eyes wide. "I bet you're having an adventure. I like adventures, except that Nanny won't let me have many."

"I'm sure you'll grow up to have many adventures, and that you'll be brave and heroic, like my older brother."

Young Fargo turned pink and grinned. "Thanks. I hope you have luck with your problem, whatever it is. Remember that it's a good idea to find somebody older and smarter who can help. That's what Dad always says. Goodbye!"

"Goodbye." Jeff turned his back so he wouldn't have to see young Fargo walking with his nanny robot in the direction of the building where someday another Wells boy would be born.

"He won't remember this," said Norby softly. "He's much too young."

Jeff started to cry. "What if there's no future for him? What if Ing succeeded? It's my fault. If I hadn't stopped Ing from conquering the Federation, he wouldn't have gone crazy and wanted to be master of a new universe."

"He probably would have anyway. It's not your fault. Come on. We'll walk for a while to clear your head."

Norby pulled Jeff along the path by the lake, across Bow Bridge and into the woods known as the Ramble. Joggers and bird watchers went by, but paid no attention to the tall teen-ager dressed in odd clothes, walking with a robot that resembled a small animated barrel. You had to be much odder than that to get attention in Central Park, at any time.

His vision blurry with tears, Jeff stumbled on in misery until he saw a blaze of crimson.

"The azalea pond! It's spring here—and look at the ruby-throated hummingbirds!"

"Too many people around," muttered Norby. "Come on."

They followed the little stream known as the Gill to the Lost Waterfall, still called that although it had been restored in the twenty-first century. The clean water splashed while small birds bathed and bluebells nodded over the banks.

Norby dragged Jeff on through the woods to the narrow opening of the Cave, a place that had also been closed for many years and still wasn't known to many people, for the way down into it was steep and its main opening was right into the lake. Jeff sat down on the stone bench inside and tried to meditate.

At first he couldn't concentrate. He listened to the bird-song, the splash of rowboaters out on the lake, and the faint hum of the surrounding city. The sounds seemed so precious, and now so threatened.

"I am a child of this universe," said Jeff. "Whatever happens to it, happens to me. I am only a small organic creature, part of the life of planet Earth, but the universe is one. All life is one, all intelligence—organic or robotic—is one. We are all responsible for helping each other . . . Norby!"

"You're doing fine, Jeff."

"I feel better, and I've thought of something. Young Fargo was right. We need wise help. We must find the Others. They are the wisest, oldest intelligent species in the universe and we must ask them what to do."

"We've met them in the distant past and in the far future, but never near our own time," said Norby.

"Try tuning in to them. I'll hold your hand and try to focus my mind, too."

Jeff half-closed his eyes, staring at the rippling water outside the mouth of the cave. He brought back the half-smile he used to help him meditate, but it vanished because he started worrying about the collapse of the universe. What could any intelligent species, even the Others, do about that?

"It didn't work, Jeff. We're still here," said Norby.

"It's different!" They were still in the cave, but only swampy ground, filled with weeds, came to the mouth. There were old aluminum cans lying in the swamp, pieces of dirty paper everywhere, and a puzzled heron sitting on the nearest branch of a willow tree.

The back opening of the cave was filled in and there was no way out except through the swamp.

"I must have gone back further in time instead of to wherever the Others are," said Norby. "Close your eyes this time, Jeff, and concentrate . . . oops!"

The cave disappeared and Jeff sat down hard on rough ground. Before him was a small muddy pond and around the shore were run-down shacks. There was only one building visible on the west side of the park, and that was under construction.

"They called that building *The Dakota* because it seemed so far away from the main part of the city," said Norby. "I've read all about it. Even your pet cave was man-made at the time Olmstead created Central Park . . ."

"Norby, we've gone back to the nineteenth century! Are we doomed to keep going further into the past? If Ing did destroy the universe in the future, is something blocking us . . ."

"Hey, you!" said a heavy voice in a strangely accented version of the English used before Terran Basic became standard. "What's in that funny-looking barrel—booze?"

A big, bearded man crashed through the trees in back of them and Jeff picked up Norby, holding him tightly.

6

AN ARTIST LOST IN TIME

There was a spinning sensation and the squatters' ground that was not yet Central Park vanished.

"Where are we? This isn't hyperspace."

"I don't know," said Norby. "I'm not sure what my circuits were doing when I hyperjumped. I just wanted to get away. It was you who shouted, 'Help.'"

"No, it was you."

"I wasn't that afraid." Norby's head sucked into his barrel so that only the tops of his eyes showed. "But I think I am now."

Jeff felt the same way, for they were in an enormous, dim room shaped like a half-moon. At the curved end was a huge photograph of a spiral galaxy, but it looked different from most astrophotographs Jeff had seen. There were no stars in the foreground, only the galaxy hanging in the black of space.

The room was so dim that Jeff didn't notice that there was a large door in the straight end, until Norby tugged at Jeff's arm and pointed with his other hand. "Look, Jeff."

The door was slowly dilating open to light so strong that Jeff could see only the silhouette of a tall figure in a flowing robe that shone green where the light filtered through the edge of it. The figure stepped forward into the room.

It was not a man. It had three eyes and two sets of arms.

"You are one of the Others," said Jeff in awe, using the language taught by the Others to two planets Jeff had previously visited.

"You know us?" said the Other. "I know that my ancestors took some creatures like you from their home planet to another planet. But that was long ago and I have never seen your kind before. Are you from that planet?"

"No, sir. I am from Earth, the home planet of my species. This is my robot, Norby, who was made by Jamyn robots who were made by the Others long ago. I will tell you the whole story and how I came to meet your species in the past, but this is an emergency. We need your help."

"Indeed. Please sit down." The Other gestured, and two low seats rose from the floor. The Other sat down and so did Jeff, with Norby standing close beside him.

"If you met my species in the past, then you must be either very long-lived, or a time traveler," said the Other, "yet time travel is not possible without a certain metal from a previous universe. We Others once had a small supply, but it was lost long ago."

"I have some inside me," said Norby proudly. "And so does another robot like me, who can't time-travel but, well, we don't know what else she can do. She's been kidnapped and we think the universe is in danger. Or has already been destroyed, up in the future."

"Are you telepathic, small Norby?"

"When I touch humans who have been bitten by the Jamyn dragons."

"Then you will be telepathic if you touch an Other, because we gave that capacity to the dragons. Come here, Norby, and give me your knowledge."

When Norby hesitated, Jeff said, "Go ahead, Norby. It's the best thing to do."

After the information transferal the Other went to consult with his colleagues in another part of the ship. While waiting for his return, Jeff tried to consume some of the liquid and solid refreshment the Other had provided. It had a strange taste and appearance, but he supposed the Other wouldn't try to poison him. Even so, Jeff was worried.

He knew now that the curved wall of the room did not contain a photograph, but plastiglass. He was in a gigantic ship traveling in space between his own Milky Way galaxy and what humans called M31, the spiral galaxy in the constellation of Andromeda. But Jeff wasn't looking at M31.

"That's our own galaxy we're looking at, Norby. It doesn't seem possible. The Others have a technology that permits this sort of travel."

"It's not *so* wonderful, Jeff. And because they don't have

any of the metal that's inside me, they can't time-travel. But, of course, they invented hyperdrive long before the Federation did."

"They were civilized long before Earth evolved life," said Jeff. "If anyone can help us, they can."

"You'd better sleep. He said it would take a while to go over my information."

Jeff leaned back, for the seat had developed a soft back as if in response to his wish. Before he knew it, he was asleep. And when he woke, he felt refreshed.

The Other was sitting near him, and Jeff smiled, feeling safe for the first time since Threezy had revealed himself as Ing.

"Jeff Wells, I am going to tell you what we know," said the Other. "We Others travel through the universe in ships like this one, exploring and learning. This particular ship specializes in recording knowledge and ideas as art forms, and I am the chief artist."

"What's your name?"

A series of musical syllables flowed from the Other's almost human mouth, but Jeff knew he could never pronounce them. "I can't say your name. Would you mind if I gave you a name I can pronounce—a name of a renowned human artist?"

"I would be honored."

"Then I'll call you Rembrandt. Please go on telling us what you Others have decided to do after learning what Norby has stored in his memory banks about Ing's attempt to destroy the universe."

"It was this ship that we are on that caught Ing's first bomb and deactivated it," Rembrandt said. "We were traveling in hyperspace at the time, and we have developed ways of detecting ships that are also using hyperdrive. Then two things happened that we did not expect. The first was that the *Quest*, as we now know it to have been, disappeared from hyperspace, though not in the usual way. Something very odd happened, and Norby's impression of it is accurate. It was as if hyperspace opened with a momentary hole that immediately shut. We do not understand the phenomenon."

"But what was the other thing that happened?"

Rembrandt laughed. It sounded hearty and human to Jeff. "We tried to pick up something in hyperspace that was not a ship but much smaller. It, however, disappeared."

"Me? I? Jeff and I?"

"Yes, Norby. Then after we entered normal space, we detected that someone was trying to reach us. We tuned into you and we helped you journey to us."

"How marvelous!" said Jeff, more awestruck than ever. These Others were incredibly powerful. Surely they could do everything—save Pera, even the universe . . .

Norby was touching Jeff, perhaps tuning into his thoughts, but not transmitting any words, just a sudden feeling of anxiety. Jeff tried to ignore it, because he was so happy that they'd found the Others.

"Rembrandt," said Jeff, "the fact that you entered normal space *after* Ing did something drastic in hyperspace, proves that the universe is still here." He pointed to the transparent wall.

"Stars—wrong," muttered Norby.

"I'm afraid they are," said Rembrandt sadly. "Our ship was thrown back in time."

"How much time?" asked Jeff.

"Jeff," said Norby, "it happened to us, too. We went back further in time than we wanted to at first, remember?"

"We have gone back very far," said Rembrandt, "so far that although galaxies have formed, there are only a few second generation stars and planets made from the elements created in the deaths of first generation stars. We here in this ship are the only life in the universe at this time."

"I will take you forward in time," said Norby, elevating his legs to full length. "Let me tie in to your computer . . ."

"We cannot return to any time where we once existed," said Rembrandt, "just as you cannot. If you help us, Norby, we will try to return to hyperspace just after we left it. We will search for Ing and if we can't find him . . ."

"Yes?" said Jeff, his heart sinking. Rembrandt looked as puzzled and worried as any human could look in a difficult situation.

"We will think about what to do. In the meantime, would you like to see some of the art forms we carry in this ship? There are too many for more than a quick survey of some of the finest specimens but . . ."

"I would like to see your work, Rembrandt," said Jeff.

"That is easily done." Rembrandt touched a switch and the

floor in front of the window shimmered. It seemed as if several objects had emerged into the room, yet for all Jeff knew he was looking at advanced holograms. Only one was easy to examine. The others—were there two?—were misty.

The clear object turned slowly, and Jeff thought he could never like anything better. It was a sculpture made of tinted crystal and light, that at first meant nothing at all; yet after a few minutes, he could see almost anything in it that he wanted to.

Then the sculpture faded, and one of the other objects became easy to see. It was chunky and rough and had jolly music coming from it all of a sudden. Jeff wanted to tap his feet in time to the music and he felt himself smiling. The thing was humorous, and he wondered if only humans would find it so.

"To amuse our young," said Rembrandt. "We have children infrequently, but we love them dearly. This particular piece is also popular with grown Others."

Jeff nodded and watched the funny object fade and a third take its place. It was a flat rectangular object and when it came into focus, Jeff gasped.

"It's an oil painting!"

"Not exactly, but perhaps the canvas, paint, and technique are similar to those humans use. We Others used this technique early in our history, and in spite of its difficulties, it is still popular with serious artists, for it requires skill which must be painstakingly acquired. We enjoy the effort to acquire such skill; at least, I do."

The painting was of a dragon cradling her young offspring, almost in the manner of a Renaissance Madonna and Child. The picture seemed to glow with the love of the mother dragon.

"I've met the Jamyn dragons," said Jeff, "but they don't remember the Others, who bioengineered them. Surely you are not that old, Rembrandt, to be one of the founders of Jamya?"

"Oh, no," said Rembrandt, smiling. "We Others live longer than humans, but not that long. The Jamyn dragons have become one of our legends, and we like to paint pictures about them."

"They would love to see you," said Norby. "If Jamya still exists. If anything still exists."

The objects of art vanished, and the room seemed colder. Rembrandt closed the middle eye of his three. He shook his head. "No, we Others are space travelers now. We do not visit planets, and we believe that it is best to leave alone those species we once helped, like the Jamyn dragons or the humans we took to the planet Izz. If they still exist."

"Don't you know?" asked Jeff, bewildered. "If they still exist, I mean?"

"Ah, young human, I see that you believe we are such superior beings that we have powers for accomplishing anything. Although we are much older than the human race, we are not all that different. All our long history of experience and technological marvels has not prepared us for this crisis. We have no machines that can give us information about the future. And without Norby's help, we cannot time-travel to find out what Ing did to the universe."

"I'm ready to help," said Norby.

The gigantic ship of the Others, so huge that Jeff had been in only small portions of it, was back in hyperspace, and had moved forward in time.

"I just don't understand it," said Jeff. "If hyperspace is dimensionless and outside time, how can we move forward in time within hyperspace?"

"We don't," said Norby, still hooked into the ship's mysteriously intricate computer. "I've never understood it either, although I *do* it, so I asked Yib here . . ."

"Yib?" said Rembrandt, while the rest of the control room crew members blinked all three of their eyes simultaneously.

"I've named your computer Yib because she's so big. I said You Immense Brain to her when I was trying to hook in—she's a little hard to get to know—and she didn't seem to mind; in fact she thinks I'm cute . . ."

Rembrandt passed one of his upper hands over his head. "We never realized that our computer had a personality. Especially a female personality. You were saying that Yib explained hyperspace to you?"

"Sure," said Norby. "Of course, a biological brain like yours or Jeff's couldn't possibly understand it completely."

Jeff and Rembrandt looked at each other in a sudden comradeship of the merely biological, while the rest of the

Others in the room smiled. Norby had already become a favorite.

"Tell us, Norby!" commanded Jeff.

"It's just that you don't move in time when you're in hyperspace, except biological time. If you stay in hyperspace, you age just as you would in normal space, but you can come out of hyperspace at the exact moment, almost, that you went in, so nothing else will have aged."

"But . . ."

"And," said Norby, "when we move further in time, as this ship has just done, thanks to my genius, it is accomplished during the transition between normal space and hyperspace."

"That doesn't make sense," said Jeff.

Norby swung his arms back and forth. "No, I guess not. I guess I don't understand hyperspace either. But I've got you here."

"We know where we are," said Rembrandt patiently, "but *when* are we?"

"Just after you left, after Ing left. After Ing blew up or something. Should Yib and I take the ship further into time and out into normal space to see if the universe is there?"

There was silence for a moment. And then Rembrandt said, "I cannot risk the ship, which contains the art treasures of the long history of the Others, as well as works by many artists now living. There must be a scouting expedition to find out what the conditions are in the universe. I will go with Norby."

"No," said Jeff. "You're Rembrandt. As good as he was, I mean. Just Norby and I will go."

Norby detached himself from Yib and walked to the center of the room. He withdrew his legs and hung in the air, staring at everyone with all four of his eyes. "No biological being should go. The universe may be lethal to them, but a robot might survive long enough to come back with the facts. I will go alone."

Jeff didn't have time to argue. He flung himself upon Norby just as the robot vanished.

7

A Disastrous Change

Jeff lay face down, staring at a floor. Something was licking the back of his neck. He sat up to see that he was in the Wells' small ship, the *Hopeful,* with Norby already seated at the control board. It was hard to see much because his all-purpose-pet, Oola, was climbing over him, licking his chin ecstatically. Loud purring rumbled under her green fur.

"Where have you been, Jeff Wells! I've waited and waited!" Rinda looked as if she'd been crying, but at the moment she seemed as angry as the daughter of a ferocious Iz-zian Queen could be. "Well? What happened to you two?"

Jeff burst into happy laughter. "We're home! The universe is safe! Everything still exists!"

"Are you out of your mind?" asked Rinda, sniffing.

"Your reasoning is logical, Jeff." said Norby, "If Rinda is here, then since Ing left hyperspace, enough time has passed for Rinda to have arrived at our apartment."

"Of course it has, you idiot," said Rinda. "I spent one day with the Admiral in Space Command while the fleet looked for you, but he and I knew you and the *Quest* wouldn't be found because you'd gone into hyperspace, and nobody else can follow. Then Yobo brought me here and we waited a couple of days. But you didn't show up, so I stayed to comfort Oola and hope that your vacationing brother would come home, but he hasn't. I've been all alone and very miserable and I don't like anything on Terran holovision and where have you been?"

She had run out of breath, so Jeff explained as fast as he could. He wound up by saying, "But Ing failed. The universe is quite all right."

"The idea was ridiculous," said Rinda.

"Of course."

"But my Pera is still kidnapped. What are we going to do about it?"

"You're not going to do anything," said Jeff. "You're going to go back into the apartment with Oola and wait until we find Ing and bring Pera back to you."

"I won't. That's why I waited here in the *Hopeful* after the Admiral and I found it parked on your apartment roof. He said that Norby might try to come back for it, especially if you ran out of air, Jeff. And you almost did. I'm glad you're alive."

To Jeff's surprise, Rinda flung herself at his chest and gave him a huge hug.

"But you can't come with us, Rinda. It'll be dangerous."

"I am a princess and the daughter of a queen and I'm going with you and that's that."

"Yeoww!" said Oola, springing to the top of Norby's hat.

"Get her off of me," said Norby. "I'm busy trying to tune back into Rembrandt's ship, and I'm having trouble."

Rinda detached herself from Jeff and picked up Oola. "Your all-purpose pet and I intend to go. Don't argue with me, Jeff. It's not a good idea."

"I'll carry you and Oola bodily down to the apartment!"

"Try it," said Rinda. She had evidently been practicing the only kind of telepathy to which Oola responded—the wish that she would change her shape in a certain way.

Oola growled and showed a set of jagged fangs in a muzzle that Jeff didn't recognize.

"Now she's a vlimat," said Rinda, "one of the creatures native to Izz. Not nice. She may not at this moment realize you are her owner, Jeff, so you'd better not try to take us downstairs."

Jeff threw up his hands in defeat, and went to the *Hopeful*'s galley to see what was available. Rinda had stocked it well with items from the apartment kitchen, including tasty dishes she'd evidently persuaded the kitchen computer to make.

He was full and leaning back in his chair half asleep when he felt the *Hopeful* toss like a ship in a storm. He tore into the control room, where Rinda was holding an irate Oola, who now looked like his pet cat, and where Norby was still at the control board.

"What happened, Norby?"

"I'm not sure, Jeff. I sent a message to Admiral Yobo, explaining that we had to find Pera, and I received a message —there it is—and decided I'd better obey him and pick him up . . ."

"You mean he wants to come?" Jeff turned on the message.

"Pick me up before you start searching hyperspace for Ing, and that's an order, Cadet." The voice was Yobo's bass rumble.

"So what is the problem in going to Space Command?" asked Jeff. "He went back there after he brought Rinda to Earth, didn't he?"

"Yes," said Rinda. "I want to see him. He's so big and strong."

Unaccountably jealous, Jeff turned to Norby again. "Why haven't you brought the *Hopeful* to Space Command?"

"I thought I had," said Norby, "but in going through hyperspace, just for the brief moment it takes on so short a trip, I seem to have gotten a little mixed up. Space Command isn't here."

"Isn't where? Where are we?"

"I thought we were in orbit around Mars, but—wait! That is Mars! Isn't it?"

Jeff stared at the viewscreen as Norby brought the *Hopeful* closer to the planet. "Sure—there's Mons Olympus, and I can see the domed cities now. For a minute I thought you'd done something wrong and brought us back in time, before Earth people went into space and started colonies in the solar system. Space Command must be in orbit somewhere . . ."

"Now hear this!" shouted an unknown male voice.

"I don't understand a word," said Rinda.

"That's a hycom message from Mars, I assume," said Jeff slowly, "but why are they speaking Martian Swahili? The language used in all space communication is Terran Basic."

"Perhaps Norby's brought us to Mars at a time when the Martian colonists had built the domes, but Space Command didn't exist yet," said Rinda.

"Impossible," said Norby. "Space Command was built first, in orbit around Luna, Earth's moon, and later moved to Mars when they began to build the domed cities. Space Command is not here, but the cities are. We couldn't have gone back in time."

"Now hear this. Now hear this." After these two repetitions, the message continued, accompanied by the picture of the speaker on holovision. He was middle-aged, wearing a peculiar dark outfit and a blank expression.

"Unregistered ship—remain in orbit until the patrol makes contact with you. Failure to comply will result in instant destruction of your ship." The picture winked out.

"Maybe we'd better do what he wants," said Jeff.

"I will," said Norby, "but I thought you'd like to hear one of their news broadcasts. I've just tuned the hycom to it."

Norby pressed a button and another voice filled the control room. It was accompanied by a picture of a large, stony-faced woman who seemed to be reading from an unseen monitor. She spoke a language Jeff had never heard.

"Is that another of the strange Terran languages used before Terran Basic came in?" asked Rinda.

"No," said Jeff. "And that one sounds almost too difficult for humans to speak. She keeps clearing her throat."

The woman cleared her throat once more and said in Martian Swahili, "Now for the translation. Mars City quotas of filracks are falling behind. If this is not rectified by next Monday, penalties will be imposed. The ration of Instant Nourish will be cut immediately. If production is not speeded up by the next Monday, the Happy Time will be increased in intensity and duration for all citizens."

The woman's face vanished and was replaced by brilliantly-colored patterns that swirled and vibrated, accompanied by oddly unpleasant music that Jeff wanted turned off but could not do so himself.

"Look at the pretty colors," said Rinda, dreamily, picking up Oola again. "Pretty, pretty, pretty. Look, Oola."

"Pretty," said Jeff hoarsely. "Turn—no—on—no—off—pretty, pretty..."

"Ow!" said Rinda, dropping Oola. "She bit me! I must have been holding her too tightly. What's the matter, Oola?"

The all-purpose pet was stalking up to the holoscreen, her green fur bushed out like an angry cat's. She spat and snarled at the screen, her snout lengthening. When the patterns continued, she sat back on her haunches and howled.

Thanks to Oola, who had captured everyone's attention, Jeff was able to say, "Norby, turn off the hycom!"

Norby did so. "What's the matter with you three?" he asked. "You look sick."

"If that's the Happy Time," said Jeff, "it hypnotizes humans, but not Oola, who obviously hates it. Didn't it bother you, Norby?"

"I glanced at it, but the patterns and music didn't do anything except give me a slight ticklish feeling in my circuits, and besides, I was too busy monitoring the approach of—that."

In the viewscreen was a small ship, approaching the *Hopeful*, and, like it, obviously built to enter planetary atmospheres and dock on land surfaces instead of in space. It did not, however, resemble the *Hopeful* nor any ship Jeff had studied during his years at Space Academy.

"It's not a hyperdrive ship," said Norby, "but it's scanning us with a very sophisticated scanner. The Federation never had any like that before. I suppose it will hail us—I've left ship-to-ship communication open . . ."

"Hey!" shouted Jeff. "What was that!" The *Hopeful* seemed to quiver and then move out of orbit.

"Traction beam," said Norby, in a small, tinny voice. "A very powerful type unknown to me. I don't like it. I'm going to try to break away." He worked hard at the control board and then said, "No use. It's pulling us to Mars."

"Go into hyperspace or back in time," said Jeff.

"Can't. Not while the beam is on. I *know* the Federation has nothing like this. Not the Federation that I know."

"Go into hyperspace yourself, Norby, without the *Hopeful*."

"I might not be able to get back to you, Jeff. I don't want to leave you in danger. We have to find out—oh!"

"Oh, what?"

"I just tuned into the hycom again and heard another message in Martian Swahili from that ship to the Mars base. It said, "Alien ship in tow. Inform the Master of Mars.""

"There is no master of Mars."

"There was something else," said Norby. "The date. I did make a mistake, after all. I didn't just go through hyperspace to pick up Yobo at Space Command. I also went forward in time five hundred years!"

8

PRISONERS!

As the captured *Hopeful* slid into a dock that clamped restraining bars around it, Jeff wondered about the five hundred years. What could have happened to Space Command, so all-important in his own time?

"Jeff," said Norby, "the tow beam's off. Shall I try to make the *Hopeful* go into hyperspace to escape?"

"Yes," said Jeff.

"Better not," said Rinda. "Would you want to carry with us what's just come in from the air lock you supposedly locked?"

Jeff turned and Norby opened his back eyes (when at the control board he usually concentrated by *shutting* his back ones). Jeff grunted as if he'd been hit, and in the next moment he was—by Oola jumping upon him and wrapping herself around his neck. She was hissing in his ear.

"I guess we wouldn't want to bring this, ah, stranger with us," said Rinda, picking up Norby, who instantly closed up. "Don't let this guy steal my doll."

"Who are you?" asked Jeff.

The stranger said nothing. If it looked at them, it was impossible to tell, because Jeff couldn't see any eyes. Slightly higher than an adult human, the alien looked like a bilious-yellow palm tree whose thick trunk ended in eight stubby legs with strange joints. The top was only superficially leaf-like, because each of its ten leaves seemed to be made of a leathery hide that ended in a thin jointed arm with terminal pinchers.

The entire creature was encased in a transparent suit with separate sections for each arm. The horn-like pinchers extruded beyond the suit and were slowly moving ominously in a way that reminded Jeff of a crab about to catch its prey.

"It smells," said Rinda, wrinkling her nose. "And since all but its claws are covered with plastic, imagine what the whole creature must smell like. Go away, Mister!"

The alien turned a sickly orange color and waved its pinchers at Rinda. A stream of syllables came out of a speaker, but no one could understand them.

There was something about the alien that made Jeff feel queasy with fear. He went over to Rinda and put his arm around her, which brought him into telepathic contact with Norby.

—Is there data about such a creature in your memory banks, Norby?

—Nothing. I don't like it at all . . .

—You can take one of us to safety. Go into hyperspace and if possible take Rinda back to the apartment . . .

—I can't, Jeff. This creature or its fancy space suit projects an electronic field that makes it difficult for me to function. Be very careful. That creature is dangerous.

They were prisoners.

"The Master of Mars has scanned your ship and says that it does not have hyperdrive. How do you explain your sudden apearance in our air space, young man?"

"Well, your honor," Jeff began, but the man behind the big desk shook his head in disapproval and the humans in the courtroom murmured.

"Use of Terran Basic is forbidden. Speak only Martian Swahili if you do not know the language of the Masters," said the thin, sad-faced man Jeff assumed to be the judge. "And I am to be addressed as 'Sir Prosecutor.'"

"What's wrong with using Terran Basic?" asked Jeff in Martian Swahili, grateful for Norby's coaching that had finally enabled him to achieve some competence in that language.

"Only regional languages are permitted. Surely you know that simple rule?"

"We don't know any of your rules, Sir Prosecutor. We have only just arrived."

The prosecutor turned to one of the human cops who had later boarded the *Hopeful* to take Jeff and Rinda to the courtroom with Oola bristling on Jeff's shoulders and Rinda carrying a closed-up Norby.

"I understand that the only occupants of that small antique spacecraft were these two children, their pet and their toy robot?'

"That is correct, Sir Prosecutor."

The alien standing beside Jeff suddenly spoke in its strange language.

After listening the prosecutor said, "I see. Then they have no grownup to explain why they violated our space without permit. They alone are guilty."

"We didn't know we were violating anything," said Jeff. "How can we be anything but innocent until we are *proven* guilty?"

"In the courts of the Masters, guilt does not need to be proven. The Masters decide. The Master of Mars has decided that you are guilty."

Rinda moved closer to Jeff so that he could touch his robot and hear Norby's telepathic message.

—Rinda, Jeff, your only hope is to say that you are from the past, thrown into this time period by some unknown force. You must go on pretending that I am merely a toy, because there aren't any robots that my sensors can find. Even the computers are small and simple. I'd guess that these aliens do everything, control everything.

"I'm sorry we have entered your space by accident," said Jeff evenly, keeping his eyes wide and his face as childishly innocent as possible. "My friend and I were playing in my brother's scout ship when the whole thing was hurled away from where we were to wherever this is."

"Your brother's ship? But humans are not allowed to own any ships, even one as small and as old as yours. Explain."

"My brother works for Space Command and . . ."

"That is impossible. Space Command was destroyed four hundred and fifty years ago when our Masters arrived."

Jeff saw that a gleam of interest was shining in the eyes of the haggard prosecutor, and that possibly there had been some cynicism in the words 'our Masters'.

Evidently the alien could understand Martian Swahili even if it spoke only its own language, for it turned orange again and talked to the prosecutor.

"The Master says that you children are time travelers and must be examined closely. First the oldest—you, boy—must learn the language. Hold still and let the Master touch you."

—Telepathic teaching [said Norby, in Jeff's mind]. Better recite nonsense poems to yourself so it won't find out anything in case it tries to probe your mind.

But as the alien's claws approached, Jeff became afraid. Although the alien still wore the transparent space suit, the odor and the strangeness it exuded were unbearable.

Oola spat and yowled and the alien drew back.

"Control your pet or it will be killed," said the prosecutor.

Jeff handed Oola to Rinda, who had a hard time clutching both an irate all-purpose pet and Norby, until Norby used just enough antigrav to make himself practically weightless. Jeff could see Rinda's muscles relax and she smiled at him. She's brave, he thought.

The alien's claws came again, and this time they touched Jeff's head. Instantly he had a terrible headache.

'Twas brillig and the slithy toves
Did gyre and gimble in the wabe. . . .'

As long as the claws stayed on his head, Jeff went on with the Jabberwocky, grateful to Lewis Carroll for providing the best nonsense poem of all time.

The claws left and his headache began to clear.

"Human, listen to me," said the alien, and Jeff understood the language.

"I could not read the contents of your brain, but that will be rectified in time. It is clear to me that you are displaced from your own time."

"It happened when Ing . . ."

"Ing, the bringer of the key," said the alien. "There is no need to discuss it. When the key was brought, the space disturbance caused the transfer of your ship to this time period. Your mind is too muddled for adequate training to make you suitable for our time. You will be destroyed while the younger child will be trained."

When Jeff saw the human prosecutor wince, he turned to him and said politely, "Please, Sir Prosecutor, perhaps you can understand that all we want is to leave. We can't possibly harm the Master, or anyone else."

Jeff spoke Martian Swahili—he could understand the alien's language, but couldn't speak it. Perhaps only a few humans could, like the holo announcer and the prosecutor. Perhaps that was why they had important jobs.

The prosecutor smiled sadly. "Where can you go? Your ship is not capable of hyperdrive, and besides, the Masters do not allow humans to travel away from home."

"Please don't kill Jeff," said Rinda in Martian Swahili that was atrociously bad, but nevertheless a tribute to Norby's skill at quickie language teaching. "He's only fifteen."

"Looks older," muttered the prosecutor. "Master, is it possible that the boy could be trained after all?"

But the alien did not seem to be listening, for its leathery leaves were waving towards Rinda. Did it want Norby? Jeff was afraid that the alien had somehow tuned into the little robot's telepathic teaching of Rinda.

Then Jeff saw that Oola's shape had changed. Horrified, he realized that he had never seen the animal she had just become, an elongated dachshund-like body with tentacles at each end and sixteen legs.

"A nununiy!" exclaimed the alien, hobbling over to Rinda and taking Oola from her.

"Our pet can be what you want it to be," said Jeff. "You must have powerful thoughts, for Oola has discovered how to be a nununiy for your sake."

Rinda giggled and immediately suppressed it, but not before she winked at Jeff. What was she up to?

The alien cuddled Oola, everyone present staring at them, except Jeff. He was watching Norby, whose head was elevating just enough for him to wink at Jeff. Suddenly Norby and Rinda disappeared.

"The little girl's gone!" shouted the prosecutor, his face grey with fear. "It is not my fault, Master . . ."

The alien waved a claw at the prosecutor, and the man doubled over in obvious pain. Jeff decided that the alien possessed the power of electronic stimulation of pain circuits. No wonder it was so easy for one alien to control a courtroom. But how did one alien control a planet? Or were there more?

"Where did the girl go, time traveler?" asked the alien. It seemed to have forgotten Oola, who was still sitting on the palm-like top. Jeff was afraid that she meant to stay the alien's pet forever.

"I don't know where they went," said Jeff.

"Perhaps not, but you know how they did it."

When Jeff didn't answer, the alien's sickly orange color deepened and it pointed a claw at him. The pain was awful.

"I won't tell you," said Jeff. "What's the matter with you, anyway? If you have to stay in a space suit, why do you bother with planets like Mars? Why are you here?"

The courtroom audience gasped. Apparently no human ever talked back to a Master.

"You dislike me, young human. All humans do, but they obey, for we train them with the Happy Hour. If you do not respond to it while you are in jail, you will be killed."

"Killing is uncivilized. If you have a society capable of the kind of space travel it took to get to Mars, then you shouldn't be interested in killing."

"You are naive. You also don't seem to realize that there is a Master for every human colony. We are invulnerable, for we protect ourselves against human stun guns and conventional blast weapons, and we have powers you humans do not possess. We are superior beings, and your puny lives do not interest us. We do not care whether you live or die, but if you live, you must serve us with total obedience."

Jeff did not answer. He was trying not to look at Oola, whose shape was changing again.

"Can you give us total obedience?"

Oola looked more and more like a cat now, and she was growing bigger, her tail disappearing to compensate for the shift in mass.

"Total obedience?" questioned Jeff, trying to look as puzzled as possible to attract the attention of the court, many of whom were beginning to murmur about Oola. "What's that?"

"Bah, you are hopeless. I will get rid of you now," said the alien, lunging at Jeff with claws outstretched.

"Wait," said Jeff, stepping backward until he was against the prosecutor's desk. "There is much you can learn from me, and perhaps I will cooperate if you just explain a few things. Why do you call yourselves Masters, and why. . . ."

"We are the only true intelligent species. All species must serve us."

Oola's fangs were growing longer. She now had a striking resemblance to the saber-toothed cat which was one of her more ferocious ancestors. But what could a smilodont do against an all-powerful alien?

"All species?" asked Jeff desperately, buying time while he hoped that Norby would return for him.

"Human imbecile! In the past some of you humans believed civilization could progress with many species living harmoniously in the same universe, but we disagree. We permit the lives of other species to continue only if they serve us. Above all, we do not permit intelligent species to travel in space. Hyperdrive is outlawed; humans stay in their own territories, making products we can use."

"But what is *your* territory?"

"Everything. We are the Masters."

"You're just a big ugly!" shouted a beloved metallic voice. And there was Norby, hovering in the air beside Jeff.

But the alien was too quick. Intense pain seared Jeff's body and Norby squeaked, falling to the floor as if his antigrav had been knocked out. The alien bent and a claw reached out to pick up Norby.

In spite of the pain, Jeff leaped upon the alien and tried to push it back, but the creature tossed him aside as if he weighed nothing.

"This robot is forbidden," said the alien. "This robot is a dangerous mechanism which must be destroyed."

"No!" yelled Jeff, trying to get up.

Oola's head reared back and then plunged down, her saber teeth stabbing into the alien's strange space suit.

The alien plucked her off its top and threw her at Jeff.

"A product of the Others, no doubt." The alien made a rasping sound that hurt the eardrums.

"The Others will punish you," said Jeff, holding Oola. Norby didn't move. Was he dead?

"Ah, then, you know the Others in your time? They are practically extinct now, for we have conquered them as we have conquered you puny humans. Soon we will be rid of any species that opposes us."

"The Others are good! They never kill. They respect life."

"Fools," said the alien. "And now, stupid human, I will take care that you never bother me again." It stepped toward Jeff again. And it crashed to the floor, its pinchers opening and closing uselessly. Inside the suit, the alien's body withered and shrank. Then it began to crumble into a grey powder.

"Oh, no!" said the prosecutor. "You have killed the Master! You have brought destruction on us all!"

"Good riddance," said Norby, jumping up and taking Jeff's hand. "It almost discombobulated all my circuits."

"You don't understand," wailed the prosecutor. "Each Master, throughout the universe, is linked with all the other Masters, and when one dies or is injured, the Masters send ships to destroy the planet or satellite where it happened. We are doomed!"

"Get into your own ships . . ."

"We have none."

"We do," said Norby. "No time to say goodbye, Jeff."

9

The Problem

The *Hopeful* was in orbit when Rinda pointed to the view-screen and said, "Here they come!"

Huge ships were bearing down on Mars. "They must have come from hyperspace," said Jeff. "There must be a great many of those Biguglies."

"Biguglies?"

"Norby named them. I refuse to refer to them as masters. Can you get the *Hopeful* into hyperspace now, Norby?"

"As you have just pointed out, the Biguglies probably have many ships everywhere, and are capable of hyperdrive. I can't just go into hyperspace. I've got to move us backward in time, to a time before the Biguglies appeared in our solar system."

"Jeff," said Rinda, "If, as you reported, the Biguglies claim to have conquered everybody, does that mean that my planet Izz has a Master, too?"

"I'm afraid so," said Jeff. "Hurry, Norby."

"I wish those ships weren't coming so fast," said Norby. "I'm having trouble hurrying. My circuits feel more mixed-up than usual."

Just as the *Hopeful* winked out of normal space, Jeff saw in the viewscreen that the domed cities of Mars were exploding.

"All those people—dead—my fault," said Jeff.

Rinda was crying. "No, my fault. I persuaded Oola to imitate something she could detect that the alien used as a pet, so the alien's electronic guard field would drop a little. I thought maybe that would free Norby's hyperdrive so we could escape back to the ship."

"I didn't realize Oola's fangs could penetrate the alien's suit, but I guess only a tiny hole was needed," said Jeff. "I don't remember wishing she would become a sabertooth, but I must have."

"If the two of you would stop heaping guilt on yourselves, let me remind you of two things," said Norby. "The Bigugly was about to kill you, Jeff. And me, too. The second thing is that none of those people we saw really exists."

"But they were real!" said Jeff.

"In a time that should not have been," said Norby. "We have just visited a false future, one that should not have occurred. Jeff, you and I have been in the future once or twice and not only were humans space travellers, but the Others were alive and well."

"Then Ing did something that caused the Biguglies to start conquering everybody," said Rinda.

"Yes," said Norby. "We must find out what he did and go back to stop it. Ing brought the Biguglies a 'key'. We must find out."

"How?" asked Jeff, feeling weary and worn out.

"And where are we now?" asked Rinda.

"We're in hyperspace," said Norby. "I'm not sure how far we've traveled in time, but at least there aren't any Biguglies sneaking into our air lock. And as to how—I don't know."

"Then take the *Hopeful* out into normal space. Then we'll find out what time period we're in," said Jeff.

"After you and Rinda get some sleep," said Norby. "Do I have to be a nursemaid as well as a genius robot who rescues everybody?"

"I guess Oola has the right idea," said Rinda.

Oola was curled up like an ordinary cat that just happened to be green. She was sound asleep.

Jeff woke with a start, for Norby was poking him in the chest.

"What . . ."

"Shh. Rinda's asleep in the bedroom and I don't want to wake her unless it's necessary."

"Why did you wake me?"

"You've been asleep six hours, which should be plenty, and I need advice."

"A genius robot needs advice?"

"Don't be funny, Jeff. Look at that."

Jeff rolled over and sat up on the mat he'd brought into the control room. He looked where Norby was pointing and saw the viewscreen.

"It's just the peculiar grey pattern of hyperspace."

"Look again."

"There's a glitch in it. What does that mean?"

"Fargo once explained to me that the viewscreen is under the control of the ship's computer, and that when another ship comes close to the *Hopeful,* the viewscreen registers it."

"Another ship? In hyperspace—Norby, it can only be the Biguglies! They've found us and . . ."

Rinda came running in, rubbing sleep out of her eyes. "I heard you shout. What's happening?"

"Nothing good," said Jeff. "I think the Biguglies . . ."

Suddenly the air lock opened and Oola leapt to her feet.

"Wowrr? Me—uuu!" Oola sidled up to the invader who had entered through the air lock. She sniffed at him, licked her paw, yawned, and trotted back to Jeff.

"Have I passed a test?"

"Rembrandt!"

It was indeed the Other whom Jeff had nicknamed Rembrandt. But he had aged tremendously. He appeared so old he was almost unrecognizable. He breathed laboriously, but managed to smile at Jeff. "When our scanning computer told us that this ship contained Norby, we could not believe that any humans would be alive. Yet here you are, as young as when I last saw you, and with an interesting animal and a beautiful young lady. You must have travelled in time, Jeff Wells."

"How much time, Rembrandt?" asked Jeff, noticing that Norby was touching Rinda with his sensor wire, presumably explaining all about the Other named Rembrandt.

"When you and Norby left our ship to enter normal space, it was just after Norby had so kindly brought us back in hyperspace to our own and your time. That was a thousand of your years ago."

"A thousand years!"

"I went forward instead of backward," said Norby. "Lucky we found you, Rembrandt."

"I don't think luck had much to do with it," said the Other. "When you did not return to us with information about whether the universe was collapsing or not, we waited many years. Finally we decided that we had to find out whether the universe was alive or dead, and we went out of hyperspace."

"I guess you found the Biguglies," said Rinda. "That's what Norby calls those leafy aliens."

A smile bent the wrinkles in Rembrandt's face. "The so-called Master Race certainly has an ugly nature, as we found out when we returned to normal space. They had conquered every inhabited planet, and destroyed every ship of the Others that they could find. They were too powerful to control, so we have unfortunately been forced to run from them ever since."

"I don't understand how you found us now," said Jeff.

"We had programmed our computer, Yib, to look for Norby in case he could help us escape the Biguglies by moving back or ahead in time. As years passed, we gave up hope, but Yib kept searching, and finally found you, with your friend."

"I'm Rinda, Princess of Izz, and I'm honored to meet one of the Others. We Izzians have legends about you, but we never thought you could live over a thousand years."

"Others live several thousand years," said Rembrandt, "but I am now at the end of my life span. Because we could not time-travel without Norby, we have lived through the past thousand years, helpless to prevent the conquest by the Biguglies. I am glad to have found you, but it is too late for us. You must go back into normal space and help your own people to recover."

"But the Biguglies will capture us!" said Jeff.

"No. In the years since you last saw them, the Biguglies have been slowly poisoned, unable to adapt to any planet where Others and humans can live. They have suffered alterations in their cells that first sterilized and then killed them. Soon they will be extinct and we'll be rid of them, but it will be slow work to rebuild the civilizations they destroyed."

Jeff ran his fingers through his curly brown hair. "But can't we help restore this time track to the way it should have been, with humans and Others all over the universe, doing well? Norby and I once visited the future ahead of this time, and that's the way it was. Why can't Norby time-travel us back to stop the Biguglies before they conquer everything?"

"I am too old now," said Rembrandt, "and I fear that the Biguglies were always unstoppable. Norby, take your humans back somewhere in time where you will be safe."

"Then there's a better solution. We'll time travel back to

stop *Ing!* Then this false future will not come about. There won't be any conquest by Biguglies."

Rembrandt shook his head. "It is true that the period of time we Others have lived through, this last thousand years, is a false time. But I fear that it is impossible to set things right. We in this last ship of the Others have tried to think of ways to solve the problem, but our research shows that it cannot be done. You cannot time-travel to change history."

"Why not?" asked Rinda and Jeff simultaneously.

"This time track will be permanent," said Rembrandt. "The original mistake that changed time cannot be corrected."

"I think I know why," said Norby. "I've analyzed all my own data and I think I know what's discouraged you Others. I'm sorry, Jeff, but we may be stuck."

"I won't believe that!" yelled Rinda. "I'm never going to give up, and if someone doesn't tell me why they *think* we're stuck in this horrible place and time, I'm going to scream."

"Rinda's right," said Jeff, putting his arm around her shoulders. "She and I are human and young, but we can stand hearing the truth. Please tell us."

"We have studied the creatures you call the Biguglies, learned their language, and listened in on their conversations. We know where they come from, and why we cannot go back to stop their invasion," said Rembrandt. "Alas, when Ing added Pera and the force of his second bomb to the thrust of his ship, the combination made the *Quest* force its way out of the hyperspaceuniverse field that belongs to our own universe. Apparently there are many parallel universes, and Ing broke through into one of them."

"Then unless we can do the same thing Ing did, we can't go to find him!" said Jeff. "Now I know what the Bigugly meant when he said Ing was the bringer of the key. It meant the key that let the Biguglies travel from their universe to ours."

"Exactly," said Rembrandt. "The key must have been Pera, and the rare metal she contains. We don't know much about that metal, but the Others suspect that it was made in the previous expansion of our own universe. Pera has it, Norby has some, and it was rumored that Others were collecting bits of it to use when our universe collapses and dies a natural death."

"My Pera?" said Rinda. "She's the key to inter-universe travel?"

"Yes," said Rembrandt. "Using the metal they stole from Pera, the Biguglies invaded our universe at the same time, billions of them, and then could not return to their own home. They conquered our universe but we cannot go to theirs."

"To find Ing," said Jeff. "To find a villain."

10

Norby's Idea

"Norby," said Jeff. "We've had a great dinner in Rembrandt's ship, and I'm beginning to think a little better."

"Dinner and sleep. I've been waiting hours for you and Rinda to wake up."

"I'm awake, and don't you dare leave me out of this conference," said Rinda, combing out her long red hair.

"This is how I see it," said Jeff. "Rembrandt has every reason to believe that it's impossible to follow Ing even if we can go back in time accurately to when, I mean just *after,* he penetrated to the next universe. The Others have lived many years on the run from the Biguglies, becoming so old and discouraged that they've given up. I used to think they were superbeings, but they have emotions and discouragements just as we do."

"I'm not discouraged," said Rinda. "I am confident that you'll find a way to sort out this mess. You and Norby." She smiled up at Jeff in a way that made him realize she wouldn't stay eleven. Her confidence in him made Jeff feel strong, powerful, and mature.

"Of course, it was really Oola who enabled us to escape," said Rinda serenely. "Not that you're not brave, Jeff, but you do fumble things quite a bit."

"Thanks a lot."

"Both of you are forgetting that if it weren't for me, you'd still be in that courtroom on Mars," said Norby.

"What do *you* suggest we do about this problem, Norby?" asked Jeff. "Since you're such a genius."

"While you were asleep I asked Rembrandt. Of course, I got annoyed when he said that the alien metal in me and Pera was dangerous and likely to be misused, because after all I have done a lot of good even if I do get mixed up at times . . ."

"Norby!"

". . . and I asked Rembrandt if the Others wanted to take the metal out of me and use it . . ."

"They wouldn't!" Jeff exclaimed.

"Right. He said, and I quote accurately, 'We will leave you intact, Norby. You are unique, and you give any universe an extra element of fun and uncertainty.' "

"Stop bragging, Norby," said Rinda. "Pera never brags."

Jeff put out a hand to stop her. "Wait. I don't think Norby was just bragging. Or that Rembrandt was just flattering him. It was a message, wasn't it?"

"I think so, Jeff. Do you want to talk to him?"

"Yes."

The air lock opened once more and Rembrandt entered. "I left it to Norby to broach the subject with you, Jeff, and after you had food and rest. We wish to borrow Norby."

"What do you mean!"

"You know, Jeff," said Norby.

Jeff did. He put his head in his hands and thought about it. "I guess the Others want to link you to their computer, Norby, so their ship will go into the Biguglies' universe."

"I'm not built exactly like Pera, so there's no way of telling if I can go through the barrier, even with all the power of the Others' ship behind me, but I'm going to try." .

"Norby and I have agreed that you and Rinda must stay in the *Hopeful*, safe in hyperspace now that the Biguglies are dying out in this time period."

"Oh, no," said Rinda. "You can't keep me out of your blasted big ship. I want to see it and I want to go where Norby goes."

"Staying behind is out of the question," said Jeff. "But I have a suggestion. Norby can take the *Hopeful* back in time to find you, Rembrandt, when your ship was young . . ."

"You are discouraged by my frailty, aren't you, Jeff?"

"Yes, sir."

"Even if I die, it won't matter. The important thing is for Norby to use our ship as it is now, for over the centuries we have made our ship increasingly powerful. If you go back to find the Rembrandt that I used to be, he will not know how to make my ship powerful enough."

"Norby might be able to take the *Hopeful* if your ship's computer augments the power of ours," said Jeff. "The link would break once the *Hopeful* penetrated the Biguglies' universe, but it might be enough to begin with."

"Too uncertain," said Rembrandt. "And without our power, how would you bring the *Hopeful* back to your own universe?"

"Isn't there the risk that if you and Norby took your ship across, you might be stuck there?"

"Yes, Jeff, but I am old . . ."

"You and your crew are the last of the Others in this time period. If anything goes wrong . . ."

"Nevertheless, we will go and you two humans will stay."

Rinda laughed. She picked up a still sleepy Oola and petted her soft green head, laughing again when Oola yawned and began to purr.

"Mr. Rembrandt," said Rinda, "You're not telling the truth."

"We Others do not lie."

"Maybe not to someone you're talking to, but how about to yourself?"

"Don't insult Rembrandt," said Jeff, embarrassed.

"Think about it, Rembrandt," said Rinda, in exactly the tone her royal mother would use when lecturing a courtier. "Perhaps the reason you don't want Norby to go in the *Hopeful* is that if Jeff and I and Norby succeed without you, then you'll die. You won't exist anymore, because this Rembrandt, the one you are now, won't ever have existed."

There was a long silence, and finally Rembrandt said, "I think you are correct, young Rinda of Izz. Perhaps I believed that somehow, if I went to the parallel universe, I would continue existing even if history were changed back. It is not logical. I am ashamed."

"Let me try with the *Hopeful*, as Jeff suggested," said Norby. "Let me use the power of your ship as long as I can."

"Very well," said Rembrandt. "We will establish the link. All of us will link with our computer and with Norby, who will then have powerful energy. I only grieve that it is likely that you will be stranded in the alien universe."

"Not if I can somehow make contact with you again, Rembrandt," said Norby. "Stay in hyperspace so . . ."

"If you succeed in the alien universe, we will not be available to you."

"But the original 'you' will be, the Rembrandt you were before, the young one . . ."

"He did not, will not, have my knowledge, especially the more recently-acquired knowledge that will enable us to use the great new power of our ship. I do not mind that my memories of battle and flight will be lost when I cease existing. I mind that all the important scientific knowledge will be lost . . ."

"Not if you give it to me," said Norby.

"You are a remarkably intelligent robot, Norby, but not even your brain could understand it."

"I'm smart—" Norby stopped, and withdrew his head into his barrel until only the domed hat could be seen.

"No, Norby. You cannot even imagine what knowledge we've learned and what can be done with it."

"All right," said Norby, "I'm not that smart, and I'm not built to record things as well as Pera, but I could record some data—like how to augment the power of your ship, and if I tell the young Rembrandt you used to be . . ."

Rembrandt's seamed and withered face smiled broadly. "You are even smarter than I thought. I will give you the knowledge, but only scientific knowledge, mainly about the ship. I do not want my young self to be burdened by the weighty, unhappy memories of an old being."

"I'm ready, sir," said Norby.

"Then let us prepare. We Others, the last of our kind in a universe gone wrong, will do all we can to send you rescuers both back—and *out*."

11

BACK AND OUT

"I don't want to be strapped into the chair," said Rinda, her cheeks so pale that her freckles stood out sharply.

"It's necessary," said Jeff, pushing her back into the chair and activating the restraining web. "Norby thinks the *Hopeful* may get shaken up when we cross into the parallel universe."

"But can't I be closer to you?" she pleaded.

"I'm going to be webbed in, too, Rinda, in this chair, but I'll leave one arm free so we can hold hands."

Oola, already encased in a padded box with a screened window, was giving her opinion of the whole enterprise by yowling and growling alternatively.

"Can't you put that animal in the bedroom?" asked Norby, fussing over his connections to the computer, which was linked to Yib in the Other's ship by means of radio waves as well as wires from ship to ship.

"If Oola claws her way out I want to be able to grab her," said Jeff.

"How can you, when you're tied up like me?" asked Rinda.

"Neither of us is tied up, as you put it. To release yourself in an emergency, just pull the string with the metal tab on the end of it, that one just over your head."

"Are you all settled finally?" asked Norby. "It's a lot of hard work to maintain these powerful connections while I'm trying to tune into somebody a thousand years in the past and in another universe."

"I don't see how it's possible," said Rinda. "How can you tune into Ing . . ."

"Not Ing!" said Norby. "I could never tune into any

human, with the possible exception of Jeff, over such a distance and time. I'm trying to find a villain by finding his victim."

"Pera," said Rinda. "My Pera."

"*My* Pera," said Norby. "I'm very fond of her. Now hush up, everybody, so I can concentrate."

"Yes, Norby," said Rinda sweetly. "We have complete faith in you." With her free hand, she reached over to Jeff, but couldn't quite make it. He stretched his arm out and caught her hand. It was cold.

—I'm just a little worried [said Rinda, telepathically]. Naturally, being a royal princess, I'm not terrified or anything . . .

—Naturally.

—But do you think Norby knows what he's doing, Jeff?

—Honestly, I don't. How can he? It's never been done before except by Ing, with the aid of Pera and a large bomb.

—But what if we get across and can't find them . . .

—Don't think about it, Rinda. Can you see my face?

—Yes. You look scared. Of course, you're not of royal blood, but I suppose we're all allowed a little fear.

—That's gracious of you, Your Highness, but watch me. I'm going to put a small smile on my face, take a deep breath, let it out and try to relax all my muscles as I do so. Watch.

—And I suppose you want me to try it?

—That's the idea.

—You do look more relaxed, Jeff. Maybe I will . . .

"Okay, Rembrandt," said Norby. "I'm as ready as I can be, considering that I don't understand Yib very well. Your computer has grown so."

"Yib understands you, Norby," said Rembrandt from the *Hopeful*'s speaker. "We are backing you up and pushing you out, all the way. It's up to you to locate yourself."

"I'm trying, I'm trying! Go ahead!"

"Goodbye, Norby," said Rembrandt. "And goodbye, Princess Rinda—I am delighted to have had the chance to know you."

"Goodbye," said Norby and Rinda simultaneously.

"And Jefferson Wells, I say goodbye to you in the hope that if you ever meet—him—please, tell him . . ."

Jeff waited.

"That's odd. I don't know what I want you to tell my

former self about me," said Rembrandt. "Just give him my best regards."

"I will," said Jeff. "Goodbye, and thanks for helping us, Rembrandt."

"The fact of my existence will be wiped out, but nevertheless I am glad to help. Somehow it makes everything worthwhile."

"You won't die in our minds," said Jeff. "There you will always exist."

"Thank you," said Rembrandt. "Goodbye."

Norby activated the *Hopeful*'s engines and said, "Hang on!"

Jeff gritted his teeth and tried not to black out. He managed to turn his head in spite of the enormous pressure and saw that Rinda's face, however distorted, valiantly kept a half-smile on it, and she was breathing slowly. Jeff tried to do the same.

And then he blacked out just after he heard Oola scream like a cougar trapped by men with guns.

"Jeff, Jeff!" Rinda was sitting on his lap, her body pressed against his, her arms around his neck. "If you're hurt I'll make my mother boil Norby and the Others in the thickest plurf she can find! Oh—you're moving!"

Rinda's tears wet his cheeks as she kissed him. "Oh, Jeff, when the ship started to go, I thought I was dying and that Oola had died, and then when I got loose I thought you were dead . . ."

"I'm alive, or I would be if I could breathe."

Rinda sat up and released her stranglehold on his neck. "Oola's all right, too. I let her out and she went to use her litter box. I feel bruised all over, especially my feelings, and I wish I were home with my parents, who are difficult but not impossible and they love me."

"Norby, have we landed somewhere or are we in space?"

"Landed," said Rinda. "You must have been unconscious or you'd have felt the thud."

"Norby?"

Rinda turned. "Where is he?"

"Wasn't he at the control board when you woke up?"

"I don't know, Jeff. I had to let Oola out and I had to run to the toilet myself, and when I came back all I saw was that you were still unconscious and I thought you were hurt. Are you?"

"No. Get off. I have to find Norby. Maybe he's repairing some damage to the ship."

But Norby was not in the *Hopeful* and did not respond to calls made on the outside speakers.

An hour later Jeff sat at the control board, feeling forlorn and lost, but hoping beyond hope that Norby might still be somewhere outside the ship, even if he were too damaged to answer Jeff's call.

In the viewscreen, Jeff studied what was outside. It was a landscape he had never seen before and wished he didn't have to look at now. Strange purplish hills were dotted with rows of odd trees that seemed to be writhing in the wind, except that the ship's sensors indicated that there was a dead calm.

"Let's go outside," said Rinda.

"No, I don't like those things that look like trees but aren't. For all we know, they are distant relatives of the Biguglies. Notice the resemblance. The ship's sensors indicate that the nearest trees are reaching out to touch the *Hopeful*. Fortunately, they look rooted."

"Well can't we at least open the air lock and get some fresh air?"

"And die."

"What!"

"You heard me," said Jeff. "Stay away from that air lock. The air outside is poisonous to humans. No wonder the Biguglies had to wear space suits when they were in air that humans can breathe."

Oola trotted into the control room and batted her paw at the viewscreen. Her claws were out and she scraped them on the plastiglass. Oola clearly didn't like the 'trees' that weren't trees.

"I bet she recognizes them as Bigugly relatives," said Rinda. "And now that we've come here, what do we do next?"

"Look for Norby," said Jeff, grasping the controls. "I've told the computer to take the *Hopeful* low over the land, back and forth to look for him. It's a good thing Fargo taught me how to pilot this ship and instruct its computer. I'm rusty, though, because Norby usually does it."

Each time the *Hopeful* came near a tree, the claws at the branch ends reached for it, but could not reach it. Jeff took the ship carefully over all the ground they must have passed when landing between two hills, but Norby was nowhere in sight.

"Computer," said Jeff, "review all incoming data again. Do you find evidence of any radio wave source that might be coming from Norby trying to communicate with us?"

"I find no evidence of the robot Norby's communications."

"Try telepathy, Jeff," said Rinda. "I know it's not supposed to work without bodily contact, but sometimes he's tuned into you when you're far away. That's how we landed in your shower, remember?"

"But I can't tune into Norby. *He* has to do it," said Jeff. "At least, he has to be trying at the same time I am."

"Can this ship's computer tell if anyone is trying to reach anybody telepathically?"

"Of course not, Rinda, it's only an unintelligent—oh! I'm the stupid one. Computer! Are there any signs of any communication that doesn't come from Norby?"

"Yes, sir. Beyond the nearest hill is a source of radio waves."

"Can you read them?"

"Yes, sir. There is a message in standard Federation code for S.O.S."

"What does that mean?" asked Rinda.

"Help."

"It's not Pera. She wouldn't use S.O.S."

"No. It has to be Ing."

12

The Sacred Grove

Jeff cautiously piloted the *Hopeful* above the tops of the tree-like creatures he thought of as Bigugly relatives. When the ship crested the hill, Rinda cried out.

"How can Ing be alive in that?"

Admiral Yobo's precious *Quest* had broken in half on impact and the outer door of the air lock was open. Jeff brought the *Hopeful* as close as he could, but there was no way to maneuver so that he could join air locks.

"Do we have any space suits?" asked Rinda.

"There's one here that fits me and there ought to be one in the *Quest*, since by law every ship must carry a suit in case somebody has to go outside to make repairs."

"Why isn't it required that there be emergency suits for everyone?"

"I don't know. I suppose the Federation is too complacent, confident that our antigrav units and strong ship hulls will prevent that sort of accident," said Jeff, pointing to the *Quest*. He opened the locker, took out the suit, and started getting into it.

"Why can't I go instead of you? Pera is my robot."

"Because Ing is dangerous . . ."

"I can use a stun gun."

"I don't have one. My brother doesn't ordinarily stock the *Hopeful* with weapons. He always says that verbal skill plus a little karate is better and safer. Besides, you can't go because the suit fits me, not you."

"Rorrrwww!" said Oola, jumping onto Jeff's shoulder just as he fastened the helmet. He lifted her off and handed her to Rinda. Then he had to speak through the suit's microphone.

"Now don't get ideas, Rinda. There's nothing you can persuade Oola to change into that will be useful this time, because whatever she looks like, her body cells are still from a different universe and won't be able to tolerate the biology of this one. I've left the radio on so we can talk once I'm over there."

"Are you hoping Norby is there, somehow trapped and unable to leave?"

She was too smart, thought Jeff, for he had indeed been entertaining that crazy idea. He nodded, waved goodbye, and went out the air lock.

There were only a few meters between the *Hopeful* and the *Quest,* but with each step, Jeff was poked and prodded and pulled by long extensible "arms" from the palmy "leaves" of the rooted aliens that surrounded the two ships. Each arm ended in pinchers that could have torn apart a suit less well made than Jeff's.

He made it to the *Quest's* air lock and saw with relief that the inside door was still closed. With difficulty, he closed the outer door behind him, sure that it wasn't completely air-tight, and then tried to open the inner door. It was locked.

"Ing!" shouted Jeff, turning up his mike to its highest volume. There should have been a pickup mike inside the air lock, but Jeff didn't know if Ing had turned off all communication from the outside when he was stealing the ship and had forgotten or been unable to turn it back on.

When there was no response, Jeff banged on the door, and after a minute, tried knocking in the S.O.S. pattern—three quick knocks, three heavy knocks widely spaced, three quick knocks again.

This time there was a click and he could open the inner door of the air lock. He did so as quickly as possible, shutting it behind him before too much of the poisonous air could enter.

"That's a Federation suit you've got on, so I assume you're human. Come to arrest me?" Ing was sitting in the control chair, one arm on the board where he had presumably just switched the air lock to open, and the other holding a stun gun aimed at Jeff. His face looked flushed and his breathing was labored.

"Rescue party," said Jeff, holding his hands out so that Ing could see there was no weapon. "Where's the suit that should be in the *Quest?*"

"So—Jefferson Wells. They sent a boy to pick me up, to take me back to one of those Federation penal colonies . . ."

"Ing, listen . . ."

The would-be destroyer of a universe coughed, his eyes bloodshot. "Take off that suit, boy, before I shoot and strip you myself. I'm going to take your ship—" He waved at the viewscreen, still operating and showing the *Hopeful* nearby.

"Ing, we're not back in the Federation . . ."

"Sure we are. I failed, but I'll try again. Thanks to that incompetent robot in the cage, we've crashed back on an idiotic sulfurous place like Io. Certainly smells like it. Take off your suit, Wells!"

"Don't trust Ing, Jeff," said Pera, peering out from the cage Ing had made from the magic box.

"Ing!" shouted Jeff. "Look at the viewscreen! Have you ever seen any trees like that? Can you believe that things grow on Io? I tell you we're not in the Federation! We're in a parallel universe, and we're trapped. All of us."

"Lies, lies," said Ing, but he coughed and the gun sagged in his hand.

Jeff's hand came down in a karate chop and the gun spun across the room. Ing lurched after it, but Jeff was quicker.

"Now I've got the gun," said Jeff. "If you want to live, at least a little longer, you'll wait quietly while I see if there's a spare suit. Get back in the chair."

Ing sat down again, coughing spasmodically. "Parallel universe? More than one? Full of life forms—how can I be a master of them all? This place is killing me . . ." Suddenly he fell out of the chair, hitting his head on the magic box.

Jeff bent over him, but the man was unconscious. A thin trickle of blood seeped out of Ing's thick black hair.

"He is damaged," said Pera. "I sense a worsening of the abnormal brain patterns."

Jeff let her out of the cage. "Pera, I'll look inside for a suit, and you explore the damaged part of the ship, but beware of the rooted Biguglies. That's what we call them."

There was no suit, and Pera reported that the drive engines were too damaged to be able to function even if they'd been able to move them to the *Hopeful*. Jeff stripped off his own suit and put it on Ing.

"Take him over to the *Hopeful*, and bring the suit back for me," said Jeff. "Rinda's waiting. Give her the gun and tell her to watch Ing. Norby's . . ."

"Missing," said Pera. "I know, because I couldn't sense him. You'll tell me about it later, after we rescue Ing."

Coughing, Jeff watched in the viewscreen while Pera held Ing's limp body and, on antigrav, propelled herself so quickly to the *Hopeful* that the Bigugly relatives didn't have time to pinch the suit.

The contaminated air made it hard to move, but Jeff methodically explored every part of the intact half of the ship. The standard emergency airtight sealing partition had done its work well, coping with the splitting of the ship. It was the faulty air lock that had let in the outside air.

Jeff salvaged what he could, and there wasn't much that was portable, only a few papers and microdiscs, for everything else was built-in. As he waited for Pera, the lights grew dimmer and finally the viewscreen winked out. With the main engines gone, there wasn't enough emergency power left to keep the computer running. The life support system would be the last to go, but the faulty air lock insured that choking to death would happen before that.

Pera entered, bringing another volume of outside air when the air lock opened again. Jeff put the suit on and, with Pera's help, was soon inside the *Hopeful*.

Ing was lying on a mattress in the control room, still unconscious, but breathing better.

"I thought we'd better have him in here so we can watch him, in case he gets worse, or if he recovers and attacks us. I can't seem to decide which is preferable," said Rinda, handing the gun back to Jeff.

Jeff did not tell her that it didn't seem to matter, since the life support system of the *Hopeful* could not continue recycling their air and water indefinitely. Eventually all three humans would die without rescue, for without Norby's hyperdrive the *Hopeful* could not go home, or even search for a better planet, if any existed in this universe.

"Pera, you watch," he said, giving the gun to her. "Rinda and I must sleep to restore our energies."

"Ing must have surgery to correct the malformation in his brain," said Pera. "Without it he may die."

"How soon?" asked Rinda.

"I do not know. Days, perhaps."

"While Jeff and I have weeks. Maybe months before we die, but then we will. I'm sorry, Pera, to leave you alone in a strange universe. After Jeff and I get some rest we'll concentrate on tuning in to Norby."

"I also," said Pera.

Jeff took Rinda's hand and they went back to the bedrooms together. She looked at him and smiled ruefully.

"Rinda, I didn't think you realized . . ."

"I may be just a spoiled little princess, but I'm intelligent and I can face dying. I think. Would it be all right if we took a nap on the same bed?"

"Sure."

"I wish I were your age. I wish we could be lovers. Couldn't we, even now?"

"It isn't that I don't want to, Rinda. It isn't that you are still very young and terribly royal . . ."

"Well what is it, then, my freckles?" She stamped her foot, and her red-gold eyebrows drew together.

He picked her up and carried her into the bedroom he always used. He put her on the bunk bed and lay beside her, holding her in his arms. "Go to sleep, Rinda. It isn't your freckles. It's that we should concentrate on being rescued."

"Oh, well," said Rinda, yawning. "We're too tired and besides, Mother would boil you in plurf."

Jeff held hands with Rinda and Pera while, on the other side of the control room, Ing the Ingrate snored. Jeff was discouraged. Even a three-way telepathic linking did not reach Norby, wherever he was.

"Ship approaching," said the *Hopeful*'s computer, in its normal dispassionate voice.

Jeff broke the link and leaped to the viewscreen.

"Norby?" said Rinda. "The Others?"

Jeff couldn't answer, for his throat seemed to clog up. He just pointed to the viewscreen. The ship was long, high, and narrow, resembling a flat box tilted on its side. It was a shiny orange color, with no discernible windows or doors, but as it hovered above the ground between the "trees," eight huge metal legs extruded from the sides of the box and plunged down to provide stable support.

"But you've never seen the outside of the Others' ship," said Rinda plaintively. "How do you know it's not . . ."

"I've been on the inside, and there's a plastiglass section in front for the control room, and one in the back for the lounge. Besides, those metal legs resemble the ones the Biguglies use for arms."

When absolutely nothing happened for several minutes, Jeff took out his space suit and put it on again, while Oola howled and Rinda protested.

"If those are Biguglies, it's not safe . . ."

"They have hyperdrive and we don't. There might be some way of using their ship," said Jeff, plucking off his chest a frantic all-purpose pet who wanted to go along.

"Oh, sure," said Rinda scathingly. "You're just going to go up to that ship and say you want it and they'll give it to you without a whimper?"

"I don't know what to do. I'm going over there so I'll find out."

Rinda turned to her robot. "Pera, we've got to stop Jeff from doing this."

"But I'm going to go with Jeff," said Pera. "Please don't order me to stop him."

"Thanks, Pera," said Jeff, shutting his helmet. "Come on, let's go visiting."

Behind them, Ing groaned, but did not open his eyes.

"Take care of Ing, Rinda, and if anything happens to me wait here."

"For what? For whom?"

"Rescue. I hope." Jeff waved goodbye and with Pera hovering on antigrav beside him, went out of the air lock.

No sooner did he step out onto the ground than lines appeared in the lower forward part of the alien ship. A rectangular section slid upward and a Bigugly came out, the first Jeff had seen that wasn't wearing a space suit.

This alien wasn't sickly yellow or orange, but a clear pale peach color, and the ten leaf-like structures at its top were larger and more luxuriant. The eight stubby legs seemed somewhat longer and stronger, while the trunk was smooth and girdled by a metal belt slung with what were probably weapons.

"Gosh," said Jeff. "I forgot that I can understand their language, but I can't speak it."

"Open your mind to me, Jeff. I will learn the language and endeavor to speak it for you."

"But there isn't time, and I'm wearing a suit."

He felt pressure from Pera's hand holding his gloved one, and then she spoke in his mind.

—Contact is contact. I will try to absorb quickly. It is my talent to record everything necessary. Try.

Jeff tried to relax and let Pera into his mind. He stared at the alien, who stood presumably staring at him, perhaps through visual organs in those odd leaf veins that Jeff had never noticed before.

Minutes passed. Many minutes. Jeff began to sweat inside the suit, but the moisture seemed suddenly cold when one of the alien's arms grabbed a pointed metal object from its belt and aimed it at Jeff.

"Lift up those two distorted extensors of yours to the sky, alien! Explain what you are doing in the Sacred Grove of the Twintas before I blast you into nothingness."

13

Enemy or Friend?

—Pera, if you're able, tell him we had an accident and need help. Tell him we didn't mean to land in a sacred grove . . .

—Not him.

—You can't translate?

—I can. I meant that that alien is not a him. It's a she. It's very clear from the slight bulge on the biggest back leaf, can't you see?

—I don't know anything about Biguglies . . .

—Yes, you do, Jeff. Search your mind while I explain to her what you said.

As Pera repeated Jeff's words in the Bigugly language, Jeff realized that he did recognize male from female Biguglies. When knowledge of the language had been given to him, so was other knowledge—of course! You had to know about the difference in the sexes in order to understand the language, because the peculiar changes in verbs often referred to slight variations in Bigugly anatomy.

"Accident?" said the Bigugly. "Impossible. There are strict rules about the use of space and you have obviously violated them. Not only that, the damaged portion of one of *your* ships has damaged one of the *Twintas*. You are in deep trouble."

"We're very sorry," said Jeff in Terran Basic, repeated by Pera in the Bigugly language. "We are new to this uni—to this area of space, and we now have an injured crewman to take care of. Have you any doctors aboard your vessel?"

"What are doctors? Your translating device, which speaks our language with an abhorrent accent, uses an unfamiliar word. Every intelligent being in this universe speaks our language—why do you need both a space suit and a language device?"

"It's a long story," said Jeff. "My body can't tolerate your air, but I do understand your language. My speech organs are inadequate for speaking it, however."

"You have not explained the word 'doctor'."

"They were beings who take care of the sick and injured, helping them heal themselves."

"You come to *this* planet, yet you ask for a doctor? You can't be *that* ignorant. You must be here to uproot and steal a Twintas. Well, we won't let you do that!"

"Then you are police?"

There was a pause while the alien absorbed the word that Pera had used for "police." In the Bigugly language it translated as "persons in charge of arrest and correction."

The Bigugly's leafy top shook as if she were shaking with a strong emotion, like rage or disapproval. Jeff wondered what he had said wrong, and then he saw that four more Biguglies were running out of the ship toward him. He tried to make it back to the *Hopeful*, with Pera pulling him, but they caught him and brought him back to the leader.

"Pera! Stay free!" shouted Jeff, not daring to struggle in the grip of the pinchers because if his suit finally tore he wouldn't be able to breathe for long.

Pera zoomed out of reach, above the pinchers of the biguglies trying to grab her.

"Miniantigrav," said the first Bigugly. "Fascinating."

"Don't go into our ship," said Jeff. "You can't breathe our air any more than we can breathe yours." Pera spoke at full volume in translation.

"You probably have much equipment we can use. And we'll take your undamaged ship," said the leader. "Tell your crew to put on suits so we can evacuate the bad air and go in. You are our hostage, so your crew had better listen to my orders. I'm the Captain and I am called Blifzz. . . ." The captain's name went on for stranger syllables than Jeff would ever be able to manage.

"We have only this one suit," said Jeff. "Please don't kill my crew by taking their air. And may I call you Blif?"

"You are a presumptuous creature, but since you are vocally inadequate, you may call me what you like." The Bigugly Captain gestured to one of her crew. "Have you scanned this ugly ship of theirs? What's inside?"

"There are two other biological creatures like this one, with two horrible long legs each, and no ortawes on top. There is also a much smaller green creature that cogitates little."

"Interesting," said Blif, "and this one is not wearing a weapon of any kind. I'm not impressed by the danger. Go get my space suit so I may investigate the aliens and their ship."

"But Captain . . ."

"At once!"

When encased in a transparent suit, the Bigugly Captain told Jeff to go into the *Hopeful* ahead of her.

Inside, Jeff took off his helmet and breathed deeply. "Where's Oola?"

"I was watching on the viewscreen," said Rinda, pale but carefully standing just in front of the low shelf where she had put the stun gun, "and when you were captured, Oola made such a fuss about going out to help you that I had to put her in the bedroom. Please, Pera, I know you have to translate Jeff's words to the alien, but come here and hold my hand so I'll understand telepathically what's being said."

"This member of your species is slightly different," said Blif, pointing to Rinda. "What is the matter with it?"

"She is female, and nothing's the matter with her."

"A remarkably puny female!"

"She is young," said Jeff, while Rinda giggled in spite of her fear. "She comes from a very important family."

"That's what anyone says who has anything to do with the M.C." said Blif.

"What are the M.C.?" asked Jeff.

"Don't pretend you don't know," said Blif, drawing a weapon. "You have obviously learned the M.C. style of our language and that makes you their creatures, or at least in their pay."

"But I . . ."

"Stand back while I learn about you from your computer memory bank [except that she actually said "the stored words"] because it has features similar to ours."

"Convergent evolution of technology," muttered Jeff.

Since Pera automatically translated, Blif heard this and paused before one of her arms touched the computer. "Do not speak as if your inferior species could in any way be similar to ours. You have probably developed your technology from the

M.C. None of it could be original." She touched the computer and was obviously absorbing information.

Rinda raised her eyebrows and said softly in Izzian, "I think this Captain Blif's personality is like Mother's."

"I hope not," said Jeff.

At that moment, Ing rolled over and jumped to his feet, snatching Blif's gun and stooping to remove his own gun from the shelf. He jammed both weapons behind the back of Blif's space-suited trunk.

"Monsters have taken over my universe," shouted Ing, "but I'll kill them all! And you, Wells—you and the girl are in league with them. You thought I was asleep, but I've been watching and waiting for my chance. Now, all of you, leave my ship so I can go . . . go . . ."

"Stop it, Ing," said Jeff, while Pera went on translating to the Bigugly. "If you damage her space suit she'll die in our air, and Rinda and I will die if you force us outside. Besides, what can you possibly do in a universe not your own? Where can you go?"

"Poor Threezy," said Rinda cooingly. "You'll be all alone in a big, lonely, strange universe and there won't be anybody to applaud when you sing and dance and juggle. Nobody to clap and laugh. So sad." She allowed a small tear to squeeze out of one eye, and came closer to Ing.

"Threezy's dead," said Ing harshly.

"Not quite. Tell me he's not," said Rinda, almost up to Ing and Blif now. "I admired him so."

"A clown!" Ing's mad eyes rolled up in the mock despair of a clown. "Stupid, when I could be a god . . ."

Rinda smiled and flipped her fist up into Ing's nose while at the same time kicking him much lower down. As he let go of Blif and doubled over, Rinda dug her thumbs into his neck at the carotid arteries until he passed out. She plucked the guns from his limp hands and gave them to Jeff.

"Mother always insisted that a Royal Princess should know how to protect herself."

"I am glad that even young human females are brave," said Blif. "I did not learn as much from your computer as I wished, but enough to know that you are called humans, and that this is not your universe, as you said."

"Blif, how much longer will your suit's air hold out?" asked Jeff.

"Two hours more."

Jeff handed Blif's gun to her. "Then let's talk. I want to tell you the truth and I want you to tell me about the M.C."

"Well—you may talk like someone of the Master Cult, but you don't act like them," said Blif. "We'll talk. I wish to know how and why the Masters taught you their style of our language without completely indoctrinating you with their point of view. You did not let the older human kill me."

"The Master Cult of your species penetrated to our universe and conquered it. Eventually *it* conquered *them* through disease, but by then everything had been changed for the worse."

"When did this happen? We have had no word of it."

"It hasn't happened yet," said Jeff, "but it will if the M.C. find us, if we don't get home somehow."

14

THE MASTER CULT ARRIVES

Half an hour later, Blif detached herself from Pera and Jeff began to worry even more. After explaining everything he knew to Blif, he'd made the decision to let the Bigugly tap into Pera's memory bank as well as into that of the ship's computer. If she were a possible ally, then knowledge was essential.

He touched Rinda's arm.

—Have I made a mistake? We know that the Biguglies will steal Pera in the future and use the metal in her to travel to our galaxy. Suppose Blif is the one?

—Pera trusts Blif, I can tell *[said Rinda, in his mind]*

—But suppose that becomes the problem . . .

—Jeff, you worry too much. Anyway, isn't it time we asked Blif a few questions about herself?

Shamed, Jeff cleared his throat and asked Pera to translate carefully what he was about to say to Blif.

"Now that you know how we were captured by the Master Cult and how they forced me to learn their style of your language, please explain to us how you differ from them."

"So you can think of me as a good Bigugly, and the M.C. as the bad Biguglies?" asked Blif, her leaves rustling so much that Jeff had the distinct impression that she was laughing.

"I forgot you'd find out from Pera what we named you."

"I don't mind," said Blif. "And I will tell you why we don't trust anyone who might be a spy for the M.C. The M.C.s were once the official spies for our government, until they took it over. Judging from the history of your species— and your Pera is remarkably well-informed—you could think of the M.C. as a sort of Central Spy Agency gone wrong."

Jeff remembered, thanks to Norby's foolishness, that Pera had absorbed information from Space Command's Secret Service files. "And what are you, Blif?"

"You might as well think of me as one of the underground, as I believe it would have been in your history. That plus a bit of a pirate, for we live in space ships and steal our livelihood from planets and ships controlled by the M.C. It is difficult and dangerous, for the M.C. have developed nasty powers including the ability to hurt creatures at a distance."

Blif paused. "Speaking of hurt, I believe I can now hear what sounds like a creature in pain."

"That's our all-purpose pet, Oola, who's started to howl. She wants to be let out of the bedroom—go do it, Rinda."

When Oola bounded in, she sniffed at Blif and began to take the shape of a nununiy. Blif petted her gingerly and said, "Amazing that this creature could have killed the Master of Mars."

Oola promptly reverted to cat form and sniffed at Ing. She sat back on her haunches and meowed.

"Ing's not breathing right," said Rinda. "I think he's going to die."

"Perhaps the Twintas can help," said Blif. "They are the life-form on this planet. Our ancient government established several such refuges for our distant relatives, the Twintas, and we visit them when we need healing. Look in your viewscreen and you will see how it is done."

Biguglies from the pirate ship had carried out two of the crew and put them down under the Twintas branches, which were now bending to grasp each injured Bigugly.

"I gave orders for the healing to proceed, once I found out that you are not spies from the M.C.," said Blif. "I have kept in touch with my ship by means of my suit mike. I'm not so brave that I would walk into an alien ship without being able to inform my companions about what's happening."

"But how can Ing be taken out there?" asked Rinda.

"I think I know how," said Jeff. He found one of Fargo's scuba masks and attached an oxygen canister. "The outside air will irritate Ing's skin, but he won't breathe it."

Later, suited up and watching the Twintas wrap branches around Ing, Jeff was touched by the now unsuited Blif, and to his surprise, he heard her telepathically.

—Our species has only rudimentary telepathy [said Blif], but those of us who have the most become leaders. I am one of them, and I wish to speak to you privately. If you think your thoughts carefully, I will understand even though you cannot speak my language out loud.

—I'll try. Why privately?

—Because, according to what you have told me, Pera is the key to the invasion of your universe. I know that I will never attempt such an invasion, for I know from your knowledge that it would doom us. In the future that you have visited, the M.C. captured Pera. The question is, when? How soon?

—I don't know.

—I fear that my ship may bring the M.C. to this planet, for we had a battle with them yesterday, wounding two of my crew. We thought we had escaped them, but they know that we must seek one of the Twintas planets for healing and if we stay here too long they will find us. And they will find you, if they dare to land.

—Why dare? Don't the M.C. use Twintas planets?

—No. The Twintas are intelligent, in spite of being rooted, and they oppose the M.C. In retaliation, the M.C. have destroyed many Twintas. That is why the M.C. are so sickly, for they have no healers. Perhaps that is also why, when they do find Pera, they will want to go to a different universe in search of immortality.

—They won't find it. What shall we do? How can we protect Pera?

—Jeff Wells, it is too late, for already they come!

Jeff looked up and saw a fleet of alien ships winking into view one by one, high in the atmosphere of the Twintas planet. These ships were also like tall boxes, but each had a curious pointed attachment like the beak of a bird.

—The hurt comes from that point, said Blif, after sending orders to her crew. They concentrate their minds to hurting and controlling . . . Jeff, go into your ship at once!

Jeff was doubling over in pain and could not move.

Blif picked him up in three of her arms.

—We have a few built-in defences against the control, but you do not.

She ran with him to the *Hopeful* and, as Pera dragged him

into the air lock, he heard Blif shout "Bring your ship into ours! It's your only hope!"

"Ing—we've forgotten Ing," gasped Jeff as he tore off his helmet and ran to the control room.

"Let me out, Jeff," said Pera. "I will get him."

"Pera, you are the danger. Can't you see that we can't let you out? We must hide you and protect you at all cost."

Seated at the control board, Jeff turned on the engines and lifted the *Hopeful* on antigrav.

"Look," said Rinda, pointing to the viewscreen. "The good Biguglies are taking Ing inside their ship. How long will his oxygen supply last?"

"Not much longer," said Jeff, turning the *Hopeful* toward the pirate ship, where a large opening had appeared in the side. "We must get there."

"Traction beams on ship," said the computer.

"Oh no! Not again!" said Jeff.

"Jeff," said Pera, "let me out and I will go to the Master Cult. They will let you go once I lead them to think that I am the only useful object here. And then I will destroy myself so that they cannot invade our universe."

"No!" cried Rinda.

"Wait," said Jeff. "Something's helping us. Something's fighting the traction beams."

"It's the Twintas!" Rinda clapped her hands. "Look—the branches are around us, and they're passing us from one tree to another, towards Blif's ship!"

15

SEARCHING FOR NORBY

Jeff, wearing a space suit, stood in a part of the pirate ship that he took to be the control room. The viewscreen was like a huge flower opened to the sun, but in the center of it he could see clearly everything going on outside.

Sheets of flames shot out from M.C. ships, pounding upon the energy shielding of Blif's ship. Below them on the planet, some Twintas withered and died, but the rest fought back in ways Jeff could not fathom. And the pirate ship fought with what seemed like old-fashioned cannonballs that turned into great crawling things that appeared to bite the M.C. ships.

—You're shooting live things at the enemy! said Jeff, touching Blif's trunk for telepathic communication.

"Everything is alive," said Blif. "And what is not, like the hulls of our ships, our guns, and certain parts of our machinery, has been manufactured by living creatures. Even what you would call our computers are all made from living organic material. We have nothing like your Pera and Norby, the purely inorganic robots you depend on. That is another reason why reason tells me that we should stay in our own universe, for here we are all connected in life."

—Perhaps even in our universe everything's connected, organic and inorganic, if it has some intelligence.

"And even if it doesn't," said Blif, gesturing to a crew member to shut down part of the ship where one of the energy shields had collapsed. "I'm sorry, Human Jeff, but I seem to be losing this battle."

—Go into hyperspace.

"I would like nothing better, for then you and your ship would be safe also, but with part of our shield down, we are in the grip of a traction beam, one of the closely guarded secrets of the M.C. Didn't you tell me that even your Norby was unable to vanish into the safety of hyperspace when the M.C. focused on the ship or on him?"

—Yes. Wait—send for Pera. She may be able to help your computer take your ship away from the traction beam. She herself has no hyperdrive, but she certainly helped bring Ing's ship here. We must try.

In a few minutes, Pera arrived from the inside dock where the *Hopeful* was moored. She hooked herself to the ship's computer, and after another few minutes she spoke.

"I cannot break the hold of the traction beam, which is growing stronger. Furthermore, the animals that make up your computer are themselves weakening, although each says it will die rather than surrender to the Master Cult."

Blif's peach coloring faded momentarily. "I did not know that the computer animals could speak as individuals."

"They can't," said Pera. "Not exactly. I'm sorry, Blif, but I can't help you."

"Then we pirates and you aliens are doomed," said Blif. "Once our shields are completely down, the M.C. will blast us with rays that destroy organic minds."

"The Master Cult must not find me," said Pera. "Please, Blif, arrange to have me destroyed at once. Since I am not organic, I would go on living when all of you are dead, and then be captured."

Jeff grabbed Pera and held her close to his space suit. The contact with Blif broken, the Bigugly reached for him—but only gently, one of her pinchers touching his helmet.

"What is it, Jeff? You seem to be thinking hard, but I cannot follow your thoughts."

—Our only hope is Norby.

"But he is lost in your own universe, or in hyperspace."

—We must reach him. We must augment our power, *my* power. Perhaps if your crew lined up, touching each other, from your computer to mine, with Pera the link between our atmospheres . . .

Blif did not argue. "Yes. It is a possibility." She gave orders.

Jeff and Rinda held hands tightly, their free hands upon the *Hopeful*'s computer. Wires led from it to the air lock's microphone, where Pera waited, touching it and a Bigugly pincher outside the open outer door. A few of Blif's crew were lined up, extending to the nearest computer terminal in the dock wall. And up in the other control room, Blif and the rest of the crew touched each other and waited.

"I'm scared, Jeff," said Rinda. "What if I can't concentrate and my uncontrolled thoughts make this impossible?"

"What if this is just a silly idea of mine and isn't possible at all?" asked Jeff. "It's crazy, like one of those old stories you see on hycom, where at the last minute the cavalry comes to rescue the wagon train . . ."

"Concentrate!" said Pera through the receptor. "I am receiving a message from Blif. She feels some of your emotions through the chain, and she says pessimism will defeat us."

"Comet tails!" said Jeff.

Suddenly Rinda grinned at him, her freckled nose wrinkling up. She leaned toward him and pressed her lips on his with a loud smacking sound. Then she chuckled, shut her eyes, and her face smoothed out, becoming calm and concentrated.

But Jeff could not relax. Something kept nagging at his mind and he felt sure he'd forgotten something important.

Where was Oola? Had he left her in the bedroom where he'd locked up the sleeping Ing?

Oola, bioengineered by robots of the Others. Pera, made by the Others. Oola and Pera. Oola and Pera and the bad human, Ing. Bad Ing. Dying—or was he going to live? Ing . . . Ing . . .

The words reverberated through Jeff's mind, while Rinda seemed to be placidly asleep and the *Hopeful* silent amid the battle still raging outside the larger ship in which it was hidden. He shut his eyes to concentrate, but he heard a noise that sounded like a door breaking open.

Ing stood in the doorway of the control room, holding a limp Oola in his hands. She looked like a dead hound dog.

"When I was a kid I had a foxhound I used to train to play dead," said Ing. "Did you know that I was giving magic acts even then?"

Oola yawned, licking Ing's hand, and jumped down. She trotted over to Jeff, becoming more catlike the nearer she approached him.

"Ing, we're in desperate danger," said Jeff, letting Oola climb up into his lap and settle down, purring. "We need help and we're trying to join minds to reach my robot, but I can't concentrate because of you."

"What is it, a big magic act?" said Ing, his arm swinging out so he could finger the stun gun that Jeff had forgotten to put in his own belt in case Ing woke up.

"Yes."

Ing yawned. "Funny thing, I can't seem to remember much except the magic tricks. Can I join this one?"

Rinda opened one eye. "Sit down, Threezy, and take my hand. Jeff, you keep your other hand on the computer. Threezy, do as I say at once!"

Ing shrugged and sat down, one hand outstretched to hers. They clasped hands and Rinda said, "Close your eyes, Threezy, and think about small robots that would make a good part of your magic act. Think hard."

It was quiet once more in the *Hopeful*'s control room.

Until Norby arrived, of course.

16

THE WAY HOME

Only Norby's voice entered the *Hopeful,* but relief swept over Jeff as he heard his very own robot shout, "Jeff, are you inside the ship that's being conquered?"

"Yes, and can you help?"

"We can," said another voice.

"Rembrandt!"

"Look at the viewscreen," said Rinda, her voice slightly shaky. "Now we know what a ship of the Others looks like from the outside."

The *Hopeful*'s viewscreen, linked to the computer of the pirate ship, showed what was happening outside as the battle was fought above the Twintas planet. And now something else had been added to the scene.

"It's enormous!" said Jeff. Rembrandt's ship was like a huge oval cloud that shimmered in the light of the planet's star. It was so big that all of the M.C. ships were in its shadow, and soon they all began to shake as if something from the Others' ship were vibrating them.

One by one, the M.C. ships disappeared into hyperspace, fleeing the unknown enemy.

"Come aboard," said Rembrandt.

Blif went with the *Hopeful* when it entered Rembrandt's ship, and walked fearlessly with the humans as they entered the vast room at the stern of the Others' enormous space ship. When Jeff sat down beside her, he was aware of a faint, pleasantly pungent odor from her suit, completely different from the sickening smell of the diseased Bigugly Masters.

Best of all, Norby looked just the same. He even sounded the same.

"I couldn't help it, Jeff."

"I know, you got mixed up."

"Maybe. One minute I was in the *Hopeful*, and the next I could feel my hyperdrive come on and there I was in hyperspace, totally lost. I couldn't find you, and I couldn't seem to get out into normal space. Fortunately, I used my superior intelligence."

"Oh?"

"I remembered that Rembrandt—the young Rembrandt—this one here . . ."

"Yes, yes . . ."

"Anyway, he could detect things in hyperspace, so after concentrating on you and not finding you, I concentrated on Rembrandt and he found me."

Rembrandt nodded. "And then we linked minds, so that I knew what had happened and a little of how to follow you. It took hard work to change our ship in the manner the old Rembrandt told Norby, but we managed. Yet even then, we would not have been able to jump through into this universe without the pull from all of you." He bowed to the humans, Pera, and Blif.

"Don't forget Oola," said Ing, pointing to the green cat curled up in Rinda's lap. "She was the first thing I saw when I woke up. She took the shape of my favorite pet and I was a boy again."

"And what are you now?" asked Norby. "Ing the Incredible Ingrate again?"

"Ing? I think he was somebody I invented. It seems so long ago. Rinda says I'm a good clown. Am I?"

"Yes," said Jeff.

"Then can I be Threezy? I like being Threezy."

Rinda rushed over to him and threw her arms about his neck, pushing her face into his beard. "I love Threezy. Please come back to Izz with me. You'll be the hit of the Palace. My father, the King, will enjoy your act, and Mother—well, when I tell Mother that you helped rescue me, she'll make you Crown Jester."

"Crown Jester!" said Threezy. "Sounds good."

"And there's always plurf if he misbehaves," muttered Norby.

"I hate to interrupt all this jollity," said Jeff, "but has anyone noticed that we're still in the parallel universe? Does anyone have any idea how we're going to get home?"

"Simple," said Norby. "The way we got here."

"Not so simple," said Rembrandt. "The changes I made in our ship to give us the power to get here, were a one-time operation. We'll have to have extra power from some other source to get back into hyperspace and out into our own universe."

Blif, listening to the conversation by holding Pera (who could translate telepathically), said, "This time we will need more than the linked minds of all of us in our two ships. We will need the whole Twintas population."

"How will we link Rembrandt's ship to the Twintas?" asked Jeff.

"Ah," said Blif. "You do not understand. I mean the entire Twintas population of this universe. They can link with each other, planet to planet, and provide enormous power, but only if they are persuaded that it is important. I will go back down to the planet below and talk to them."

Rembrandt leaned forward. "Is it dangerous?"

"How did you know that?"

"I surmised that it must be, since I would guess that you have not done it before, not even to save yourself from the Master Cult."

"If I link my ship and yours to the Twintas of this planet and they link with the other Twintas planets, the force may be enough to send you to your own universe. But it may not."

"I meant is it dangerous to you?" asked Rembrandt.

"I do not know. The Twintas are strange creatures, opposed to our enemies, the Master Cult, and willing to heal those of us who are hurt. But perhaps they would prefer that all of us Biguglies became extinct, leaving them alone in this universe."

"I will talk to them," said Rembrandt, adding, "with Jeff's and Norby's help."

"Mine?" said Jeff.

"We have the memories of Rembrandt as he might have been," said Norby. "We are linked to him closer than anyone else. Let's go, Jeff."

Jeff and Rembrandt, both in space suits, followed Pera and Blif as the pirate led the way from the Others' lander to the

central grove of the Twintas. Jeff's gloved hand touched
Rembrandt's for telepathic contact.

—Rembrandt, for some reason Blif reminds me of you.

—Possibly because I am descended from pirates.

—I can't believe it! The Others are so good . . .

—Jeff, the Others have had their own social history, including a period of tyranny that was eventually overthrown by
an underground that called themselves pirates. Tyranny is
always possible when an intelligent species becomes too pop-
ulous and too powerful before it becomes wise.

—But that must have been long ago. You Others have become so very wise . . .

—We now have enough wisdom to control our population
and our power, and we strive to learn and grow, for improvement is always possible, young human. Never become self-
satisfied. I learned from Norby that the Biguglies who
conquered our universe in the false future thought they could
be all-powerful, but they succumbed to disease at last. Nothing is invulnerable. There's always change.

—Sometimes I've seen so much change that I feel we
humans won't learn to cope with it.

—Don't cope. Move with change and enjoy the ride. Rembrandt laughed.

—Is your art part of the way you enjoy the ride?

—Yes. I hope that those who see my art discover that the
living universe is wonderous and should be cared for.

Blif halted in front of an immense Twintas that looked like
the oldest specimen on the planet.

"Ancient One," said Blif aloud, while at the same time
touching one of those oddly jointed arms that Jeff still thought
of as branches.

"We need your power. You Twintas who remain alive on
this planet know that the aliens helped drive off the Master
Cult ships. Now these aliens must return to their own universe, but this requires much power. Can you help us?"

Jeff could understand the conversation, although Blif spoke
in what was probably an archaic form of the Bigugly language. He could hear no answer from the Twintas.

Blif waved one of her rear pinchers in the direction of Jeff,
Norby, and Rembrandt, who stood hand-in-hand behind her.

"The Twintas say they will not help, for in touching you

aliens, they have learned what will happen if you cannot get home. The M.C. will return, take Pera, and leave this universe for yours. The Twintas want this future to come into being."

"It isn't the correct future for our universe!" said Jeff.

"The Twintas say that is no concern of theirs. They wish to get rid of the Master Cult completely, and this is a way."

"But not the only way," said Rembrandt. "I can show the Twintas how to concentrate their power, not only to send us back home, but to protect themselves from the Master Cult." He turned to Norby. "Please go to my ship and return with my crystal-light sculpture."

Norby left, while Jeff wondered what could possibly persuade the Twintas to help, when helping meant staying vulnerable to the Master Cult's attacks.

"Here it is, sir," said Norby, his arms stretched as far as possible to hold the sculpture. "May I join it?"

"Yes, Norby."

Jeff saw, with horror, that Norby had somehow melted into the sculpture, that the sculpture had apparently become fluid enough to wrap itself around Norby.

"Norby! Come back!"

"I do not understand," said Blif.

"Wait," said Rembrandt. "I create works of art to be enjoyed by all. And Norby is also, in his way, a work of art. The two can join, and then . . . watch!"

It seemed to Jeff that Norby was frozen inside the crystal sculpture, but he was still alive, for the robot's eyes shut, and then opened. The crystal began to spin, sending out fine tendrils that glittered in the sunlight. When it stopped, Norby was no longer visible, for the crystal was cloudy.

"What happened to Norby? Bring him back!" shouted Jeff.

The Ancient One of the Twintas seemed to bend as all of its pinchers grasped the crystal tendrils. The nearest Twintas touched the trunk of the Ancient One, and reached with their own arms to touch comrades who were further away.

Suddenly Jeff felt that the whole planet was united, each Twintas touching another, perhaps communicating mentally with the rest of the Twintas planets. But was Norby dead?

And then, so easily that it seemed ridiculous, the crystal sculpture shook itself and Norby dropped out.

"Hi, Jeff—were you worried?"

"Oh, Norby, you're all right?"

"Of course I'm all right. I just gave all my knowledge to the Twintas, courtesy of that peculiar object Rembrandt devised. It's going to be a permanent part of this planet now, and no Master Cult will ever be able to touch it."

The crystal sculpture had taken the shape of a Twintas, some of its tendrils pushing into the ground and the rest of them wrapped around the trunk of the Ancient One.

"My gift to your universe," said Rembrandt, Pera translating again for Blif. "We Others believe that your universe is developing in an interesting way, with a technology based on living creatures that voluntarily join with you. My crystal-light gives you knowledge and increases the power of the Twintas to protect themselves and you pirates from the Master Cult."

Rembrandt paused, both sets of arms outstretched toward the Ancient One. "Oh, Twintas, the elders of this universe, will you not help us return to our own universe? We do not wish to contaminate yours, and you should not try to get rid of the Master Cult by aiding them to invade ours. You now have more power. Help us!"

Jeff held his breath, for the Ancient One seemed to shiver, the vibration passing from one Twintas to another. It seemed to last forever.

"It's okay," Norby announced. "They say yes."

"How do you know, Norby?" asked Rembrandt.

"I can understand them. They're not so bad. They appreciated all my knowledge. There's only one trouble."

"They want you to stay—is that it?" asked Jeff. "Well, I won't have it. You've got to come with me, Norby..."

"Oh, they don't want *me,* now that they have my knowledge. They want to see Threezy perform. There are no jesters in this universe—yet."

"We must remedy that," said Blif. "Humor and song are valuable aspects of a universe, and although we have them, a professional minstrel and jester would be a useful addition."

Rembrandt must have given orders through his suit mike, for the next thing Jeff saw was Ing/Threezy, inside a transparent flat-bottomed bubble big enough for him to stand erect and move about a little. The bubble floated out of the Others' ship

and was passed along to the Ancient One by the nearest
Twintas.

"What in blazes is going on?" roared Threezy, his beard
quivering and his handlebar moustache flaring out. "Those
three-eyed, two-armed bandits shoved me into this thing—
say, Jeff, can you hear me?"

"Loud and clear," said Jeff. "If you can hear me, please
listen carefully. A universe is at stake. You must perform for
the—ah—trees. They are intelligent and will help us go
home if you do."

"Well I won't!" shouted Ing. "I've remembered being Ing,
and why should I become Threezy to please a bunch of idi-
otic-looking monsters who can't possibly have the power. . ."

Norby disappeared, reappearing almost immediately inside
Ing's bubble. "What ho, villain!" said Norby. "What's it to be,
a duel to the death, or a dance for our supper?"

Norby bowed, or rather his jointed legs did, and he fell
smack on his face, two-way feet waving behind him.

There was a rustling sound, and Jeff saw that Blif and all
the Twintas were vibrating their leaves and arms, apparently
with laughter.

"Don't get in my act, robot," said Ing.

"I'm a better clown than you," said Norby, rising on antigrav and spinning slowly, his domed hat rising and falling.
"And I can sing, too."

"This universe's a funny place,
But so's the one we know,
Therefore I think it's no disgrace,
To laugh at friend or foe . . ."

Ing grasped one of Norby's hands and began to spin too.

"You sing off key, you robot twerp,
Your villany is weak,
My place on stage you can't usurp,
For Threezy is unique!"

Jeff saw that Pera was holding one of Rembrandt's hands,
and also touching the Ancient One, probably giving them both
a telepathic translation of the words.

Ing took a couple of silver disks from his pocket, picked up
Norby, and began juggling all three of them, aided, of course
by Norby's use of antigrav. Norby winked at the Ancient One
every time he bobbed upward, and for some reason it was
very funny, especially since Ing kept singing.

"From worlds down here to space above,
There's danger, death, and doom,
So sing of happiness and love,
And take away the gloom."

Ing snatched the balls out of the air and made them vanish, while juggling Norby with his other hand. He grinned fiendishly at everyone, stood on his hands, and kept on rotating Norby with his feet.

"The Master Cult's a silly bunch . . ." sang Norby, off-key as usual.

"Ridiculous riff-raff!" warbled Ing in falsetto,

"So when they come to punch and crunch—" sang Norby,

"Defeat them with a laugh!" finished Ing.

The show went on, and Jeff began to relax, for the Twintas were obviously pleased, and Ing was obviously Threezy after all. He was laughing at Norby's next antics when he felt the mind touch of Blif.

—How did they know?

—Know what?

—That the Twintas gain power when they laugh.

—I guess none of us knew that, but maybe it's true of anyone in any universe.

Norby and Jeff stood on the carpet in front of Admiral Yobo's desk in the great rotating wheel of Space Command. The Admiral scowled at them.

"So you didn't capture Ing."

"Well, we did, sort of," said Jeff, "but Rinda wanted to take him back to Izz and the Queen thinks he's cute . . ."

"Bah," said Yobo. "I will suspect the worst. And by the way, Fargo's back and wants to know if you've been taking care of Oola, because she's missing from the apartment."

At the sound of her name, Oola opened her eyes and meowed at the Admiral. Then she yawned and went back to sleep in Jeff's arms. Evidently she thought traveling from one universe to another an exhausting business.

"I suppose I'll have to hear all the boring details of why you brought the *Hopeful* to Space Command for repairs to the hull. Looks like you'd shot her out of a cannon."

"Not exactly, sir," said Jeff. "You see, when we found that Space Command didn't exist . . ."

"What!"

"I mean, in the future that wasn't, or wouldn't be . . ."

"Cadet!"

"Wait," said Norby. "I will explain everything, in one simple sentence."

Yobo groaned. "Go ahead, Norby. I'll regret I let you, but go ahead."

"Okay, sir. I—Norby the Magnificent—saved the universe!"